The Naked and the Dead
Barbary Shore
The Deer Park
Advertisements for Myself
Deaths for the Ladies (and Other Disasters)
The Presidential Papers
An American Dream
Cannibals and Christians
Why Are We in Vietnam?
The Armies of the Night
Miami and the Siege of Chicago
Of a Fire on the Moon
The Prisoner of Sex
Existential Errands
St. George and the Godfather
Marilyn
The Fight
Genius and Lust
The Executioner's Song
Of Women and Their Elegance

Pieces

NORMAN MAILER

Pieces

LITTLE, BROWN AND COMPANY BOSTON · TORONTO

FIRST EDITION

LIBRARY OF CONGRESS CATALOG CARD NO. 82-082202

MV

Designed by Janis Capone

Published simultaneously in Canada
by Little, Brown & Company (Canada) Limited

PRINTED IN THE UNITED STATES OF AMERICA

For my sister, Barbara

Contents

Pieces

Our Man at Harvard   1

An Advertisement Advertised   6

Are We in Vietnam?   9

Of a Small and Modest Malignancy, Wicked and
   Bristling with Dots   13

Two Letters from Frank Crowther   82

Miller and Hemingway   86

Papa & Son   94

My Friend, Jean Malaquais   97

Narcissism   106

Tango, Last Tango   115

The Faith of Graffiti   134

A Harlot High and Low   159

Pieces

Our Man at
Harvard

⚓

Let me tell you about the Somerset Maugham party that we gave at *The Advocate* in the spring of 1942. The magazine was housed then in a dark gray flat-roofed three-story building across the street from the stern of *The Lampoon* (and indeed we were much aware of being in their wake — *Lampoon* editors usually went to *Time*; ours to oblivion). In those days *The Advocate* building was as ugly from the exterior as it is now. A few small and dingy stores occupied the ground floor; some mysterious never-seen tenants were on the second; and *The Advocate* offices took up the third. They were beautiful to me. One climbed a dull, carpeted staircase as dusty as a back road in Guerrero, used one's *Advocate* key to go through the door at the top, and opened the suite, an entire floor-through of five rooms, five mystical chambers full of broken-down furniture and the incomparable odor that rises from old beer stains in the carpet and syrup-crusted empty Coke bottles in the corners. It is a better odor than you would think, sweet and alcoholic and faintly debauched — it spoke of little magazines and future lands of literature, and the offices were almost always empty in late afternoon, when the sunlight turned the dust into a cosmos of angels dancing on a pin. Magicians would have felt a rush of aphrodisia amid all this pendant funk and mote. Maybe I loved the *Advocate* offices more than anyone who was taken in my competition — I spent the spring of sophomore year at Harvard drinking Cokes by a table at the window that faced on *The Lampoon*, and I read old issues of the magazine. Once I was an authority on the early published work in *The Advocate* of T. S. Eliot, Edwin Arlington Robinson, Van Wyck

Brooks, John Reed, Conrad Aiken, E. E. Cummings and Malcolm Cowley — it must have been the nearest I ever came to extracting genealogical marrow from old print. Occasionally Marvin Barrett, the president, or Bowden Broadwater, Pegasus, would come through the office, give a start at seeing me at the same chair and table where he had glimpsed me on the last visit and go off to do his work.

The following academic year, '41–'42, Bruce Barton, Jr., was elected president and John Crockett became Pegasus. We had troubles instantly. Barton, called Pete, was the son of Bruce Barton, Sr., an advertising magnate as well known in his period as was Nicholas Murray Butler, and for that matter one could find similarities. (Barton must have been the last of the advertising tycoons who believed passionately in a strenuous Jesus with muscles.)

His son, in compensation, was a gentleman. Pete Barton was the nicest guy a lot of us met at Harvard, and with his blond hair, good if somewhat pinched features and fundamental decency, he could have passed for Billy Budd if 1) he had not gone to Deerfield, which left him a little more patrician than yeoman in manner, and if 2) he had had more beef. But he was gentle, he was quietly literary, and his father had millions. Since *The Advocate* was in its usual cauldron of debt, no other man would have been so appropriate to serve as president. Barton might even have had a benign, well-financed and agreeable administration if not for the new Pegasus, John Crockett, a man as talented as Claggart and equally riven in his soul by detestation of our Billy Budd.

Being innocent of Crockett's propensities for literary evil, we were a happy group coming into the office. The magazine would be ours. We would print what we wished. Our first issue, therefore, consisted of each of us putting in his own story. Crockett then took our gems to a printer in Vermont. This was, I think, in November. By February we still did not have a magazine. Crockett kept assuring us the printer would soon deliver. None of us ever called him. Crockett had promised us that the inexpensive rate he had managed to extract from the Linotype mills of the Vermont woods would be ruined forever if we broke any of our voices on the printer's ear. Therefore, we waited. Nervously, impatiently, suspiciously, we waited for the issue with our stories.

Instead, Crockett came back with the seventy-fifth anniversary edition of *The Advocate*, a little work of love Crockett had gotten together by himself over the last year — in truth, a prodigious push of

Pegasus-manship — collecting poems, pieces and comment from the fine ranks of Wallace Stevens, Horace Gregory, Djuna Barnes, Marianne Moore, Robert Hillyer, Frederic Prokosch, Mark Schorer, John Malcolm Brinnin, Richard Eberhart, Bowden Broadwater, William Carlos Williams, plus a poem by John Crockett, "The Sulky Races at Cherry Park." It was a mammoth virtuoso literary crypto-CIA affair back in March of '42, and none of us on *The Advocate* had had the first clue as to what Crockett was cooking. As for the issue with our stories — Crockett promised to get to that next. The expression on his young but sour face told us what he thought of our stories. Crockett, incidentally, while not as well-featured as John Dean had a great resemblance to him — I remember his tortoiseshell glasses, high forehead and thin pale hair.

Pete Barton had been agitated for weeks at the long wait on our first issue. Painfully aware of his father's weight in the world, he was invariably overscrupulous never to push his own. He had suspended himself into a state of forbearance worthy of a Zen warrior considering the immense agitation the late appearance of the magazine had caused. When the anniversary issue appeared (to rich critical reception in the Boston papers, worse luck!) Barton finally demonstrated his father's blood. He called an emergency meeting where he calumniated himself for his derelictions of attention, took the full blame for the financial disaster of the issue (it had cost something like three times as much as more modest issues; our debt on the consequence had doubled overnight) and — Billy Budd to the last, absent even to intimations of a further notion to evil — stated that he would not ask for Crockett's resignation if he could expect his cooperation on future projects.

Crockett replied with a nod of his head and a profound turning of our collective head. Having heard, he said, that Somerset Maugham would be in the Boston area during April, he had sent an invitation to Maugham to come to a party that *The Advocate* would be happy to throw in his honor, and Maugham had accepted. Maugham had accepted.

This piece of news ran around the ring of Cambridge like a particle in a cyclotron. Nothing in four years at Harvard, not Dunkirk, Pearl Harbor or the blitz, not even beating Yale and Princeton in the same season for the first time in years, could have lit Harvard up more. Not to be invited to that party was equal to signifying that one had mismanaged one's life.

The literary grandees of the faculty sent their early acceptance:

F. O. Matthiessen, Theodore Spencer and Robert Hillyer in the van; the officers of *The Lampoon* sucked around; housemasters' wives asked how things were *going* at *The Advocate*. On the night of the party, four hundred souls in four hundred bodies as large as Patrick Moynihan's and as delicate as Joan Didion's came to the small rooms on the third floor and packed themselves in so completely that you ended by bringing your drink to your lips around the wrist of the strange forearm in front of your face. The noise of cocktail gabble anticipated the oncoming shapings of time — one would not hear the sound again until the first jet planes fired up their engines at an airport. Drinks were passed overhead. If you did not reach at the right time, another hand plucked the drink. It did not matter. More was on its way. Glasses bounced like corks over white choppy Harvard hands. From time to time, word would pass like wind through grass that Maugham had just entered the building, Maugham was having trouble getting up the stairs, Maugham was through the door. Maugham was in the other room. We formed phalanxes to move into the other room; we did not budge. A phalanx cannot budge a volume that is impacted. The lovely smile of resignation was on the lips of faculty wives: It is the establishment smile that says, "Life is like that — the nearest pleasures are not to be tasted." After a half hour of such smiling into the face of a stranger as one brought one's arm around her neck to get at one's drink, the wind came through the grass again. Maugham, we heard, was at the door. Maugham was slowly going down the stair. Somerset Maugham was gone.

Hands passed drinks above the impacted mass. Eyes flashed in that hard gemlike smile of pride retained when opportunity is lost. In another half hour, there was a lessening of pressure on one's chest, and bodies began to separate. After a while, one could walk from room to room. What was the point? Maugham was gone.

It was only on the next day, after the claims of liars had been checked against the quiet evidence of reliable witnesses who had found themselves analogously empretzeled in every room and on the stairs, that the news came back. By every sound measure of verification, Somerset Maugham had never been in *The Advocate* building that night. Crockett, now confronted, confessed. Out of his unflappable funds of phlegm, he allowed that he had known for weeks Somerset Maugham was not coming — the great author had been kind enough to send a telegram in answer to the invitation. "Certainly not," it said.

It was too late to ask Crockett to resign. Due to the war and an accelerated graduation, our term as *Advocate* officers was up; the new president and Pegasus were in. Because of the party, we left with a debt that had just doubled again. *The Advocate* has never been solvent since.

A postscript: Pete Barton became a Navy officer and commanded a ship, came home, worked as quietly for *Time* as if he had been a *Lampoon* man, and died before he was forty. The only time I saw John Crockett again was about ten years ago in New York on a reunion at the Harvard Club. He was now in the State Department and had been stationed for years in Yugoslavia. He told delicious stories about idiotic conversations with Madame Tito at banquets in Zagreb. He looked to be as wicked as ever. Our cause was being well served in Yugoslavia. It occurs to me that the mag across the street never knew what a talent it missed when *The Advocate* got Crockett. Rest in peace, Pete Barton.

An Advertisement
Advertised

‿ꞈ

The *Deer Park* is the book which taught me how to write, but *Advertisements* followed, and it was the first book I wrote that had a style I thought I might be able to call my own. It was forged out of a continuing recognition of how difficult it was to put words together when writing about oneself.

Style, of course, is what every good young author looks to acquire. In lovemaking, its equivalent is grace. Everybody wants it but nobody seems to find it by working directly toward the goal. On the other hand, unless born with grace or style, nobody seems to get there without working hard in some direction or other.

Advertisements was written at the end of the slowest and most morale-disrupting kind of work. I didn't begin the book until 1958, ten years after *The Naked and the Dead* was published. In between had come *Barbary Shore* and *The Deer Park* and I never want to have two novels as hard again to write.

I did not know what I was doing. As I have explained now and again, I had been divorced by success from any intimate sense of my identity and had a hard time getting halfway back. Apart from that psychological vertigo which will attack any athlete, performer or young businessman who has huge early success, I had my own particular problem, a beauty — I did not know my métier. *The Naked and the Dead* had been written out of what I could learn from James T. Farrell and John Dos Passos with good doses of Thomas Wolfe and Tolstoy, plus homeopathic tinctures from Hemingway, Fitzgerald, Faulkner, Melville and Dostoyevsky. With all such help, it was a book that wrote itself. It had a style-proof style. That is to say it had a best-seller style, no style. Very few people failed to read that book with some interest.

I knew however it was no literary achievement. I had done a book in a general style borrowed from many people and did not know what I had of my own to say. I had not had enough of my own life yet. The idea could even be advanced that style comes to young authors about the time they recognize that life is out there ready to kill them, kill them quickly or slowly, but something out there is not fooling. It would explain why authors who were ill in their childhood almost always arrive early in their career as developed stylists: Proust, Capote, and Alberto Moravia give three examples; Gide offers another. This notion would certainly account for the early and complete development of Hemingway's style. He had had before he was twenty the unmistakable sensation of being wounded so near to death that he felt his soul slide out of him, then slip back.

The average young author is not that ill in childhood nor that ill used by early life. His little social deaths are overcome by his small social conquests. So he writes in the style of others looking for his own, and tends to love words more than rhythms. In his haste to dominate the world (rare is the young writer who is not a consummate prick) he tends to use words for their precision, their ability to define, their acrobatic action. His style often changes from scene to scene, from paragraph to paragraph. He knows little about creating mood and the essence of good style is that it sets a mood thick as a theatrical piece, and then alters that mood, enlarges it, conducts it over to another mood. Every sentence, precise or imprecise, vaulting or modest, is careful not to poke a hyperactive finger through the tissue of the mood, nor do the sentences ever become so empty of personal quality that the mood sinks to the ground of the page. It is an achievement which comes from having thought about one's life right into the point where one is living it. Everything that happens seems capable of offering its own addition to one's knowledge. One has arrived at a personal philosophy or has, at least, reached the rare plateau where irony rather than philosophy serves to sustain each day. At that juncture, everything one writes comes out of one mood, one's own fundamental mood.

Some such development may have gone on in me over the ten years from the publication of *The Naked and the Dead* to the commencement of work on *Advertisements For Myself.* Maybe I had come to realize that authors died from the reception of their books, literally began to die a little, and every dishonesty in oneself added gangrene to the wound. So *Advertisements* became the book in which I tried to separate my legitimate spiritual bile from my self-pity and maybe it was the hardest continuing task I had yet set myself. What aggravated every problem was that I was also trying to give up smoking, and as a corollary of kicking nicotine, I was thrust into the problem of style. In those days, my psyche felt as different without cigarettes as my body felt in moving from air to water. It was as if I perceived with different senses, and clear reactions were blunted. Writing without cigarettes, the word I looked for almost never came, not in quick time: in compensation I was granted a sensitivity to the rhythm of what I wrote and that helped to develop my style, no, rather say it proceeded to turn my nose in the direction of style. I began to learn how difficult it is for a prose writer to move from the hegemony of the word to the resonance of the prose rhythm. That can be a jump greater than a leap into poetry; maybe it is analogous to changing one's religion.

I suffered, anyway, prodigies of brain-curdling, and educated myself all over again how to write, write without cigarettes, and found the beginnings of a style that might begin to express the way my own mind (as opposed to other writers' minds) was ready to work. So, *Advertisements for Myself* was a book whose writing changed my life. Let us hope that is conceivably for the better.

Are
We in Vietnam?

꙳

This is the only novel I ever finished under the mistaken belief I was writing not this kind of novel but another. Living in Province-town on the edge of those rare, towering and windy dunes which give the tip of Cape Cod a fair resemblance to the desert of the Sa-hara, I had begun to think of a novel so odd and so horrible that I hesitated for years to begin it. I did not like the story; it came to me with fear. I imagined a group of seven or eight bikers, hippies and studs plus a girl or two living in the scrub thickets that sat in some of the valleys between the dunes. Only six feet high, those thickets were nonetheless forests, and if one could find a path through the thorns and cat briars, nobody could track you, not in a hurry. So I peopled the thickets with characters: my characters were as wild as anyone who ever came to Provincetown. It is not a tame place. Years ago, a First Lady was once told it was "the Wild West of the East," and that is not a bad description. The tip of Cape Cod curls in on itself in a spiral — the long line of the dunes comes around like the curve of one's palm and fingers as they close into a fist — it is one of the very few places in America where one comes to the end of the road for a more profound reason than real estate ceasing to be profit-able. In Provincetown, geography runs out, and you are surrounded by the sea.

So it is a strange place. The Pilgrims landed there before they went on to Plymouth — America began here. The Pilgrims lost interest in scrub pine, mournful winds, and sand in the land. They moved on, left ghosts. Whaling captains settled in later, left ghosts. In winter the town is filled with spirits. One can go mad in that rainy climate waiting for March to end. It is a place for murderers and suicides. If decades went by without a single recorded homicide, that record ended abruptly with a crime of true carnage. A few years ago, a young Portuguese from a family of fishermen killed four girls, dismembered their bodies, and buried the pieces in twenty small and scattered graves.

That catastrophe was not a good deal worse than anything I had already contemplated for my gang, since I conceived of them making nocturnal trips from the dunes into town where out of the sheer boredom of an existence not nearly intense enough to satisfy their health, they would commit murders of massive brutality and then slip back to the dunes. Motiveless crimes. I saw a string of such crimes.

I was, as I say, in fear of the book. I loved Provincetown and did not think that was a good way to write about it. The town is so naturally spooky in mid-winter and provides such a sense of omens waiting to be magnetized into lines of force that the novel in my mind seemed more a magical object than a fiction, a black magic.

Nonetheless, I began the book in the spring of '66. It attracted me too much not to begin. Yet because I could not thrust Provincetown into such literary horrors without preparation, I thought I would start with a chapter about hunting bear in Alaska. A prelude. I would have two tough rich boys, each as separated from social convention as any two rich boys could be — Texans I would make them out of a reserve of memories of Texans I had served with in the 112th Cavalry out of San Antonio. The boys would be still young, still mean rather than uncontrollably murderous — the hunting might serve as a bridge to get them ready for more. They would come back from the Alaskan hunting trip ready to travel — Provincetown would eventually receive them.

Now, anyone who reads the book which this preface serves will see that nobody ever gets to Provincetown. The chapter on hunting becomes a half-dozen chapters, a dozen chapters, it ends up being all of the book. If I wrote those chapters wondering how long it would take to extricate myself with novelistic integrity from all the elaborations of the hunt I seemed more and more bound to get into, it was not until those boys were back in Dallas and I was getting ready to move them East that I realized two things.

(1) I had nothing further to say about them.

(2) Even if I did, I could no longer believe that Tex and D.J. could still be characters in the Provincetown novel. They had another quality by now.

So I lived with my manuscript for a few months and ended by recognizing that I hadn't been too bright. I had written a novel not a prelude. The book was done. Later, a number of readers would think *Why Are We in Vietnam?* was far and away my best book. I thought I had never written a funnier one.

In retrospect, I was less certain, however, of the humor. For when Sharon Tate was murdered in the summer of '69, and the world heard of Charles Manson, I could wonder what state of guilt I might have been in if I had written that novel of desert murderers. How then could I ever have been certain Manson had not been sensitive to its message in the tribal air?

But then writing has its own occult force. At its best, we never know where our writing comes from nor who gives it to us. If Jack Kennedy's name is invoked in the first sentence of *An American Dream*, nine lines farther down that page, a man named Kelly is mentioned. Later in the same chapter we learn Kelly's middle name is Oswald — Barney Oswald Kelly. That chapter appeared in *Esquire* about a month after the assassination, but it had been written three months earlier, a coincidence to force one to contemplate the very design of coincidence.

So, too, had I written in *Barbary Shore* about a secret agent named McLeod who had been, in his time, a particularly important Soviet agent. He lived in a cheap room on the top floor of a cheap rooming house just across the hall from the narrator. Writing the book, I always found it hard to believe that such a man would be found in such a place, and the simple difficulty of not quite believing what I wrote did not help to speed the writing of the book. A year after it was published, I rented a room in a dank old building with high ceilings called Ovington Studios on Fulton Street in Brooklyn not a half mile from the rooming house in *Barbary Shore,* and on the floor below during those ten years I kept the studio was Colonel Rudolph Abel, the most important Soviet spy in America — or, at least, so was he described by the FBI when the arrest was finally made.

We will never know if primitive artists painted their caves to show a representation, or whether the moving hand was looking to placate the forces above and the forces below. Sometimes, I think the novelist fashions a totem just as much as an aesthetic, and his real aim, not even known necessarily to himself, is to create a diversion in the fields of dread, a sanctuary in some of the arenas of magic. The flaws of his work can even be a part of his magical strength, as if his real intent in writing is to alter the determinations of that invisible finger which has written and moved on. By such logic, the book before you is a totem, not empty of amulets for the author against curses, static, and the pervasive malignity of our electronic air.

Of a Small
and Modest Malignancy,
Wicked and Bristling
with Dots

✌

This summer I took my family on a motor trip through the West, and left the highway for a one-hundred-mile jog to pick up some fossils for my boy. This took us to Hurricane, Utah ... around the Zion Park country. A great vastness, magnificent. ... It is three in the afternoon when we get there, to a house, the fossil-seller we read about in the Museum of Natural History magazine operating out of his cellar. It's a gorgeous day, just right, and we go in — into a small living room with about nine people in it, all staring at that square of light: they're watching a game show, three generations of them, the grandparents (American gothics, blooded, stolid) down to the near-infants, wired, a funny show, I guess it's supposed to be, at least "joyous," but no one is laughing, no one is smiling even; they're just fixed there in their places, staring (not looking, mind you, in the way that Sontag separates looking and staring: by God, this is "silent" art for the populace). Well, the feller sends us down to the cellar to pick around in his stuff and goes back into the living room. We're down there almost three hours; my boy can't make up his mind, and my wife is no help: and when we come back up, they're there, same postures, no change; a soap opera, I think it was, running. ... It leaves you feeling something about the force we are talking about, its power to de-nature.

— out of a letter from Gordon Lish

13

Channel 1

Limbo was a house of many mansions. Mailer's spirits, while hardly free — they whipped around his soul like electrons orbiting a ring — began, nonetheless, to awake. The telling monotonies of Limbo (all those faceless fornications that rang in the ears, those stupors that drifted like bad weather, apathies piling on apathies like old newspapers, the crackle of static, and the playback of cocktail gabble, the gluttony of red wine taken after white wine on top of harshly cooked food, or the holes in one's memory now plugged with electronic hum, plus the horror of contemplating drops from heights where one did not want to find oneself, and all the stations of the cross of feeling empty while waiting for subway trains and airline shuttles and waitresses in busy lunchrooms) all such items having been so far experienced in Limbo as direct punishment, now began to partake of ecological logic. It may be that Lish's letter had something to do with it.

Mailer began to believe that this enforced immersion in every sensation, episode, glut, glop, and repellent handle of experience (his vision filled with nothing but the faces of digital watches, the smell of pharmacies, the touch of polyester shirts, the wet wax-paper of McDonald's hamburgers, the air of summer when traffic jams, and shrieks of stereo as the volume is mis-laid, the little nausea that plastic highball glasses will give to the resonance of booze) were not necessarily items to scourge him around one eternity before dispatching him to another, but might be instead his own natural field of expiation. In place of his soul expiring, or suffering some whole damnation now, he might still be part of his own karmic chain and going through a purification of those misspent hours before being thrown back into the contest again. A joke resounded in his ears. "It's a great day for the race," said the elevator operator in the acrylic uniform in the Formica-paneled cage. "What race?" said the passenger. "The human race," said the elevator operator and laughed his way up the ascension.

All who died were guilty. In part, at least, they were guilty, and conceivably they were innocent in part, and Limbo, thought Mailer, might even be the charity to suppose that innocence, if it wanted to go back to the race, was in need of education. Limbo, on the consequence, took all those moral stances embedded in concrete, and wrenched them askew. In the mansion, there was that human, for instance, who held the award for the most faithful church attendance over two decades in the American Midwest; now, he was pissing and moaning up a storm at the injustice of being here. Still, he was guilty. The inhabitants were all judged by one fine measure: had they or had they not wasted more of the soul's substance than was required by the exigencies of their life? Since the first perception offered here was that the most consumable substance of the soul was nothing other than time; that Time, whole and mysterious bed of light, electricity, and force, was invested, like the true fund of the realm, in every soul, it followed as a consequence that Time was not to be wasted, but rather, whatever the warp of one's upbringing, was to be spent, all neurotic, psychotic, screwball, timid, stingy, spendthrift, violent or fear-filled habits taken into account, was still to be spent as wittily, cheerfully, and/or bravely as possible.

That was the standard of Limbo. Time was not to be wasted. It came over one, even on emerging from the first stupefying sleep (and therefore beginning to suffer monotony, apathy, and the boredom that comes from being out of Time) that this dreadful experience, these appalling emptinesses of the spiritual gut which now made up the hours — could one presume to speak still of hours: rather was one not living in seamless non-dark non-light units punctuated by no breath? — was, while a doleful experience, steeped in torpor, still a course in orientation over spiritual ills. For instance, the Midwestern churchgoer now inhabited a cell (in this penitentiary of the heavens) next to one of the world's worst cons, a man who had killed three prisoners before dying himself over the twenty years of his Lewisburg stretch. Yet the con was here for another kind of crime — he had put in more man-hours watching TV than any other convict in the federal system. All the same, the two were installed side by side — their crimes against the cosmos were apparently not dissimilar. They had both wasted their stuff, and egregiously. The churchgoer had perpetrated this by the brute sterility of his attendance: the complacency of his performance (that is to say, the spiritual stagnation at the center of his complacency) had been a powerful miasma to lay on the spirit of three young ministers who in succession grew old at accelerated rates looking into his professionally empty eyes — he had certainly spoiled more of existence than he sustained. The con, in his turn, had poisoned the livelier possibilities of many a young wolf and punk whose burgeoning shit-oriented libidos would somehow drain out of them after saun-

tering past that corner of the inmates' lounge where the con was en-
sconced by the set. Considering how immense was his potential
violence, just so flattened had been the mood by that act of his will
which chose to do time quietly, watch TV, and get out — at which,
in fact, he failed, for he kept killing other convicts. The con's real
mission in life, and he knew it, was to outwit guards, stifle alarm
systems, and climb unclimbable prison walls. The logics of Limbo
were not easily available, and yet the message, as one took it through
the now non-corporeal equivalent of one's pores, was that something in the cosmos could have prospered more if the con had
climbed the wall instead of imbibing TV, even as the churchgoer
could have stirred beneficial forces in the universe by catching an
X-rated movie or two.

Given the iron law of such logic, Mailer came to recognize that he
would have done better in his life to go to church once in a while on
Sunday (not even Limbo suggested a synagogue for him!) rather
than increase the total of his appearances on television.

Indeed, it was this particular piece of moral knowledge he was
obliged to ingest right after his emergence from the first stupefying
sleep-out. It was to recognize that every dull thing one had done to
the universe (filling out crossword puzzles one did not wish to fill,
taking the Eastern Airline shuttle when other transportation was
available) every hour one had voided thereby of its fresh and keen
desire to be used, the air around one, in consequence, suffocated by
psychic exhaust, had now to be breathed again, the air of the stifled
past to be swallowed, digested, suffered, and then stuffed into the
ongoing baggage of one's karma. This mansion of Limbo was here to
bring you face to face with those sins for which there are no tears,
even as a husband and wife cannot weep if they lose a potentially
heartfelt piece of ass by watching TV all night; yes, this corner of
Limbo (a clean and well-appointed place whose appurtenances were
suggestive of the interior of a picture tube on a black-and-white
set — that is, all curved, silver, and gray, an odorless impalpability
of fluorescence in an eternity of flickering) was now apparently
ready to teach him, that is, teach his soul, something new. That
meant, on reflection, that he might still have a soul. Something in
himself exactly like the Old Center seemed certainly not to have
ceased, that part at least of himself he had always thought wiser
than the rest of him (that part which took pains to mash an invisible
egg on his head after a rotten remark) was coming to recognize that
his tour through Limbo (if indeed a tour and not an ongoing pun-

ishment) would ask him to meditate at length and presumably to purpose on those yaws and palls of his life which had passed through TV. He was going to be obliged to regard his own wretched collaboration with the multimillion-celled nausea-machine, that Christ-killer of the ages — television. (Let us say it takes a Jew not wholly convinced of the divinity of Christ to see that is who the tube is killing.) And he shuddered through the now-familiar, if minimal, retchings of Limbo while remembering how on numerous occasions with each of his seven children he had closed the doors of his own resistance to TV and let the little fuckers keep looking at the screen because it *pacified* them, which is to say took the lividity of their five-year-old nerves and slowly (that is, faster than sight) and buzzingly, cauterized their nerve ends just the right bloody bit, no blood seen. Again the guilt that cannot be alleviated by tears stirred like sludge in his own small part of the great cosmic gut. Yes, there was a malignancy present in the bowels of communication, and it was video.

So could he meditate now for his next karma, or at least for this part of his next karma, by brooding over the nature of television. As soon brood over the nature of cancer gulch! Might they not be the same? A piece of plastic in the tissues of communing, a pollution in the avatars, good old anti-matter living next to matter.

He prepared therefore for the meditative journey that proves most excruciating in Limbo, a rounding through the past, a trip back! It is a venture full of perils. For the glassy sluggish surface of the past, once disturbed, would offer every encouragement to mosquitoes, insomnia, the rash which issues from deodorants, and more Limbo.

To meditate on TV would prove equal, however, to writing a recollection of an enemy one had never met and could not quite believe in. How can one conceive of an enemy who is without personal animosity? It is like writing a memoir on an oxymoron. Limbo set its tasks.

Channel 2

Mailer, nonetheless, had a few tricks. The virtue of having lived as a professional writer was that one's soul — much punched-out bag — had acquired a little craft for dealing with the peculiar properties of context. One knew what to guard against. Not all events were, for example, equally extricable from the past. It was not unlike hunting for odd-colored stones in tidal flats. Some would come up at the touch of one's fingers. Others stirred with a fury and threw off clouds of black sand full of anathema. A root of blatwort (or any weed with some such name) would be discovered beneath, embracing the stone. On the other hand, those attractive pebbles that came up free, tended also to be slick. Like good anecdotes that had no roots, they soon lost their charm. Whereas, a real piece of the past always seemed to connect to an underground creeper that went on forever.

Writing about what had happened, therefore, could put you into difficulties worthy of Proust or Einstein. Hoping to evoke an event, one could not expect that the act of finding the facts would fulfill the job. It was more elusive. The event might have a fine mood created by the facts that went into it, but it was another matter to get one's writing to prove equal to the mood. A poem does not describe a movement of a bird in flight so much as the unaccountable stir from one syllable to another will allow us to feel the thrust of a wing.

This glimpse of the intricate nature of his craft left Mailer, however, with only a small glow. Limbo was adept at dimming the rosier emoluments of reverie. There came the gloomier conclusion — a pure artifact of Limbo itself — that if his memories of TV were without roots, they were also without mood. The inner taste of his experiences on TV tasted like aspirin to him.

He might have a problem, therefore, equal to the size of this mansion of Limbo. It would be to take his soul through the leachings of its experience in fifty, or was it a hundred, or two hundred TV appearances (the promiscuous are not those who know too many lovers so much as those who no longer count them) and extract from the memory of these outings, not the moral lesson, but the way to absorb back into himself the excrementitiousness of his TV past.

Yet he could not even know that this was his task. He found, out of the thousand papers he might have managed to smuggle across with him, nothing in Limbo but a letter from Gordon Lish, an editor he hardly knew; on the evidence of this letter, Lish had a style whose carefree disjunctions were much like the author's own, and that was swell. That was company on a long trip.

On the other hand, Mailer had small trust in Limbo. There was no way of knowing the certifiability of what you could remember.

Lish's letter seemed to propose an immense essay: *"Treat television,"* Lish had written, *"as pure phenomenon, purest form . . . open the eye onto television without comment, without attitude, without the particularities that constitute the content of the thing as it is."* So went a couple of the phrases. To the degree that Mailer thought he understood what this meant, he thought he understood it well: ". . . *television will be displayed wholly in terms of its existence as the all-pervasive environment, the universally felt national experience . . . an awesome, omnipresent force, the object that has penetrated and now fused with its subject . . . a revelation of TV as gestalt, form, power."*

What if he had written the piece already? What if it had been a good piece, and he had only brought Lish's letter along to remind himself of a nice achievement. The most damnable property of Limbo (other than its nearness to Damnation itself) was how one's memory was more appalling than a hangover. It certainly felt as if he had written such a piece, or was it only that on every day in the past when he turned on a television set, he had felt the emotions Lish was exhorting him to put upon the page: *"the immense circuitry, something is beaming, beaming, beaming."* Yes, he thought of that every time he was near a set. It was a most unpleasant *something.* So unpleasant, that over the years he had virtually stopped looking at TV. Even the study of professional football games on Sunday afternoon in a room full of good friends and Bloody Marys had begun to pall. The company was good, the drinks were fine, but *something* was in the room, and he could feel its presence eating them all. Yes, you did not make love to your wife after watching TV for an evening. *Something* had entered the blood; *something* had been busy eating the sweetmeats out of the seed.

It was true. It was a personal phenomenon. He had stopped watching TV. He had no interest even in what was supposed to be good. Once he turned on *Mary Hartman, Mary Hartman* and could see what was being talked about, yes, it was tastefully written, it took chances, was offbeat, but *something* was right in there with it and he didn't like Mary Hartman enough to keep the taste of aspirin in his mouth. *Roots* went by; he never took a look. "It's a cultural phenomenon," friends argued with him. He was experiencing his own phenomenon. No more TV. Unlike cigarettes or booze, TV was the easiest habit in the world to give up — once it had leached you out. Every night, or almost every night, even three nights a week for twenty years, the vampire that lived at the center of *some-*

thing had come out of the set and sucked his blood; so it was small surprise that *something* had no interest left in him either, not after twenty years of getting his blood ready for Limbo. The vampire of video obviously preferred to live on young blood. TV was not the altar of modern medicine for nothing, bloodletting was still the secret agent in every debilitating cure.

There were, of course, no TV sets in Limbo. Indeed, how could there be, if it was understood that for the duration of one's stay in the mansion, one was supposed to gather back from the air those vibrations one's TV sets had once put into it!

Still, he would not have been above turning on a set for an instant now if only to give himself a clue as to whether he had written his detestation of TV already, or if the task was yet upon him, and if so, then it would never be done; he now had the misery of comprehending that he would do no writing in Limbo; nothing further to add to the ideational glut of the world. Instead he would rest here, a cow digesting and redigesting the waste he had injected into human stuff, that *"small living room with about nine people in it, all staring at that square of light . . . no one is laughing, no one is smiling even; they're just fixed there in their places, staring . . ."* It was part of the malice of Limbo that Mailer now began to brood on the possibility that these people in the little Utah ranch house were looking at himself, were stupefiedly studying his own electronicized limbs and lineaments in a replay of some godawful afternoon show ten years old — what else would they choose to replay for these black-and-white sets on the desert? "Norman," said Joey Franklin beaming in the midday sun of the TV lights, "you're a great writer I hear, he's a great writer, folks, he writes books! And I don't read books much, don't have the time, so tell me what's the name of a good book?" Into the silence, Joey says — he has a pipeline into *something* — Joey *asks:* "Is *Alice in Wonderland* a good book?"

It cannot be a put-on. Franklin's eyes bounce like marbles.

"Yeah," says Norman Mailer, "it is a good book."

"How about *Rebecca of Sunnybrook Farm,* Norm?"

"I would guess that's not as good." When this is over, Mailer tells himself, he will kill the publicity girl from New American Library who put him on this show in the first place. It will sell books, she had promised him.

Out in Utah, are they taking it all in?

Is he more guilty for having appeared on TV shows than those who only refused to turn off their sets?

Channel 3

In the years before he ever went on TV himself, he used to watch it religiously; after a while, sacrilegiously. It started in the winter he was first smoking marijuana. He smoked it with all the seriousness of what was then his profoundly serious heart. It was 1954, and the drug was more important than any love affair he had ever had. It taught him more. Making love to different women, he would attempt to find that place where marijuana had last left him. It was the arena of the particular sensation he chased, as though he had been given a lovely if ineluctable emotion while watching a bullfight, and so went to the Plaza the following week to look for the same emotion — it did not matter altogether who the bullfighter was.

Since he was then in the opening-out of a career that would later provide a false legend of much machismo, he was still timid. Being deep in pot, and relatively full of life, certainly full of every intimation about himself, he was nonetheless too timid to go out late at night and see what the bars would provide. Since his second wife, not unlike himself in her jangled relations to bravery and cowardice, had usually and prudently gone to bed, he would be up alone at night, his mind teeming, and he would watch TV till the stations shut down. In those days, he made monumental connections on pot. He had to see no more than one animated spiral inserted by a commercial into the guts of a washing machine, a lively spiral that would tunnel right up the tube, and he would try to explain to his friends next day that the advertising agency was promoting the idea that their washing machine was congenial to a housewife's cunt. His friends thought him mad. He examined automobile commercials by the same light and saw that they were no longer selling the car by way of the pretty girl sitting on the fender as once they did; now, they were selling the car itself. The car was the fuck. "Dynaflow does it in oil," the announcer would say of an automatic transmission. So, he would tell his friends. His friends would think him mad and try to dissuade him from smoking too much pot. Marijuana was regarded differently in those days; it offered echoes of *Reefer Madness*.

He would watch Ernie Kovacs and Steve Allen late at night and would recognize that they knew what he knew. They saw how the spiral worked in the washing machine commercial, and why Dyna-flow did it in oil. Years later when Motivational Research was presented to the world, and everybody was ready to tell everybody at a party that an automobile was not used by a man to get a mistress, but was the mistress; and a housewife liked to identify the health of her washing machine with her own genito-urinary harmonies — speak no ill of the bowels! — Mailer was merely glad that Vance Packard had done the job. He was behind on too many of his own jobs. Marijuana had flung the separate parts of his brain into too many vivid places. In those days he had perceptions on every subject; was convinced, on the consequence, that he was a genius. He was getting very little writing done.

Still, he clung to his set. It explained the world to him. He was getting hip to everything, and the beauty was that he did not have to venture out.

It would not occur to him until six years later, when he would stab his wife, that it was not timidity which had been his first vice, but violence, a murderous nest of feeling so intransigent that he did not dare to go out at night for good cause, and did not know how to sleep at night without Seconal for even better cause — there was too much hatred at the distance between what he wished to do and what he was able to accomplish. Since his wife, faced with the choice of going to sleep early, or entering on a claustrophobic quarrel, would, of course, go to sleep, he would sit by himself from midnight until two in the morning when the last show would go off the air, the flag would ripple in the wind, and The Star-Spangled Banner would be played. In those days, he got to hate The Star-Spangled Banner all over again. It sounded like the first martial strains of that cancer he was convinced was coming on him, and who knows? If he had not stabbed his wife, he might have been dead in a few years himself — the horror of violence is its unspoken logic.

So, in those early mornings when television was his only friend, he knew already that he detested his habit. There was not enough to learn from watching TV. Some indispensable pieces of experience were missing. Except it was worse than that. Something not in existence was also present, some malignancy to burn against his own malignancy, some onslaught of dots into the full pressure of his own strangled vision. Often, when the stations would go off the air and no programs were left to watch, he would still leave the set on. The audio would hum in a tuneless pullulation, and the dots would hiss in an agitation of what forces he did not know. The hiss and the hum would fill the room and then his ears. There was, of course, no clamor — it was nearer to anti-noise dancing in eternity with noise. And watching the empty video, he would recognize it was hardly empty. Bands of gray and lighter gray swam across the set, roll-overs swept away the dots, and something like sun-spots crackled forth. Then the set went back to the slow scan of the waves and the drone of the audio. He discovered at last that such use of TV was a species of tranquilizer and could deaden the sharpest edge of his nerve. Blunted, impalpably bruted by a half-hour of such odorless immersion, he would with the aid of his Seconal be a little more ready to go to sleep.

A few years later when McLuhan would torment the vitals of a generation of American intellectuals with the unremovable harpoon that "the media is the message," Mailer could give his agreement. The message of TV was the scan of gray on gray and the hum of the sound when there was neither music nor a voice. Much later, in the Fall of '72, he would set out to make audiences laugh by comparing President Nixon's then featureless but disturbing personality to a TV screen that is lit when nothing is on the air. Nixon was there, he would remark, to deaden the murderous mood of the Republic. In-deed, it was the best explanation for why a man so unpopular was going to win by so great a majority. If Nixon did not make anyone very happy, neither did the TV set. Its message was equal to Nixon's: I am here to deaden you — you need it!

Maybe America did need it. Brooding over America of the Six-ties, that insane expanding America where undercover FBI men were inspiring (wherever they were not committing) the most vio-lent acts of the Left, brooding on that rich and powerful country where puritanism was still as alive as every Baptist, that corporate land with no instinctive response to aesthetics engaged now in the dissemination throughout the world of the worst applied aesthetics in the history of the world, its superhighways the highest form of strip mining, its little buildings kin to shoeboxes, its big buildings scaled to the module of one cardboard carton piled on top of an-other, the U.S. skyline thereby deserting the high needles of Man-hattan for the Kleenex boxes of Dallas; that food-guzzling Republic that froze its food before it would overcook it, and liked to lick ketchup off French fries so soggy they dropped from your fingers like worms — the worst food in the history of the world! — that sex-revolutionary Republic where swinging singles were connecting up with like-units — every other Baptist! — that sadistically revolutionary Republic going into black leather, S-M, and knocking off gooks in rice paddies, defoliating the foliage, digging the hog-resonance of motors between one's legs, and flame-throwers and comic books, and Haight-Ashbury, hitting golf balls on the moon, yes, that America, full of dread, could certainly use TV — I am here to deaden you, you need it!

Those were legitimate feelings for 1972. One had had a large fraction of a life by then watching TV, and one had long ago had the education of putting oneself on shows. Back in '53 and '54, however, stoned on pot, wafted up and down on Seconal, jammed with ambition, terror, and the common lust to learn the secrets of the world some easy way, the immersion into TV was profound. By it, one could study the world, and the tricks of the world.

So, for instance, would he examine people as strange to him as Igor Cassini who had a show in those years for snobs and it was hard as fiberglass. TV proved to be more interesting then for you could see a genuine article regularly, well-groomed, Republican, rich enough to own horses, sexy enough to marry up, and empty enough to find any topic of conversation amusing provided it was void of content. Those were Igor Cassini's guests. Mailer would on such occasions peer right into the tube to get a little nearer to the novelistic wealth.

Or: studying the tourist, he learned much about American fellatio. TV was scintillating for that. Next to the oil of Dynaflow and the spiral in the washing machine, came the phallic immanence of the microphone. A twinkle would light up in Steve Allen's eye as he took the mike and cord down the aisle and in and out of impromptu interviews with his audience, snaking the rounded knob right up to the mouth of some starched skinny Middle West matron, lean as whipcord, tense as rectitude, a life of iron disciplines in the vertical wrinkles of the upper lip; the lady would bare her teeth in a snarl and show a shark's mouth as she brought her jaws around to face and maybe bite off that black dob of a knob so near to touching her tongue.

A high school girl would be next, there with the graduating class on a trip to New York, her folks watching back home. She would swoon before the mike. She could not get her mouth open. She would keep dodging in her seat, and Steve would stay in pursuit, mike extended. Two nights ago she dodged for two hours in the back seat of a car. My God, this was in public.

A young housewife, liberal, sophisticated, happy to present her congenial point of view, compliments Mr. Allen on the quality of his show. "We watch you regularly, Steve, and like to think we're not too far behind the times up in Norfolk, Connecticut. That's right, Norfolk, not Norwalk." Her mouth, which has regular lips, is held a regular distance from the microphone. She shows no difficulty with it, no more than she would have with a phallus; two fingers and a thumb keep the thing canted right. There can be nothing wrong, after all, in relations between consenting adults. So speaks her calm.

Then there is a big heavy-set man who owns a grain-and-feed store in Ohio. He prides himself on imperturbable phlegm, and some thrift with words. He is not quite aware of the mike. If a man came into his store and proceeded to expose himself, this proprietor would not see it right away. He might, after all, be explaining the merits and demerits of one feed-mix to another; since he chews no gum when he walks, neither does he offer attention to tangentia as he talks. Now, singled out from the audience to be interviewed, he is stiffnecked, and responds only from that side of his mouth adjacent to the cheek on which Steve is asking the questions; he allows, "New York is a good place to visit, but, yessir, I'll be glad to start up for home," then, bla-looh! he sees it, black blimp-like little object! he blinks, he swallows, he looks at Steve: "I guess I've had my say, Mr. Allen," he says, and shuts up shop. Later he will tell a pinochle partner about the crazy people in New York. "Yes," the friend will acknowledge.

"You bet, Steve," says the next fellow, "I'm awfully glad you selected me. I've always wanted to talk to you." He is fully aware of the mike and what it portends. "Yes, yes, I'm a male secretary, love the work." "It doesn't bother you," asks Steve, "if people say, 'What is that, a male secretary, isn't it supposed to be women's work?'" "Oh, Steve, that doesn't bother me a bit. Here," he says, reaching for the mike. "Do you mind? I'm much more comfortable when I hold it."

"Help yourself," says Steve.

"Oh, I intend to," says the guest. "Life is a feast, and I think we should all get what we can, don't you?"

Hip! Mailer, building dreams of future power in the darkness, saw it all. America was getting hip. In the center of marijuana was the secret of how to do it. You needed the audacity to take your step.

In those days his life was simple, if much debilitated. Exhausted from writing *The Deer Park*, frantic from trying to do his columns

for *The Village Voice,* used-up from the terror of his central political premise — he believed that the orgy was the salvation of
America (he still did not know that the average swinger was about
as militant as the average tennis player, and in an equal rush to save
the cosmos!) — he was, if three times exhausted, nonetheless a
demon of psychic r.p.m.'s. When his brain was not in torpor, it felt
like an immense dynamo running at top speed in an empty shed in
the middle of the woods. He knew what it was to feel like electricity,
and understood the profoundly depressing statement in *Being and
Nothingness* that consciousness was the nihilation of Being. For his
brain worked at a great rate (half as fast it must be on occasion as
Jean-Paul Sartre's) and he felt the full dimensions of the void his
consciousness was generating in his brain cage.

Still, he was also possessed of an idea. It would go through many
changes and verge on becoming the opposite of itself, but it would
remain the idea of his life — it was (to take it by the most dangerous
premise first) that criminals were nearer to God than cops; corollary: a good cop was therefore a work of art. It would also conclude
that love was as rich a mystery as death, and perhaps as indecipher-
able; you could hardly know more than whether you had a love that
was good or bad for your orgasm. In consequence, the idea would
state that fine justice could be found only once in one's life, and that
was in the hour after death; something quite the opposite of *something* looked at you then from the other side.

He had the confidence that ideas such as these would eventually
thrive, unless the liveliest nerve of the mind was doomed. If such
doom was a real possibility, and the totalitarianism of the twentieth
century was not the shadow but the reality, and one lived beneath
it, well, society was not yet dead, and he still saw a great mission for
himself: it was to save the nerve of Being.

Since he had also to recognize that nine-tenths of what went on in
television looked to kill the nerve, his sense of mission grew larger.
It was the backstretch of the Eisenhower years. There was not
much hope on any horizon. Not a clue on how to stir. Since he did
not know that a revolution was beginning in America which would
live for a little while on an exchange of consciousness between
blacks and whites, and a beat generation would yet poke holes in the
American middle class, and a civil rights movement shift the nature
of the laws, he thought in the measureless vales of his vanity that he
was obliged to do the job himself, and he had mental experiences
out on marijuana that were so harsh, so arrogant, so lonely, so tor-

mented, and so demon-ridden — as if twenty devils could pull his chariot when ordered — that he was left with the confidence for years to come that he could write about the inner states of men like Hitler and Napoleon, Lenin and Castro and Cortes. It is a vanity to keep a young writer alive.

Of course, it also made him look on every action as immense with consequence — the early steps of a great leader! He did not forgive friends lightly for failing to see the transmogrificational significance of his thought, nor would he forget, he told himself, their lack of alacrity to follow him. He felt like a general without any army; his attention when he watched TV was not for his pleasure, therefore, but his martial art. He studied Ernie Kovacs like Moltke read Clausewitz, certain his hour was coming. The first TV show on which he would ever appear would be a call to the first battle, and he would fire a shot to ring around global village.

Channel 4

The first show happened to be *Night Beat*, Mike Wallace the host. Mailer got ready like a Depression fighter going into the main bout at the Garden on Friday night. Since his anticipation of such experiences had been formed by films of the Thirties, and his wife would in fact have their first baby in two weeks; since he also saw his opponent as tough, the pressure might be immense, but, as he saw it, he had to win. On just such trinities as poverty, babies, and tough opponents had John Garfield's movies been built.

Two decades later, Norman would not bother to think about a TV show until he was on it. He had learned over the years that the inner condition for projecting a firm and agreeable presence for TV was to be bored. Ideally, it was best to feel no more desire than a prostitute toward the tenth client of the night. This abyss between the luminosity of the outer appearance and the void of the inner dark was a phenomenon unique to TV participants, and might be the very health of the malignancy; it was certainly what kept television such a formidable foe. How could one battle a process that accommodated the emptiest space in oneself?

Of course, on the afternoon before his first television appearance, Mailer was hardly in possession of such wisdom. Rather, he was as tight as a man going to the electric chair. Trying to relax on his bed, adrenaline would take the best of him, and he would pace the room, and proceed to interrogate himself, asking the worst questions Mike Wallace might dare to ask, then search himself for the best of eight possible answers, a true fever! Young fighters dropped fights by squandering adrenaline before they reached the ring; they, too, were overcome with the monumental significance of whether they won or lost. Mailer, possessed of all the innocence of a protagonist who had never been on TV, did not understand he was entering no main event, but seeing the floor plans for a future mansion of Limbo; how was there a way to comprehend that he would not make history, but probably stifle it a little more?

It was a natural error to make. He could not, after all, get beyond the idea that he would be on the virgin air. If one said what one had to say with wit, conviction, and passion, if one said the unsayable, if people therefore heard something for the first time, passions ought to commence, buried sentiments could take life. But first he must be able to hold his own with Mike Wallace, and given Mailer's massive incapacity to stay cool, that was not automatic.

Wallace had become a success by way of a personality considerably at contrast to other TV hosts. His manner was not friendly but adversary. His straight black hair and craggy face gave off a presence as formidable as an Indian in a gray flannel suit. To this he added a humorless mind of which he was utterly unashamed, and used therefore as a weapon — no wit could slow his attack. His badly pitted skin suggested the unremitting stubbornness of a district attorney bitten hard enough in his youth to offer little mercy now. He was obviously not, like other interviewers, full of the very lard of companionability. Instead, Wallace gave the impression of wanting to interrogate further than the family manners of television permitted. Something of solemn, even heavy, purpose came off him, a distrust of human nature that was ready to focus on the probable insincerities of his guest. It was therefore a show to attract jokes about the masochism of people who would accept invitations from Mike Wallace, but Mailer, having studied the format for months, saw it as a rite of passage. If one wanted to make an impact on TV, *Night Beat* was the proper test.

By now, his own approach was as humorless as Wallace. He had so fired up the household, that his wife, in her ninth month, also took it as a test and put on a low-cut black velvet dress, thereby mustering her best appearance. Her hair was as black as Mike Wallace's and being a real Indian (Peruvian) she did her best to help her husband make a decent entrance. Indeed, she looked splendid and sent out the beauty of her pregnancy like a promulgation of status. Her mate might have been happier to come into a real ring with a trainer to massage the back of his neck, and he certainly had the ravenous flare in his throat that only true desire for whiskey can bring, but he also knew the happiness of the fighter — at long last, love! even if love is the pow of a glove and the rocketing of the ring lights. He felt equal to expectation itself — maybe he had never been as aware before of all of America out there — a pregnancy in the night itself equal to his awareness of a million homes tuning into *Night Beat.* In later years, when everything was taped, he would not often feel the sensation that everyone was listening as the sounds came out of his throat.

Now, the program began, that is, they took seats that had been set out facing each other, chatted a little — it was a false and most unnatural kind of chatting, like fighters meeting at a weigh-in — and then with thirty seconds to air-time, to Wallace's small but somewhat superior annoyance, Mailer poured his water back into the carafe, took a small flask of gin out of his pocket, and decanted half of it into the empty glass.

He was sipping the gin as they went on the air. Since his mind had been overworked for hours, the liquor did not relax his tongue so much as disconcert his head and burn his stomach.

"*Life* magazine accuses your novel, *The Deer Park,*" said Wallace in his opening and hortatory tones, "of dealing with immorality, alcoholism, perversion, and political terror in Hollywood. Why do you emphasize these themes?"

Mailer laid out the rights of a novelist to choose his subject, but his answer went on too long, and Wallace merely looked quizzical, self-centered, and superior in his lack of comprehension even as Norman said, "Only hypocrisy and insincerity are dirty. *Life* magazine is a dirty magazine."

So he felt uncomfortable through the early questions, going too long for one answer, too flippantly for another, only to be brusque on the third reply. He was like a tight-muscled fighter and could not seem to fake Wallace the least bit out. His voice began to grow dogged. On the other hand, Wallace did not seem comfortable either. Before one could expect it, the first commercial had come. One-third of the show was over, and it wasn't going as he had hoped.

He raised the ante. Mailer had an instinct for the wicked. If evil was to discover what was good, and proceed to destroy it, then how many people could ever learn enough to be evil? Wickedness was more available. Wickedness would consist of raising the ante without knowing what the consequences might be. It was a way of asking for peril without a clue to who would be hurt. Wickedness was what he leaped into tonight. It was as if the only means for dealing with Mike Wallace's imperturbable certainty that the people who ran things knew more than the people who didn't was to keep raising the ante of his replies. Before long, he was saying, "America is a great and prosperous country, but it is not a brave or noble country. Our leaders are drowning in conformity and act like *women.* "

(May it return a full sense of the Eisenhower period to recognize that our author was not near to suspecting a powerful movement would arise one day to banish men from public life for failing to refer to women as persons.)

Wallace, being equally ignorant of the future, looked awfully confident. "Who in high office," he asked in his deepest voice, "would you say is so feminine?"

Mailer came back with the first happiness he was ever to know on television. "President Eisenhower is a bit of a woman," he said into the ring of night around them, and was certain he could feel the instant when the heart of a million TV sets missed a beat.

Wallace never looked more like an Indian. His eyes grew as flat as the eyes of a movie Apache who has just taken a rifle bullet to the stomach.

"Come off it," he said. He, too, was listening to the silence in the living rooms.

"I mean just that," said Mailer.

They went on. The atmosphere was not dissimilar to the tension in a bar when a glass has been shattered and no apologies are made. They went through the half-hour to conclusion, and Mailer did a little better, and Wallace might have done a little less well, and the show came to its end. Mailer felt a great glow. He was immensely pleased with himself. In the elevator, going down to the street, his wife said, "Maybe we'll be dead tomorrow, but it was worth it." It is possible they never had a better moment together. They had been with each other for years, yet always fought in the animal rage of never comprehending one another. On this night, however, with the baby two weeks away, they were ready for one hour, at least, to die together. For once Mailer felt like a hero. In those days saying something bad about Dwight D. Eisenhower was a not great deal less atrocious than deciding Jesus Christ has something wrong with Him.

Our new TV talent waited therefore on large and scandalized results from this Wallace show. Nothing seemed to happen. Occasionally he would run into an old friend who had happened to see it, and would chuckle over his remark. Weeks later, he learned that James Hagerty, the Press Secretary to President Eisenhower, asked for a transcript. That was all he ever heard. The phone did not ring with invitations from network executives to discuss a new show built around his controversial personality. Indeed, he was not invited on other shows for a while. It was more than another year before he was asked by David Susskind to come on *Open End* with Dorothy Parker and Truman Capote.

Channel 5

In Limbo, it was becoming less difficult to understand why he always felt an instinctive distrust of the memoir. Part of one's share of anathema was to recollect the past in a style now analogous to the sentimental and streamlined details of the memoir. The final insult to one's life came by way of recognizing that one was here reduced to viewing the moral lessons of one's past through a film of slick. All the real, important, and (now that one was in Limbo) desperate meanings of one's acts slipped by, vague and smooth, almost without evaluation. The agreeable readability of the memoir (that property which made it perfect for the kind of magazines laid on airline passengers) was exactly what made it a torture now. Living among the glossy walls of Limbo, moral facts were hard enough to hold without the frictionless surface of a memoir.

Ergo, the author found himself shuddering — even if he did not know why — at the recollection, let us say at the reconstitution, of his experience on *Open End*, shivering indeed in that feverless ague where boredom is at last revealed as the ultimate protection against dread; yes, what better explanation for that family in the Utah desert staring at the video glass than precisely their awful if unstated decision, so gloomily made, that boredom was better than dread, that even an unpalatable mixture of boredom and dread was better than dread. Anything was better than that immense on-sliding

American dread. For here, on this northern half of the continent, where the uprooted had looked for every frontier that could be broken (since people without roots discover peace in the sound made by tearing up the roots of others — how else account for the glee of airplane designers at the sound of jet engines sucking up the promise of the nearby air, or the joy of a young criminal breaking into a home?) yes, here, dread was the ongoing uneasiness of those whose roots were cut (which automatically made America the country most possessed of dread, since how many in this country could find the house where they were born?) Yes, if dread was the communal American experience (how better account for the prodigious American fear of communism in those years after the Second World War when the USSR was at its weakest?) yes, if security against dread was the subtext behind every political movement in America, everything from right-wing fear of a conspiracy in high financial places to destroy Christianity forever, all the way over to the liberal terror that a violence was coming which would not be controlled by even the most sophisticated and enlightened social planning, then, given a dread so immense, it was easy to see why a man should be chosen for President so late as 1976 by way of a number of television debates that presented to the nation the first proposition of American politics: "When it comes to picking a President, Boredom is better than Dread!" So said the debates, and the power that was finally elected, the political movement whose real fortunes were advanced, was television itself, yes, television, with its silent radiating argument that it was the best political program yet found for the tranquilization of dread — "I will deaden you a little bit; you need it!"

Contrast these grim conclusions, arrived at in the bowels, that is to say in the glassy coils of Limbo, and compare them to the innocence of Norman's early assumption that television was a platform from which to incite an ideological riot, a God-given opportunity (offered by the complacency of the Establishment) to get the truth out; perhaps, we can learn, after all, why he shuddered at the recollection of his appearance with Dorothy Parker and Truman Capote. He was now suffering from the derision of Limbo; few souls offend it more than the actor who believes he is becoming a protagonist when he is only turning into a comedian, and this unpleasant thought now as unable to move out of his head as a jellyfish fixed on the sand, he was able for a space to feel the grit of reality, and thereby found himself thinking again, and with considerable pain, of the expression on Dorothy Parker's face when he first saw her standing on the studio floor in Newark waiting for the arrival of Capote and himself. She had earlier been picked up in Manhattan, as they had been later, by a dark Cadillac limousine, furnished by the studio, to carry them to New Jersey for a few hours, and the expression in her eyes suggested that that was outrage enough in itself — to be found in Newark!

Dorothy Parker was not to shine on this night. It was to be her first appearance on TV (and probably her last) and never may a video camera have been less disposed toward a talented writer. She was not, in person, a large woman, nor by the measure of her literary wit, a bold woman. Anyone who had read Dorothy Parker, and was expecting therefore a lady of immaculate wit and elegant savagery of tongue, would feel on the consequence when meeting her, a discernible shock. She was tiny, and she tended to be plump. She had bags under her eyes (from the fatigues of three good decades of drinking) and these bags touched the heart in a way few middle-aged women and only a very few middle-aged men with wondrously lugubrious bags can so touch us. (Perhaps it is by way of the sorrows they have bottomed out on while drinking.) Dorothy Parker looked like a bird at the mercy of every beast with teeth, a flurry of feathers up in a tree with wonderful bags under her eyes. And in the middle of her sad little face, sad as the ghost of tenderness itself, was her nose, the tip of which was always overpowdered. She would dust it once with a swipe to one nostril, and again with a swipe to the other, the overlay thereby suggesting the white painted button of a clown who is more lugubrious than his bulbous red-tipped colleagues.

She also wore a series of black shawls and garments to give her the appearance of a British witch. The garments looked to have come from an attic. Since Norman met her first in Los Angeles, seven or eight years before the evening they went on in Newark, he could not imagine at the time where she found her clothes. Los Angeles was a city whose homes were conspicuously without attics.

She also had a manner that was gentle, full of praise, and treacherous as a scorpion. The day he was introduced, an agent who would later be powerful enough to deal with the memoirs of presidents and kings was in Dorothy Parker's room at the Chateau Marmont, and she gave the agent nothing but compliments, sweet compliments in a tender threadbare little voice that spoke of his energy, (boundless!) his good-will (Christly) and his genius (large enough to sell one of her poor scripts; he, he alone, could do it!) and the agent having left in all the happiness of being given these compliments by a great American writer — he was still a young agent, pushy, and prematurely bald — she said, so soon as the door was closed, "Agggrhh" — a clearing of the throat in pure facsimile to that first blast of the interior when vomiting — and added, "What an awful man. What a dreadful dreadful man!"

After that meeting, Mailer always did his best to be the last to leave Dottie Parker's sitting room at the Chateau Marmont. Once, confessing to Lillian Hellman his concern at how Dorothy Parker might describe him in his absence, Miss Hellman laughed with the happiness she always felt in being generous, instructive, and superior to the innocence of her friends, and said, "Norman, everyone knows that Dottie will talk about you after you leave the room. It will amount to no more than the compliments she's just given you. Everybody who cares about Dottie knows that's the price to pay." And she laughed gaily.

Still, Norman wanted Dottie Parker's real affection. He wanted the lovely things she said to him on one side of the door to be repeated on the other. Since they got along very well, and he was always proud to invite her to his rented house, and pleased to be invited back to her poor suite at the Marmont (she had no money in those years — all the splendid short stories and no money!) he even entertained the illusion that she might offer a dispensation.

He would never find out, however, because of her dog. She had a Boxer, not a year old, named Bruce, who had been badly mistreated by his first owners, and now whimpered at harsh looks. Dottie did her best to give the dog more courage — she raised him like the child she had never had, ready to take Bruce up each rung of the mile-high ladder that climbs from abysmal cowardice to transcendental courage; she would tell her friends of each new advance Bruce and she had made. One would learn that Bruce had gotten up his nerve sufficiently one day to take a walk around the block with her.

These methods seemed intolerably slow to Norman. He kept telling her that she ought to bring Bruce over to meet his dog. Since Dorothy Parker had by now made friends with Karl, she was tempted. Timid people were invariably proud of such a friendship for Karl was a black German Shepherd, huge and ferocious to strangers. Since his first allegiance was to the house, his master became whoever lived in the house (and incidentally fed him). Norman, renting the place, was therefore the master and thus became the only man in Laurel Canyon who could drive up to the house, get out of his car, and not be attacked. No one else dared. Our best-selling young author used to run out to the driveway when guests came; otherwise visitors were obliged to cower inside their vehicle while the dog would lunge at the windows. Once Norman got out, however, and barked, "Karl!" the Shepherd immediately subsided. He could now recognize that these intruders would be acceptable to the house. After they were admitted to the living room, Karl would even go over, sit down on the floor, and make a point of shaking hands with them. Delighted that the dog had become well-disposed, the new arrival would make much of this. Karl would extend his paw for a second greeting. His tongue would loll and he would pant a little. After the third handshake, Karl would get a hard-on. "*Karl!*" his master would say, and the hard-on would go away. Under such circumstances, it became easy to think of him as an overrated danger.

So when Dorothy Parker finally decided that she might bring Bruce to the house, Mailer thought it was a terrific idea. He would take care of bringing them together peacefully, he promised. Good to his word, he put Karl away in the bedroom before Dorothy Parker arrived with Bruce. The Boxer, however, did not want to quit the car. He could hear the other beast.

"It'll be all right," said Mailer cheerfully, "once Bruce is inside. Karl is really lonesome."

Coaxed within the house, however, Bruce urinated on the carpet. It was not difficult to forgive him. In the bedroom, Karl was making that sound a cat will make when a dog is near, and she is ready to fight for her life. It is a more awesome sound when it comes from a large hound.

"Don't you think this is a mistake?" said Dottie Parker. "I can put Bruce in the car and go home now."

That would be a loss for Bruce, he answered. "Why don't I put Karl on a leash, and bring them together slowly? It'll be so good for Bruce if he and Karl can make friends."

This liberal and romantic expectation prevailed. Karl was brought out of the bedroom. The dog came quietly on his tether, and looked at Bruce without a sound. He sniffed the other's nose. A pause. Bruce peed. Karl's head went off in a roar as loud as a howitzer. His mouth opened into shark's teeth and flayed the air with strings of saliva; at this point his master was sufficiently outraged to yank him back by the neck, and manhandle him to the bedroom. In the space this took, Dottie Parker was out the door, and in her car. Before she could drive away, Norman came running out to find Bruce collapsed in the rear seat. The dog's limbs were vibrating. It was that quiver which will not cease until the nerve dies.

"I said it wouldn't work," said Dottie Parker face to face. She imparted this in a tone of whole reproach as if to tell him that the worst damage a friend can wreak is to convince you to be brave when you know you are right to be cautious, and then proceed to prove that indeed you were right. It throws you back even further upon yourself when that is no place to be.

As she drove off, he knew that he had wanted to bring Karl from the bedroom because he wished to show how well he could control the dog. Besides he had been curious on the outcome. He noticed that he did not feel very sorry. Only chagrined. But then the wicked are famous for offering small remorse.

Channel 6

He was not to see Dottie Parker again until this evening they would meet on *Open End* eight years later, and when he arrived at the studio in Newark, and saw her waiting, older, more fragile, close to desperately nervous and certainly not cordial, his feelings were only in a small way hurt that she was not happy to see him again, and showed an obvious preference for Truman Capote. He was, by his own measure, not the same writer she had known before. He had met her, after all, in the season after *The Naked and the Dead* when he went out to Hollywood, and much had been made of him. Now, after this early success, he had gone through a number of years in which people spoke of him as a failure. Since he had written two novels, *Barbary Shore* and *The Deer Park*, which he thought had received unfair reviews, he had a view of himself that was at odds with others, and he did not like to be snubbed by people who had been friendly to him ten years ago. All the same, it gave justification to his anger. So her unfriendliness left him in a well-balanced position. If it came to it, he would not have to be too friendly on the show.

David Susskind also gave small welcome. "We met a long time ago," Susskind said.

"I remember."

"I do, too," said Susskind in a chilly voice. It had been at a party on a very hot summer night in 1948, and they had talked on a Manhattan roof. Susskind was then a young agent, and he had wanted to sell *The Naked and the Dead* to the movies. Mailer had made fun of him. "Don't you understand?" he had said to Susskind, "*they* can't make it into a film, and I don't want it made."

Of course, years later, he sold it after all, and *they* had made a very bad film. So he felt at a disadvantage now with Susskind and said, "Maybe I should have listened to you."

Susskind's face showed what he thought of people who were rude years ago and ready to flatter now. Their relations for this night were certainly not off to a good start.

He had only Capote. They had gotten along well on the drive out to Newark, each — they had not met before — intensely curious of the other. Since Mailer's wife accompanied him again, and again was looking her best, he had made a point of having her sit between Truman and himself. Since she was twice Truman's size and had the overpowering sexuality, on occasion — this was such an occasion — of her burgeoning Latin blood, it had been an advantage equal to playing on one's home court.

Truman did much complaining on the trip out. "I didn't want to do this show," he said in a dry little voice that seemed to issue from an unmoistened reed in his nostril, "I told Bennett Cerf it was a mistake, but Bennett thinks television is going to be very important for selling our books. I hope he's wrong," said Truman Capote and laughed.

Once the show began, Norman thought himself splendid. Unlike the night with Mike Wallace, he felt at his best, thoughts came clearly, he was full of energy and the others seemed bewildered. Susskind labored in the early minutes to put Dorothy Parker at ease but he was not able to succeed; she simply would not trust him. She spoke in a pained and quavering voice, hardly able to make herself heard. Truman did not add much, and Mailer, pleased with his powers, began to take over. Soon he and Susskind were doing most of the talking, that is, most of the debating, for it was obvious Susskind was irritated by what he had to say. Whenever Norman would launch on a flight of what he considered well-stated criticism of society, Susskind would make a point of looking at his watch. Whenever he could, Susskind tried to give time to the others, but it did not work. The others seemed apathetic. Once, while executing a panegyric about politicians, Norman Mailer flew so high as to say, "They're all whores."

Dottie Parker interrupted then to say with a little real force, "That's a sweeping remark."

"Well," said Mailer, "it may be sweeping, but it certainly is true."

It put Dorothy Parker back into silence — who was she, after all, to defend politicians? — and it irritated Susskind more. After close to an hour of TV time that felt wholly enjoyable to Mailer, he began to grow irritated at Susskind's efforts to slow him up. Since his host seemed determined to shut off this most interesting part of the show, Norman could see no reason not to allow the host to hang himself, and so he ceased speaking. Susskind began immediately to draw upon Truman Capote, and Capote, having digested a few of the peculiar processes of this odd medium, and measured the possible fit for himself, began at last to speak, and was, Mailer thought, not unamusing. He laughed encouragingly at Truman's remarks; he offered attention. Truman was so tiny that something gallant came to you from the fact of his existence itself. Mailer felt generous indeed. Few moods are as charitable as this sensation of being physically superior to everyone in the room.

In such a state, feeling handsome, vital, and more interesting than anyone had a right to be, he got into a discussion with Truman about the merits of Jack Kerouac. Since Mailer was not without his jealousy of the large attention paid Kerouac that year, he gave a defense of *On the Road* that was built on the basis of calling Kerouac, Jack — that is, he was two-thirds for Jack's virtues and one-third against Jack's vices.

Capote detested Kerouac. As Mailer grew benign, Capote grew precise. He rose at last to his own peroration and invoked the difficulties of the literary craft in contrast to Mr. Kerouac's undisciplined methods of work. Finally, in a tone of fearless and absolute severity, Capote said: "It is not writing. It is only typing."

"I agree," said Dorothy Parker in a hoarse voice.

"Well, I don't," said Mailer, only to give a limp defense. He was empty of vast indignation at this dreadful put-down of Kerouac. He even decided it might look good to let Truman have his winning little moment, certainly better than trying to hog the show.

Open End came to a finish. As they walked off the set, a few technicians were studying the kinescope of what they had just done. Therefore, Parker, Capote, Susskind, Mailer and Mrs. Mailer stopped to watch a minute of it.

Dorothy Parker did not look good on TV. She took one peek at herself, gasped, and said to Susskind, "No, I really don't want to see another instant of it." Solicitous as St. Peter, Susskind led her away.

In contrast, Norman Mailer had the pleasure of seeing himself as he wanted to look. The kinescope caught him as he was making a point, and his face looked forceful, his language was good, yes, he appeared even better on TV, he thought, than in the mirror. "Didn't I tell you," said Truman, "that you're terrific on this? You're *telegenic!*" It was true. But then, in every intermission, Truman had been telling him how splendidly he was doing.

Truman groaned when the camera shifted to him. There was a medium shot of Truman looking a hint bewildered at the beginning of the show, and he winced as he heard his voice. "I told my publishers I shouldn't go on," he declared with annoyance.

In the limousine on the way back to Manhattan, Truman kept saying, "I shouldn't have done it. I didn't want to, I've never appeared on television, not once — even though I've had many invitations — and I certainly oughtn't to have been here tonight. What I can do is special, it's *very* literary, and I shouldn't attempt to *intrude* my personality. I'm not good at that like you, Norman. Television is good for you."

Mailer lay back in the limousine, enjoying a winner's ride, and his wife said encouragingly to Capote, "You were good, too, Truman. You really got better as it went on."

"Do you think so?" asked Truman. "Do you really think so?"

Now, both Mr. and Mrs. Mailer assured Truman Capote that he was better than he thought he had been.

"Well, at least," said Truman, "I was better than poor Dorothy Parker. When she looked at herself afterward . . ." He shuddered in sympathy. "Wasn't that *Disasterville?*" They laughed, but not in pleasure at her woe so much as in wonder at the clear lines of Judgment itself.

Truman could not quite get out of his bad mood, however. Before they said goodnight he suggested they have a drink with him at El Morocco. Before long, they thought to have supper. Despite all the sandwiches served on *Open End,* they were starved. Truman insisted on treating. A prince, he seemed to hint, must play the host after a sorry loss — it is the only way to come close to one's blood again.

It was late on Sunday night and they had the place to themselves. Under the solicitousness of the waiters and the captain, and finally the manager himself, who all came over to assure Capote of their unremitting attention, under the spell of this wholly superior service Truman was obviously accustomed to receiving whenever he went into El Morocco, his spirits not only revived but turned charming, and he began to offer an attention to Adele Mailer that had her believing in the unique properties of her attractiveness and her wit; yes, Truman was charming. Mailer saw why he had become the in-house author of the most important hostesses in New York, and envied him honestly, the way one good athlete will have respect for another. Just as a pitcher will think, "If I had as much stuff to my curve, I'd win more games because of my superior ball sense," so did Mailer think wistfully that if he could get to a few of the select parties Truman got to, why, boy, he'd have more to say about society. Of course, how could you be a radical yet intimate to the top drawer of the world — that was the iron warp of irony itself.

They had a fine time. They discovered unexpected points of agreement, and lively places to disagree; they had each had such curiosity about the other after all these years — their first novels had come out within a year of one another; both had been celebrated almost instantly. It was a grand evening, and at the end, Truman announced they would be great friends forever, and thanked them for taking him through what would otherwise have been a terribly depressing night — "God, was I awful on that show," he said as they parted, and he made a face to simulate the gargoyle of godawfulness.

There were not many nights when Norman Mailer went to bed so pleased with his wife, himself, and what they were able to do for each other as on this evening. He woke up early in the morning, enjoyed his breakfast, and could hardly wait for the phone to ring, and the praises of his friends to begin. But when he had heard from his parents (who loved the show) from an aunt and uncle (loved the show) from his sister who liked what he had done ("generally") and was somewhat taken with Truman, "what an interesting personality he has really," she said; and when he had gotten tired of waiting for friends to ring, and called up one instead, there was a pause at the other end, and then the friend said in sorrow, "Oh, man, did Truman take you!"

He called other friends. They seemed not to have seen the show and left a pall equal to the message of the medium itself. He went out on the street for a walk; since he was living in Greenwich Village, it was not hard to run into a few acquaintances. One stopped, saluted, and said: "It is not writing; it is *only* typing," and gave a long phlegmy laugh as he went on down the street. Another said, "Truman; too much!" A third said, "Could you get me to meet Capote?"

More serious friends were balanced. "In terms of polemical points, I think you made the most. Of course, Capote does suggest real authority."

He called Truman a couple of days later.

"Yes," said Capote, "isn't it the *strangest* thing? Everybody has been telling me how marvelous I was. I can't believe it. 'Norman Mailer is the one who was marvelous,' I say to them, and they reply, 'Truman, you were *wunderbar*. Don't sell yourself short.' 'Honey,' I told this friend, 'I been short all my life,'" Truman guffawed with pleasure even more profound than the night at El Morocco. "It certainly is a mystery," he said with complacency.

Mailer couldn't bear it. He finally called *Open End* and asked to see a kinescope. It became his first introduction to our hypothesis that television is not a technological process that reproduces images of real life by way of electronics, but is rather a machine (more or less cosmically operated) to anticipate the judgments and/or anathema of Limbo; the technicians pitch in with camera angles.

He discovered that the nice close-up he had seen of himself immediately after the show was one of the few close-ups they had chosen to give him. The more he talked, and the more Susskind looked at his watch, why the more they relegated him to medium shots and long shots. There is something pathetic about a man speaking at the bottom of a long shot: he does not sound convinced by himself. He is, after all, at the end of the tunnel.

In contrast, they gave many close-ups to Truman. Capote did not look small on the show but large! His face, in fact, was extraordinary, that young-old face, still pretty and with such promise of oncoming ugliness; that voice, so full of snide rustlings and unforgiving nasalities; it was a voice to knock New York on its ear. The voice had survived; it spoke of horrors seen and passed over; it told of judgments that would be merciless.

Watching the kinescope, Mailer realized at last what an impact Capote had made on the television viewers of New York. They had never seen anyone remotely like him. Once Truman finally opened his mouth, the camera never left his face. The camera would turn to Capote even as Norman was speaking.

His own arguments that sounded so forceful to him a few nights ago now seemed vague, and with his beard, pious. (He shaved off

the beard a week or two later.) Talking about large matters on television with all the passion and all the lack of specific detail these immense theses encouraged, speaking in a voice that came out of the
depths of a medium shot proved to be not nearly so exhilarating to a
viewer as it had felt for him in the middle of articulating his
thoughts. His obvious pride in his ideas now seemed fatuous. His
physical superiority was gone. He was only intense, vague, and a bit
out of focus. Whereas Capote took his unforgettable personality and
added to it, practicality, common sense, and pride. In so misty a
medium, the best gift a guest could provide was pearls. The certainty of a pearl! Yes, to light upon a problem and come up with a
good one-line answer was to produce a pearl of the mind. How
much interest could viewers have in a point that took five minutes to
make? That was something they could not do. It spoke of too good a
college education. So they preferred people with a one-line answer,
barroom knockouts, one-punch pearls. There is no man or woman
on the street whose mind will not produce a pearl from time to time.
They loved Truman because he had given them "It is not writing. It
is only typing."

From now on, thought Mailer, he would not try to show how intelligent he was; he would look for pearls. That became his latest
hypothesis: the light from a TV screen was flattering to a pearl.

Of course, he was always miserable without an hypothesis. The
hypothesis could later prove invalid, but it had to be interesting
enough so that he could live with it for a while. That the orgy would
benefit humankind more than the family was one of his early hypotheses, Bolshevist as hell. That the war in Vietnam was a bad war
because rich boys should not fight poor boys unless there was equality in the weapons was another, and that offered the best of conservative principles: the rich had better be terrific. Whether the particular hypothesis was good or bad, however, he leaned on it. There
was something so rigid in his upbringing that for reference he had
great need of a straight line — a straight line is, after all, the very
first of the hypotheses (and, according to Einstein, wholly incorrect,
since no line can run straight in space given the curly route of a light
wave and the oval field of magnetic force). Mailer sometimes wondered if he was one of the first to recognize that 186,000 miles a second was not the true speed of light, but only its calculated progress
along a nonexistent straight line. If you measured the speed of light
by the time it took to wind through the waves, then a beam might
travel up to 1,000,000 miles a second in order to traverse 186,000

miles. That, doubtless, was one more reason why the sum of a million was magical to Americans.

Such were a few of Mailer's conclusions after his defeat by Capote.

The next time they met, Truman had a new assurance to put on top of the old one. In these few weeks, he confessed, there had been numerous invitations, all turned down, to appear on other shows; a difference in Truman's idea of himself had begun to appear. That personality he had presented, with all his early bravado, to a most special part of the world, was, it seemed, going to be accepted by all the world. He obviously felt stronger already. And Mailer, stunned as any confident contender who has been abruptly knocked out, now felt, measure to measure, weaker. It was obvious to him (for no one understands the future reactions of a snob so well as an unsuccessful snob) that never again would Truman spend a night trying to recoup the losses of his ego out of *this* Mr. and Mrs. Mailer.

Channel 7

Years later, Norman would decide that television was one of those hostesses who were most impressed if you were somewhat unimpressed to find yourself in her home, and that was easy enough to handle. It was just that on television, your real hostess had to be the spirit of the electrons. While nobody was in command of enough physics to explore the idea that some men and women tend to attract electrons, while others most certainly repulse them, it seemed reasonable to suppose that electrons might conduct relations with more than a few forces, satanic and divine, and so could be working in unseen harness to focus or ruin your TV appearance. Translated, that should be able to state: The telegenic have good bioelectric relations with the tube, and these relations may yet be measured. Of course, Norman, biased to the depths of his unexpected defeats, was convinced that zombies were the first to benefit from such relations.

These were conclusions he came to with reluctance. He was plagued in those years by the divide between his absolute, if somewhat improbable, sense of intellectual mission, and his incapacity to work at anything like the necessary pace to accomplish his wonders. He thought, without admitting it to himself, that television might be a way to express ideas that would otherwise never reach an audience, not if they had to wait for the writing. (Obviously, he wished to lift himself to heaven by the power of his speech — a little misapprehension of cosmic reality that he only came to recognize when his later writing, so well praised, raised him no higher than Limbo.)

Of course, he had an idea not easy to express under any quick circumstances, and hardly by way of the pearl: he saw a conspiracy in society to destroy existence. Being blessed with no ear for the finer sounds of nature, he did not hear the drip of pollution in the conduits; he only felt the stifling of his own existence. That, of course, is enough. It may be even a sign of health to sense danger to nature in every little death to oneself.

So he wanted to be on TV; so he told himself; he would be on it to shout the alarm. So he saw every appearance where he did well as a decent effort committed to his side of the gods; yes, he would do his best to get the great dialectic of society unfrozen once more — that was the dialectic where the people knew enough to affect even the most skillful manipulations of the establishment — he would, yes, try to get such a dialectic going. A mature democratic society was worth zero without it. He did not understand that *something* was calculating how to cancel more than one dialectic.

Still, these were the early years of TV. He had a few moments when he felt as if he broke through. It was not entirely a string of disasters. He had, after all, the illimitable freedom (in early 1960) of saying late one evening on Irv Kupcinet's show in Chicago that he thought J. Edgar Hoover had done more harm to America than Joseph Stalin, and so had the pleasure of being the center of attention one early morning in Chicago; Kup's show by 1960 was big news to the local audience, for it had an ability to gather all the visiting firemen passing through. An amazing number of people would therefore come home on Saturday night and go into four A.M. of Sunday morning watching *At Random*. This was March in 1960, after all, nine months before Jack Kennedy was inaugurated, and how many in Chicago had something better to do at that hour if they could not sleep?

"Yes," Norman repeated, "J. Edgar Hoover has paralyzed the imagination of this country in a way Joseph Stalin never could," and the other guests put their hands in the air to state that they were not opposed to J. Edgar Hoover. The former president of the B'nai B'rith was a guest, and the Lord Mayor of Dublin was another; a chief from the national police of Sudan made a third; a woman reporter who had traveled with Eisenhower in South America composed a fourth; they all were in a hurry to swear their allegiance to Hoover.

Later, after the show, he heard that a large number of calls had come in, forty-eight in fact. He had always assumed that thousands of calls came to such shows every night. He did not yet know that television did not send you to the telephone, let alone the barricades. Still, forty-eight calls had come at two in the morning. Twenty-eight had opposed what he said; twenty approved. Since no call was counted unless you left your name, it meant that twenty people (with whatever number of false names among them) had been ready to agree. That count was as agreeably astonishing to Norman Mailer on that night as Gene McCarthy's forty percent against Lyndon Johnson's forty-eight percent in New Hampshire would seem apocalyptic to the media in '68. Mailer felt an intimation for the first time that the Sixties might bring a few changes to the old game.

Eighteen years later, obtaining his FBI file by way of the Freedom of Information Act, he would discover that out of three hundred xeroxed and highly deleted pages sent to him, more than thirty were devoted to his single appearance on Kupcinet's show. Let us depart from Limbo long enough to see how language sounds in the real world.

TO: DIRECTOR, FBI
FROM: SAC, CHICAGO
SUBJECT: NORMAN MAILER, PANELIST
                IRVING KUPCINET
                "AT RANDOM" TV PROGRAM
                MARCH 20, 1960
                INFORMATION CONCERNING

NORMAN MAILER is an admitted "leftist." He is also an author, his most popular work being the novel "The Naked And The Dead." His remarks clearly reflect his animosity toward the Bureau.

The enclosed text clearly reflects that other noted panelists on the program definitely and specifically disagreed with and refuted his observations.

A number of persons in Chicago have personally commented to me that MAILER made an ass of himself on the program, and all such comments received have been definitely pro Bureau and anti MAILER.

RE: NORMAN MAILER

During the program, the participants engaged in a discussion relating to the Federal Bureau of Investigation. These remarks are being included below in summary form and at pertinent places verbatim.

MAILER talked of the United States as the most powerful nation in the world after World War II with the exception of Russia, and both these countries, who had no tradition of ruling, fought about who would rule. The United States began to ape the methods of Russia with the tactics of the Communists being taken by Madison Avenue, the term used to indicate the advertising agencies who run the mass media. MAILER went on to say:

> I said the other day in an interview that we have a very subtle totalitarianism here, a pleasant totalitarianism, in that we don't have concentration camps. We don't have a secret police everywhere. We do have an FBI which is one of the two religions left in America. There's the FBI and medical science.

ELAINE SHEPHERD: And hooray for the Federal Bureau of Investigation.

MAILER: Well, I would say three cheers against them. I am for putting them down. I say let's have no more of the FBI; they are running the country.

SHEPHERD: You can't be serious.

MAILER said he had only one more comment to make with regard to Miss SHEPHERD's saying the Communist aim is to make America soft.

MAILER: This country was softened up but not by the Communists. It was softened up by the FBI, by Joe McCARTHY, by the House Un-American Affairs (*sic*) Committee, by the peculiar, subtle psychological reign of terror that went on in this country five years ago. . . .

KLUTZNICK: People have abused J. EDGAR HOOVER, and there are times when I have been angry at him myself for some things he said, but let's put it this way. He has given us a kind of police administration that people like Inspector Hamid and others all over the world respect because of its efficiency, and more than its efficiency, its peculiar devotion to staying within that law which it is permitted to stay within and nothing more.

SHEPHERD: At really comparatively low salaries. These are dedicated men.

KLUTZNICK: This is very important to remember.

MAILER: This is marvelous, but I would like to say something. You speak of efficiency. You speak of the low salary the people have who work for it. . . . I will also say that the concentration camps at Buchenwald were run in exactly the same way; they were terribly efficient.

KLUTZNICK: This is not true.

MAILER: They were efficient. The people who worked there received low wages relatively, and they probably kept within the directives that were issued to them.

SHEPHERD: Now, that is beneath the dignity of sophistry.

There was a momentary digression with some remarks on the meaning of sophistry.

KLUTZNICK: No, but look. I read the records of Buchenwald —

MAILER: Now, I didn't say — I didn't say —

BRISCOE: You said they were efficient and with low salary.

MAILER: I didn't say that the FBI is a Buchenwald. I only said that the virtues you ascribe to the FBI can be ascribed to the concentration camps.

The discussion turned to the proposition of the police as a necessary evil.

MAILER: . . . the man in the street does not have a specific knowledge of the right things and the wrong things that the FBI does. He has a general knowledge of them and a general fear of them and a general respect for them which, I say, is too great. Because what I am getting at is this. There has been so much damn fear in this country for the last five or ten years . . . that people in this country are being worn down and they are being softened, and they are turning apathetic, and there's getting to be very little passion left in American life, and this was about the most passionate country in the history of the earth at one time, and the most adventurous and the bravest and the boldest, and it has become a cowardly, sleek, soft, fat country.

KLUTZNICK: I would agree with some of that.

MAILER: What I am saying is that this is exactly the climate which the Russians adore, and if they ever come over here, the first thing they would do is that they would have their secret police chief get together with the FBI, and you would be amazed at how little time it would take — We are exactly creating a totalitarian climate in this country which will make it possible for the Russians to come over and take us with no pain at all.

SHEPHERD: You are questioning the patriotic integrity of our federal agents?

MAILER: That they are patriotic I would not deny for a moment. I am sure they are all passionately in love with America, and maybe a little bit too much in love with America. The thing is that I distrust it.

KUPCINET: I can agree with NORM that we should stand back and take a look from a distance; don't be swelled up by anything you read about anything. Ask questions about everything, and this would be a better democracy.

In another part of his file, Mailer found a letter from SAC, New York, to the Director of the FBI. It was dated March 25, 1960.

Information has been received that Mailer, in an appearance on the Chicago television program, "At Random," on 3/20/60, advocated the abolition of the FBI. He said the FBI was too efficient against communism and was connected with McCarthyism and the House Committee on Un-American Activities. He also said that the FBI's efficiency "created a psychological atmosphere on the part of the public and that the public is being protected from communism" and that the public, and not the FBI, should be allowed to decide for itself what is good for it.

You are requested to bring the investigation of Mailer up to date.

Channel 8

He could hardly have known the FBI was taking such interest in his few remarks — he did not really believe in his own paranoia — yet somewhere in those market places of sleep where the knowledge of one dreamer passes over to another, in those psychic flights that lift from the mind and are on the air, maybe we reach another human despite all the crackling and confusion and outright din of all those amplified waves electronically induced by torture of the air itself, maybe our own thoughts, often so noble as to originate out of the magnetism of human mood itself, also pass back and forth like radio waves and come into our sleep despite the interference of every electronically communicating machine, yes, come to us through all the jammed air and defoliated fields of lost prayer. (Is that any more difficult to believe than that one corporate machine can pass a message to another when they do not touch?) So some obscure but real message may have come to him that the FBI had bit on his words and he had pricked their blood; afterward he was fortified in the notion that TV could be a forum for ideas, at least for ideas that came in the shape of pearls — J. Edgar Hoover has done more harm to the minds of America than Joseph Stalin — and you could change people's lives and give a shift to society; you need only be good enough to do it.

So, he kept the idea that he would yet learn to handle himself on the most obdurate and repellent medium in which he ever worked. He certainly kept appearing on TV shows. As the years went by and a little more literary work began to get done, there seemed always a new book for which it was natural to go on TV. Of course, TV did not help his books to sell — not with his personality! — but still he went on. He learned that an appearance on TV left you feeling as agreeable as a session with a doctor and an X-ray machine; he learned that the taste of aspirin (was it ashes?) would follow in the mouth; he learned that you formed no friendships with other guests on a show for everyone split the moment a program was done as if they had all been participants in a bloodless sexless and faintly disgusting orgy — some high whinny of sanitized shit was in the sniff of the air. He learned that the pioneer days of TV were indeed over, for only one experience on TV had been great, and that was to be on *live*, on to feel the unfelt oncoming reaction of millions of people all at once — that was gone. Now, every show was taped, which is to say ninety-nine out of a hundred shows were taped, and the others were either early in the morning, or news shows, and the anchor men read their texts. It meant that you were usually recorded at ten in the morning or six in the evening for a show that might go on at midnight that night, or on a night next week, or in half a year, and so you were skewed out of time. The subtle emotions of a previous day and another hour would go into the midnight perceptions of an audience who would be obliged to assume — even when they knew better — that you were speaking to them at that moment even though you were not, and that was a subtle poison to slip into the perceptions of anyone studying a TV set, not to speak of the chop laid into the waves on wherever was the sea of time.

Yet if nearly everything but the early morning shows were now taped, and even the *Today* show had a seven-second lag between what you said and the instant it reached the audience's ear, time precisely for fuck-the-President to come out as "Bleep the President" — sounds in any case that only a madman would be able to make at seven twenty-two A.M. — if you knew as you got on the air, therefore, that the air was not the air, no more than the last shiver of a transcendental act is going to pass through the lining of a condom; if some technician had his fingernails on a knob between you and the air, then you were not live, you were captive. Words good enough or conceivably great enough to move the doors of history in any future time of stress would never get into the transmitter. If a subtle totalitarianism or an outright fascism came to America, then the instrument to control TV had already been installed — your words were taped, and on occasion they were bleeped. Even a hero looked like a chicken when his words were bleeped.

Still, he went on shows. He could not rid himself of the notion that it was a technique worth learning. Besides it is pretentious to look for virginity in the midst of the promiscuous. So he went on Joey Franklin, and on Mike Douglas and David Frost and Cavett and Merv Griffin and Carson and even appeared on Steve Allen in a ghost of the old show. He went on CBS and NBC and ABC, he went early in the morning to be taped live, that is with a seven-second hitch, and went in the late afternoon to be seen in the middle of the night and he went on Channels 5 and 9 and 11 and 13, and station KNET in Los Angeles, some such letters, and other letters for Detroit and Houston and San Francisco and Cincinnati, New Orleans and Chicago, Denver and Atlanta and Toronto and Washington and Philly, he went on with athletes and singers and dress designers and comedians, with ingenues and the inventors of novelty products, with doctors who knew diets and doctors who could speak of sex, he went on with worthy and self-serving politicians and lawyers for newsworthy rights, and once he even went on with Mother Teresa and Malcolm Muggeridge; he took what was offered, seeking to refine a technique whose first lesson he might never have learned, yet something in his stubbornness insisted on keeping the idea; he must use every means to advance his idea, and rarely did. And over the years, his idea changed. For if in the beginning he had seen a conspiracy by society to stifle existence, he came in time to think there was a conspiracy in one part of the cosmos to destroy the existence of the rest of the cosmos, and how do you get such an idea across, when it involves a train trip to Philadelphia, a half-hour with Mike Douglas and Rocky Graziano, and back again? He could have been a wrestler working one night in Atlantic City, the next in Pittsburgh, he took falls that would have broken his back if he had

had a literary sensibility left, he listened to Joe Garagiola once on the *Today* show reading from *Why Are We in Vietnam?* "Bleep," said Garagiola pretending to read from the novel, "I want to bleep-ing tell you that that's bleeping bleep when the bleeps hit the bleep." It was proper payment for going on the *Today* show to try to advance the fortunes of *Why Are We in Vietnam?* On the other hand, it was just a wrestler's loss; he was supposed to lose that event.

He went on wherever they invited him. He would go on Bob Cromie's *Book Beat*, and act like a gentleman, he would go on Susskind again, and again, he was on with Buckley once in '64, and Buckley finally allowed that Russell Kirk was right in calling Norman Mailer a freak, and Mailer in simple pain (you weren't supposed to get hurt in wrestling) said, "If you think I'm a freak, why did you invite me to dinner?" and Buckley shrugged and said, "No matter," and Mailer never forgave himself for not throwing a punch at that moment (except he wanted to get over the reputation he threw punches at people). He waited for the next show they were on together — it was Les Crane who had the new interview show that year — and Mailer called Buckley a very bad word, and Buckley, as if he had been waiting a year for this, calmly raised his hand to Les Crane and said, "I assume you're cutting this out of the show," and Crane said of course he would, and a few hours later, since Buckley was drinking with Mailer in the best good-will, Norman apologized, for he knew the word he had called Buckley was not true, or in any case — how was one to know of anyone? — not fair, and finally probably not a sin, and Buckley accepted in good grace. Hours later, Mailer began to brood over the little fact that Buckley had not apologized in turn and then he began to wonder if one of the reasons for the Buckley family fortunes was that they did not go around exchanging apologies for too little. Buckley invited him once to *Firing Line* and he had the pleasure of telling Bill that he thought Fidel Castro and Charles de Gaulle were the only heroes he could find in the modern world, and Buckley may even have missed a breath on that remark. Mailer was beginning to take pleasure in his pearls. Like an old pederast who keeps warm with the memories of a few divine young phalluses he has seen, Mailer lived with the memory of a few of his remarks. Once, in London, on David Frost's *Saturday Night* show, on the night he met Frost, David had come at him like a British heavyweight mauler, no great skill, but plenty of shove, "All right, Norman Mailer, you've written that sex can be killing. What do you mean by that?"

"David, I don't think one should talk about sex on TV."

"Why don't you?"

"It's like talking about your wife."

"Now, Norman, you said sex is killing, you wrote that right here, and we want to know: What is so killing about sex?"

It was a live show. They still had live shows in London in 1970. He could feel half of Britain gathered around the hearth; the other half were right next to their TV sets. He was getting ready to speak to this other half.

"Tell us, Norman. Don't be coy. What is punishing about sex?"

"David, do you want me to unzip, and lay it on the table and show you the welts and the warts?"

It was his best shot to a TV interviewer's eye since he dropped Eisenhower-is-a-woman onto Mike Wallace. Frost looked like a British heavyweight who has just been tagged but somehow does not go down. His eyes blinked. They sat there looking at one another over the sputtering of the British hearth.

Frost went on to do the rest of his show and do it well, engaging in a dozen arguments with a panel of management and labor union men, he took a good punch, and Johnny Carson gave a good punch (in the clinches) as Mailer would also discover on the occasion in '72 when he announced he was for McGovern while sitting next to Carson. During the break, as the canned commercial went on, Carson leaned in and said, "You really like McGovern?"

"Yeah," answered Mailer.

"Nah," said Carson. He leaned in at the advanced angle of a slim man about to slip you a tip on a horse, "I was talking to six friends, and on an impulse, I don't know why, I stopped and said to them, 'Who does McGovern remind you of?' What do you think all six said?"

"What?" asked Mailer.

"Liberace," said Carson and leaned away. They were on the air again. "Norman," said Johnny, "you were about to give us your views on McGovern."

He did his best but Carson had taken two percent forever from his genuine respect for George McGovern.

Yes, in the middle of metaphorical visits to Dr. Something, our national radiologist, out of the sum of spiritual wrestling matches and invisible boxing-fests, out of that accumulation of hours over the years that felt like exposure to the subtlest cancer of them all (and had they ever done a correlation between the purchase of TV sets and the rise in cancer — no, *they* hadn't; no, *they* wouldn't!) he came, more and more (to his own embarrassment), to treasure his TV pearls. They took some of the taste of the aspirin away; they had to; nothing was so depressing as those predictable draws TV encouraged; you were polite, the host was polite, an idea went back and forth and died. All the while, out in the vast pall, *something* was coming out of the sets. In such a pass, pearls took on the luster of small and pleasurable drinking habits. He even came to think of pearls the way an Irishman will live with legendary put-downs of one protagonist by another; and that was sad because Norman knew pearls appealed best to people who couldn't bear questions that took longer than ten seconds to answer. He was catering to TV addicts.

He would discover this all over again in that place where one may always learn something — in the middle of an event that has gotten out of hand. One night on Merv Griffin, back in 1967, he attacked the war in Vietnam as an evil war that would bring every horror in this country up from the sewer, and went on to describe America as a huge drunk staggering down a road while covered with his own vomit. The studio audience began to hiss with real anger; he looked back in equal anger and said: "Did you all go to high school?" The remark came out faster than his mind, and it was cruel: it went to the heart of the secret. For this audience had a common denominator. Something in their faces spoke of high school as the summit of their lives, the end of their development. These lumpy, dull-necked, dead-eyed people with their flower print blouses and acetate shirts, their big-beamed slacks for the women, and pinch-cheeked slacks for the men, were living in the kind of torpor that encouraged spending three hours on line to get into a TV show, yes, high school had been the most exciting few years of their life, and just as they hated him for scoring such an unhappy secret, so did he hate them because he never had a good time in high school and felt deprived for thirty years afterward.

Merv Griffin had his work that afternoon. If a studio audience was normally a TV host's prize cow, the cow was acting on this occasion like a bull. The disturbance did not cease, and Mailer, hardly about to hush his views on Vietnam, kept answering the audience's gibes with his own, until he could feel the moment when Griffin must have wondered if the time had come at last when a few dozen people were going to leave their seats and charge on stage. They never did, they never would, but Griffin couldn't be certain that day, and so, for years, whenever he invited Mailer back on his show, he would introduce him as "one of America's best-known brawlers, although he's really a very nice man."

After a time, Dick Cavett began to do something of the same. Once, when Norman suggested he was not a brawler, Cavett gave his fine Venetian smile: "A brawler is a guy who's all marked up after a fight — is that what you object to?"

The audience laughed, and Mailer nodded. Cavett owed him one. Cavett, indeed, owed him more than one. Once, on Cavett's program, Norman said he thought David Frost was the best TV interviewer in America, and proceeded to explain to the studio audience that while he had been drunk when he said it, the remark had its merits. Carson, he would explain, left you feeling like a horse that has been taken through its paces by a no-nonsense jockey, and Griffin, while cordial and decent, was more comfortable with singers and comedians.

"What is my fault?" asked Cavett, as if hoping there might still be a joke at the end.

"You're fine."

"No, tell me my flaws. I only invite you on, after all, to give my masochism a fighting chance."

The audience laughed, and Norman was annoyed enough now to pass over Cavett's merits. So he did not say that he thought him the most literate of television hosts, and admired him for trying to keep wit alive in the Sludge (which is the name of the great TV river) but instead said next, "Well, Frost is a good listener." It was true. Frost's gifts were personal. He listened better than other hosts, and so left his guest feeling forceful. "Frost is fun to be on with," Norman concluded.

"I'm not?"

"Oh, I like you."

"I don't care if Frost is better than me," said Cavett, "just as long as you like me." The audience roared.

They moved on to other matters, and in the intermission, Cavett said, "Did you mean it?"

"I said it on Frost's show last night."

"Well, why do you tell me now?"

"This show will go on tonight, but David's won't be heard for another week. I thought it would be unfair to come here, have a good time, and then let you find out later what I said." He paused. "I was going to tell you in the intermission, but it seemed the cheap way to do it."

"Yes, you bet," said Cavett. "David Frost, Jesus Christ!"

The next afternoon crossing a street in Chicago — Norman was in Chicago to do more TV to promote the sales of a book that no one who watched TV would ever be likely to buy: could it have been *Of a Fire on the Moon?* — he heard a stranger yell out from across the street, "Hey, Norm, how could you ever do that rotten thing last night to Dick Cavett?"

It took years to recognize that he had uttered no little harm; across the seasons, whenever Cavett might have a fight with his network, one or another executive hostile for certain to Cavett's subtle superiority to TV itself, would be able to say, "After all, Dick, even your friend Norman Mailer thinks David Frost is better than you."

Still, he did not come to understand how often the entertainer could have thought about that remark until the night he was on the Cavett show with Janet Flanner and Gore Vidal. It would prove to be an evening where no one would come out well, unless it was Janet Flanner, but it was a night, nonetheless, to convince Mailer that he was incapable of learning how to conduct a feud on TV.

Channel 9

From a letter to *Women's Wear Daily:*

Sirs:

It has come to my attention that Gore Vidal has been speaking in your pages of my hatred of women. Let me present the following items.

Number of times married:	Mailer 5	Vidal 0
Number of children:	Mailer 7	Vidal 0
Number of daughters:	Mailer 5	Vidal 0

These statistics of course prove nothing unless it is to suggest that the reason Vidal may have married no lady and fathered no child is due perhaps to his love of women and his reluctance therefore to injure their tender flesh with his sharp tongue.

Yours sincerely,
Norman Mailer

Until this letter, Vidal and Mailer had managed to keep a public peace for years. They had each decided long ago there were more profitable wars in the literary world, and so maintained the professional pact not to speak ill of each other for too little.

Probably this peace had exacted its small price. It is difficult for certain authors not to say terrible and/or accurate things about each other in print. Mailer might hear occasionally of a nasty remark Vidal had made in private, but ignored it on the assumption that Gore, tuning up for a little writing, was once again confusing malice for precision.

Still, Mailer knew his own career had become too popular for the pact to continue. Sometime after *The Armies of the Night* won a couple of prizes, Vidal began to sour in public. Condescending and somewhat righteous references to Mailer began to appear in Vidal's interviews. That was a clue to the temper of the time. Vidal was one literary politician with an impeccable nose for ripe liberal issues, and he was now rushing into the most useful denunciations, politically speaking, against machismo, and was quick to attach to this theme the-hatred-of-Norman-Mailer-for-women as if that were a well-established fact known to most of the citizenry.

Since Mailer was fond of repeating that there were four stages to comprehending a woman's character, and you could not claim to know her until you had passed through the four, that is, living together, being married, having children, and going through divorce, since he might therefore like or dislike a lost mate in a given season, but finally thought that was equal to approving or disapproving of Paris or London after you have lived there for many years, a woman indeed equal to a culture, so that you could hardly pass through four such stages with her and be left with nothing, he thought (as we can see by his letter to *Women's Wear Daily*) that it was kind of gross of Gore to declare that Mailer hated women when (to be downright crass about it) it was not Vidal, dig! who had spent his life in the collective arms of the powerhouse.

Of course, in compensation, Gore had taken up a seat in the power of print. If people saw something in a magazine, they liked to believe it. That much, Vidal knew. Stupid people! So, some time after his letter to *Woman's Wear Daily*, Mailer picked up *The New York Review of Books* one summer day and read a review by Vidal of a book by an author named Eva Figes in which the young-old critic stopped long enough to say, "There has been from Henry

Miller to Norman Mailer to Charles Manson a logical progression. The Miller–Mailer–Manson man, or M3 for short, has been conditioned to think of women as, at best, breeders of sons, at worst, objects to be poked, humiliated, killed. . . ." Vidal, going on from here to speak of M3 as if the case were made — well, in truth, even as Mailer knew that Vidal was looking for just such a result, just so did something blow in his brain.

"Why," asked Mailer in his mind of Vidal, "didn't you have the simple literary decency to say, 'This literary progression, extreme as it may sound at first, will engage my best efforts to show that there are startling and frightening similarities between Manson and Miller and Mailer'?"

Instead, this arrogance! Vidal, with his insensitivity to nuance, would not even make a suitable valet for Henry Miller.

And then, there was himself! He had not been writing for thirty years to be called M3. Mailer could hardly wait to catch up with Gore Vidal.

Yet the opportunity, when it came, did not give good anticipation. Indeed, he hardly knew whether the meeting would take place. He had been invited to appear on Cavett, then he heard Vidal had also been invited, then was told Vidal had dropped off the show. Finally he was informed Vidal was back again. It seemed Cavett would now have one more guest: Janet Flanner. The assistant producer who offered this piece of news said she was formidable.

Mailer had never met Janet Flanner but was used to seeing her pen name, Genêt, in *The New Yorker*. She had been doing a column on Paris for as long as he could remember (for decades it seemed before the real Genet came along) a firm gossipy *feuilleton.* It is the kind of writing whose merit is not easy to evaluate unless you know as much about the subject as the author; ergo, he had been less impressed with Janet Flanner's literary abilities than by her power to keep a job for a lifetime.

"I assume she's Gore's friend," Mailer said.

"It's more like he's her doll," replied the assistant producer.

"Thank you very much," said Mailer.

It did not bother him. Formidable people were often not formidable under video. Indeed, there was never a reason any longer to be bothered with what was awaiting you. By just so much had Mailer's opinion of television's importance changed. By now, he saw no point in being splendid on a TV show — it did not contribute to the sort of meaningful career where every step was on the staircase, in fact one rarely had an idea of when one was good and when terrible. Mailer had appeared on shows where he felt splendid and full of energy, yet looked uncomfortable to himself, even agitated, when he watched it afterward; conversely, he had come into many a studio feeling lifeless and later looked a model of cool deportment. The secret on TV, if there was a secret, was not to do too much.

Yet it could never be as simple as that. Sitting next to Johnny Carson, for example, was like setting up camp next to an ant-hill. Carson never stopped fidgeting. None of his nervousness, however, passed through the tube. Finally, one was at the mercy, Mailer expected, of this as yet undiscovered psycho-electronic valve that filtered vices out of certain people only to distort enthusiasm into the appearance of hysteria for others.

Of course, if you could not control how you would appear, if it was up to the valve, then there was no point to getting charged-up for a show. Mailer had come to believe in the old Hindu saw: Do not spend time worrying about matters you cannot affect.

So he made other appearances that day, other radio or TV — he could no longer remember — it seemed from the vantage of Limbo where old dates were quietly curved (so that you slid in memory around one winter over to another) that he may have been making some kind of effort on *The Prisoner of Sex* — was it for the hardcover or the paperback? and had, in any case, done a show already, and gone to a cocktail party where he enjoyed three or four drinks to the hilt. Mailer had the operative definition of *to the hilt:* it was the state where a carelessly lit match sent you up in flames.

When he arrived at the studio, they rushed him to makeup. Vidal had been supposed to go on first, but hadn't arrived. Would Mailer object to taking his place? He had hardly given his assent before he was informed that Vidal had arrived after all. Would he now mind if Mr. Vidal went on as originally planned? Since Mailer had formed the little vice when appearing on Cavett, of comporting himself as the star, he could not pretend to happiness at finding himself on the shuttle. Still, he kept his mouth shut. He did not wish to jostle his liquor.

At this moment, alone in the Green Room, he felt a tender and caressing hand on the back of his neck. It was Vidal. Vidal had never touched him before, but now had the tender smile of a man who would claim, "It doesn't matter, old sport, what we say about each other — it's just pleasant to see an old friend."

Mailer answered with an open-handed tap across the cheek. It was not a slap, neither was it a punch, just a stiff tap.

To his amazement, Vidal slapped him back.

Norman smiled. He leaned forward and looked pleasantly at Gore. He put his hand to the back of Gore's neck. Then he butted him hard in the head.

"Are you crazy?" asked Vidal.

"Shut up," said Mailer.

"You're absolutely mad. You *are* violent," said Vidal.

"I'll see you on the show."

He was, after Vidal left (and that was quickly enough), obliged to pace about. Other people came into the Green Room, saw him, and went away. It was obvious; he did not feel like speaking.

The show began. Cavett did his monologue, and it was a good one. "A lot of critics knock television. They have a kind of snobbish attitude towards TV and they think it lacks culture," he said with a smile. He had the only smile that came through the valves of video looking wicked and angelic at once.

"Tonight," continued Cavett, "I have three people on who are important in writing; they've done other things too, but they're all well-known writers. Just to prove to them that television has figured in the thoughts and writings of people of some stature among the literary profession, I asked my research department to come up with a few things that have been written about this program from some prominent figures. In a couple of cases I have a tendency to do it in the voice of the well-known person. This is from an unpublished work of William F. Buckley, Jr. entitled, 'A Felicitous Discourse on Epistemological Incunabula,' subtitled, 'God: The Man and The Myth.' " The audience applauded his smile with laughter. "The quote is: 'One of the less onerous duties incumbent upon a quondam political journalist is the occasional appearance on sundry quotidian chat programs that proliferate these days like Liberals at a hundred dollar a plate dinner for the poor. Not the least in stature, though clearly the least in stature actually, is a jovial dwarf named Cavett,' " — they roared — " 'who fortnightly forays into — or nightly actually — all fields of erudition and these forays are unblemished by the slightest knowledge of any of them.' That's old Bill." There was laughter.

"Here," Cavett went on, "is a paragraph by women's liberationist Kate Millett entitled 'Little Pig, Big Mouth.' " (Laughter) " 'Let's look at the facts. In the past year, sexist talk-show host Dick Cavett has welcomed several hundred guests on his show. Why have these not included one woman Supreme Court justice, one woman admiral, one woman pro-football player,' " — he stopped for the laughter — " 'one woman-father, husband, king or rapist? I'll tell you, sisters. Because Mr. Cavett, like all arrogant, ignorant, hypocritical, selfserving, pompous, rotten male chauvinist pigs, is simply . . .' and then she goes on to become slightly insulting." The audience adored him. "I don't," said Cavett with his finest smile, "want to read that part to you."

A question period with the audience followed, and he was asked "Do you dye your hair?"

"No," Cavett replied, "I tint my body a little to set it off."

Vidal now came out, and was as sluggish as a club-fighter who is looking for his mother.

> VIDAL: You're looking very well. Do you tint your body? (*laughter*)
> CAVETT: Funny, that was going to be my first question to you.
> VIDAL: That was it exactly, yeah.
> CAVETT: You heard all that?
> VIDAL: I was overhearing the audience, yeah.
> CAVETT: The audience was giving me a bit of time there, as we say in America.
> VIDAL: As you say in America. Well . . . love it or leave it.
> CAVETT: I haven't seen you in a long time. Do they say that in other countries — love it or leave it?
> VIDAL: Well, yes. Amsterdam, love it or leave it. No, no, you're free to come and go.

Vidal, however, was not a professional for too little. After the commercial, he began to rally; indeed Mailer was finally obliged to admire how Gore was able (wonder of wonders) to recover from the head-butting. Having been taught this informal martial art by a retired black Light-Heavyweight named John Bates who worked for a spell in the late Fifties as a bouncer in the Cafe Riviera on Sheridan Square — Bates' head felt like a cannonball! — Mailer knew the aftermath; nausea, and an ongoing vacuum in the brain.

Still, Gore was only showing a few bad effects. Of course, his head had been somewhat harder than expected — writers' heads tended to be more rock-like, for example, than actors', who suffered disproportionately from even a tap: head-butting may be ultimately a question of how heavy an identity (authentic or false) one is able to support — but, even so! Mailer knew how hard he had hit him. (Between half and three-quarter throttle.) Of course, Gore had given his television routines on so many shows that he could probably recite the same lines, with the same wit, same timing, and same turn of delivery, under sodium pentothal. Moreover, Vidal was not one to forget an effective remark; he never used a new thought so long as the old one could still seem new; it was obvious he had no respect for Mailer's long-held belief that repetition kills the soul. On the contrary, if such a law was in force, Gore would decide it was best not to have a soul. The soul was most famous, after all, for getting in your way — this much cynicism had Vidal absorbed from world literature!

Therefore, the only evidence, at present, that young Gore had passed through a contretemps in the Green Room — that is, had his head smashed — was his gesture, repeated somewhat frequently, of bringing up several fingertips to gently massage the skin of his forehead, same fingers indeed that had so recently offered to caress the back of Mailer's stiff neck. Other than that, Mr. Vidal was getting around to presenting a first-rate picture of himself.

He was speaking of his friendship with Mrs. Roosevelt. He and she had interests in common, including the protection of the Hudson River from further pollution. For Cavett's liberal audience, there was no name, Mailer decided gloomily, more calculated than Eleanor Roosevelt's to give the wholly satisfactory sensation of having one's buttocks stroked with velvet. To be given intimate glimpses of the lady! Even though he sneered at such crowd-pleasing tactics, Mailer was as taken as anyone in the audience. His only contact, after all, with Mrs. Roosevelt had been at long distance in the Fifties when he saw her printed reaction to a statement he had made in Lyle Stuart's *Exposé* that white southerners did not wish to give the Negro his equality because — he had been quick to explain — Southern Whites felt they had their social superiority and Negroes had their sexual superiority, and that — thought Southern Whites — was fair enough. Eleanor Roosevelt's short statement read: "I think Mr. Mailer's remarks are horrible and unnecessary."

Vidal's life with Mrs. Roosevelt transpired, however, on less troubled waters. He spoke of their first meeting with tender éclat. "I drove down," he told Cavett's audience, "to Val-Kill Cottage where she lived. It was a summer afternoon. The place was absolutely empty. Front door was open, walked in, nobody there. 'Anybody home?' She was a little deaf. No answer. So I went to the — the nearest door was half open, so I opened the door and there to my horror was Eleanor Roosevelt — very tall woman — standing in front of the toilet bowl. And I thought, 'Oh, my God.' And she gave a terrible cry, and then she turned around and she said, 'Well, I suppose you'd better know everything.' And she had some gladiolas in the toilet bowl which she was arranging. She said, 'It keeps them fresh.' " The audience laughed happily. "So we began with perfect intimacy, Mrs. Roosevelt and I. I knew everything from then on that was in the bathroom."

Clever Vidal! Out of the twenty-eight routines suitable for an appearance on Cavett, Gore had chosen to disclose Eleanor Roosevelt's watercloset. How could the audience not believe they had divine relations?

> VIDAL: (*ruminatively*) What I liked about her was there was nothing human that she felt human ingenuity wouldn't sense and right action could fix it, and she really believed that, and many people found her very boring because of it. I found her very inspiring. Gosh, I've been with her four in the morning in Schenectady trying to get a bus someplace when we were out campaigning, and on and on she would go, this old woman, quite sick, because she felt it was worth doing. And what's gone wrong in the world now, I think a great many of us feel that things are now irreversible, you know. They're never going to make the rivers clear and clean again, they're not going to save the land, they're not going to do anything about Detroit, the American empire is not going to liquidate itself. And there's beginning a sense of despair. You cannot turn it back, and Eleanor was the last person really who said, "Oh, we can, and we must."

Janet Flanner now came on. She was not a large woman, but she was old and grand and had an air of giving short measure to fools. By the manner in which she sat down next to Vidal, and laid her white-gloved hand on his arm, it was also apparent that she was authoritatively fond of him.

Cavett began to say that the last time he had had Janet Flanner on his program, she had told of finding Ernest Hemingway in her bathtub.

"He was stealing my warm water, that's what he was doing. Sheer theft is what I called it," said Janet Flanner.

She had a nice crust to her personality. It was like the crust on good bread that lets out agreeable sounds when a piece is broken off for you. The audience was tittering to show their approval. It hardly mattered how much she said since she could give you a lesson in deportment by the clearing of her throat.

Cavett asked: "Can you bury once and for all the tired old myth of the Frenchman being the sexual marvelous athlete of all time? . . ." And she replied: "Well, I've only buried a few so I can't tell about all the rest of them." In the midst of the applause, it was now obvious that Cavett, in his turn, was certainly fond of her. His manner seemed to suggest that the only reason he had ever wanted to have his own show in the first place was for the honor of introducing a lady so splendid as herself. He was actually laughing with happiness at her remarks.

For that matter, Mailer was obliged to admit all three were getting on very well:

> VIDAL: Did you know that George Washington used to take his false teeth at night and put them in a bowl of Madeira wine?
>
> CAVETT: No.
>
> VIDAL: I thought you would like to know that, Dick.
>
> FLANNER: As they were made of wood they must have been quite tasty by breakfast. (*laughter*)
>
> VIDAL: It was his brunch that he would put in the next morning.
>
> CAVETT: Madeira wine. Why? What's the effect of that on the false teeth?
>
> VIDAL: I think he liked the taste and they were made out of elephant bone and wood.
>
> FLANNER: And out of bone. The elephant bone is a new trick to me.
>
> CAVETT: I thought they were always wood. I always wondered — I pictured his dentist saying, "I have bad news for you — termites," or something. (*laughter*)
>
> FLANNER: Oh, you're a wicked boy. (*laughter*)
>
> CAVETT: Am I? (*laughs*) Where are we going?

In the Green Room, Mailer — like that general he could never become — was contemplating the military chances for entering an ambush of such delicacy connected to such strength. The only answer was attack. Shatter all prepared positions. Go out, he said to himself, and smash that fucking tea-house.

Channel 10

Those watching would see Norman Mailer emerge on the screen in a dark and disheveled suit, bow heavily to Janet Flanner, shake hands with Cavett, and pointedly not shake hands with Vidal. People in the studio audience would comment audibly at this display of discourtesy. Mailer would glare at them. Cavett would ask why he did not shake hands. Mailer would reply that he did not approve of Vidal, and thought him shameless in intellectual argument.

The camera would cut to Vidal's face. He would look composed on occasion, less composed on other occasions. Occasionally, Janet Flanner would touch his arm in reassurance, as if to signify that she would protect him from ruffians. Vidal was obliged to simper at that. It takes real machismo to look stern when your protection is seventy years old.

Under these loads, the next minutes progressed unevenly. Mailer was wound-up, and Vidal was silent. Cavett did not seem to know whether to put Lanolin on a rash, or pull cocks' feathers. Given this sort of prompting, Norman managed to get in a few words he had written about Vidal in *The Prisoner of Sex.*

> MAILER: I said that the need of the magazine reader for a remark he could repeat at dinner was best satisfied by writers with names like Gore Vidal.
> FLANNER: All those writers called Gore Vidal.
> VIDAL: I know. There are thousands of them, yeah.
> CAVETT: Writers with names like Gore Vidal.
> MAILER: There are two or three, you see.
> CAVETT: Who are some of the others?
> MAILER: I don't know.
> CAVETT: Who wants to host the rest of this show for me? (*laughter*)

Who had butted who in the head? Mailer now asked himself. After this exchange, his ability to mount a sustained argument, never impressive at best, was hardly robust in the face of Cavett's wit, and Flanner's deft interruptions. In short time, the audience turned unmistakably against him. When he said that the contents of Vidal's stomach were "no more interesting than the contents of an intellectual cow," they began to boo. He turned to them, and said, "You boo before you know what the man has done." They booed him again. He knew that he must move the conversation over to how Vidal had characterized Miller, Mailer and Manson as M3, but there was nothing routine about scoring a point when you were debating one on three, or, since Gore was so silent, one on two-and-a-half. During each commercial, Mailer would sit heavily in his seat, staring with a dead eye at Vidal, but this time — air-time certainly racing away — he handed Cavett a page he had torn out of *The New York Review of Books* with Vidal's review, and asked him to pass it over to be read aloud. As the show proceeded, however, Vidal did not read it. Norman began to upbraid him further.

"You go in for intellectual adulteration," he said to Vidal, and then with no great display of coherence added that Vidal was welcome to rip apart any piece of his writing. "By God," Mailer vowed, "I may be writing on the floor, but if you taught me something about writing, I'd look up and I'd love you for having taught me something about writing. But when you only teach me something about the tricks of adulteration," Mailer shook his head. "You say the rivers will never be clean again and you pollute the intellectual rivers . . ."

"I wasn't," Vidal drawled, "setting myself up as the Famous Writers School, you know." He drew the chortles he must have anticipated for that.

> MAILER: Why don't you try to talk just once, Gore, without yuks? Why not just talk to me instead of talking to the audience?
> VIDAL: Well, by a curious thing we have not found ourselves in a friendly neighborhood bar, but both, by election, are sitting here with an audience, so therefore it would be dishonest of us to pretend otherwise. (*applause*)
> MAILER: All right, Gore, look. We are here with an audience by choice, but let us at least — let us at least —

He wanted to grapple with him in argument, get him to read his own words. In the confusion of trying to get to Vidal with one hand and keep Cavett and Flanner off with the other, he was planning to say, "At least, read your own words," when Flanner whispered half-audibly to Gore.

> MAILER: Hey, Miss Flanner. Are you workin' as the referee or as Mr. Vidal's manager? (*laughter*) I'm perfectly willing to accept you in either role . . .

CAVETT: Can we afford you both talking?

MAILER: But my mind is fragile and I find it very hard to think and if you're muttering in the background it's difficult.

FLANNER: I made only the slightest mutter. (*laughter*) You must be very easily put off center.

MAILER: It's true, you made only the slightest mutter.

FLANNER: A tiny mutter.

MAILER: Yes, yes. But I listen to you spellbound —

FLANNER: I won't bother you anymore.

Norman was beginning to wonder if anything would work. He made a small vow never to drink again before going on TV. That valuable paper with Vidal's invaluable comments on Manson, Miller and Mailer was now in Vidal's pocket, oh that fine review with such plums as "M3 is on the defensive, shouting names; he thinks that to scream dyke is enough to make the girls burst into tears. . . ." "It was in those years that M3 was born, emigrated to America, killed Indians, killed blacks, conned women. . . ." "Miller–Mailer–Manson. Women, beware. Righteous murder stalks the land. . . ."

In the absence of any substance to Mailer's attack, Vidal was taking on strength. The show was past the three-quarter mark and Gore was coming alive. Yes, Gore was now saying avuncularly, the good thing about Norman "is his constant metamorphosis. He does rebear himself like the phoenix, and what the next reincarnation will be, I don't know."

MAILER: You seem to have figured out that the next reincarnation for me is going to be Charles Manson.

VIDAL: Well, you left yourself —

MAILER: Why don't you read what you wrote?

VIDAL: You let yourself in for it, and I will tell you — I'll give you a little background here — that Mailer has —

MAILER: We all know that I stabbed my wife years ago, we do know that, Gore. You were playing on that.

VIDAL: Let's just forget about it.

MAILER: You don't want to forget about it. You're a liar and a hypocrite. You were playing on it.

VIDAL: But that wasn't a lie or a hypocrisy.

MAILER: The fact of the matter is that people who read *The New York Review of Books* know perfectly well — they know all about it and it's your subtle little way of doing it . . .

VIDAL: Oh, I'm beginning to see what bothers you now. OK, I'm getting the point.

MAILER: Are you ready to apologize?

VIDAL: I would apologize if — if it hurts your feelings, of course I would.

MAILER: No, it hurts my sense of intellectual pollution.

VIDAL: Well, I must say, as an expert you should know about such things. (*laughter*)

MAILER: Yes, well, I've had to smell your works from time to time and that has helped me to become an expert on intellectual pollution, yes.

VIDAL: Yeah, well . . . let's — I was going to say, I —

FLANNER: Not only do you insult each other, not only in public, but you act as if you were in private. That's the odd way —

MAILER: It's the art of television, isn't it?

FLANNER: It's very odd that you act so — you act as if you were the only people here.

MAILER: Aren't we?

FLANNER: They're here, he's here. *I'm* here, and I'm becoming very, very bored. (*laughter, applause*)

MAILER: You still haven't told me whether you're Gore's manager or the referee.

CAVETT: If you make history here by punching a lady . . . (*laughter*)

FLANNER: I won't have it! I won't have it!

MAILER: Now, look, you see the sort of thing that goes on. Now you say I make history by punching a lady. You know perfectly well — you know perfectly well that I'm the gentlest of the four people here. (*laughter*)

CAVETT: I just hope it lasts through the next whatever we have left. (*laughter*)

MAILER: I guarantee you I wouldn't hit any of the people here because they're smaller.

CAVETT: In what ways? (*laughter*)

MAILER: Intellectually smaller.

CAVETT: Let me turn my chair and join these three. (*laughter, applause as he moves his place*) Perhaps you'd like two more chairs to contain your giant intellect. (*laughter, applause*)

MAILER: I'll take the two chairs if you will all accept finger-bowls.

This remark was sufficiently gnomic for Cavett to chew it and get to no witty place.

CAVETT: Who wants to grab this on our team? (*laughter*) I nearly have it, it means something to me. Fingerbowls. Fingerbowls. Things you dip your fingers in after you've gotten them filthy from eating. Am I on the right track? Am I warm?

MAILER: Why don't you look at your question sheet and ask a question.

CAVETT: Why don't you fold it five ways and put it where the moon don't shine.

It was received as the remark of the evening. Boborygimous was the laughter. Mailer sat there, contemplating a region in the depth of his rectum. "Mr. Cavett," he said, "on your word of honor, did you just make that up or have you had it canned for years and were you waiting for the best moment to use it?"

"I have to tell you a quote from Tolstoy," said Cavett, and the laughter continued.

Mailer turned his chair away from the guests and toward the theater. "I want to ask all of you something," he said to the audience. "Are you all really truly idiots or is it me?"

The audience replied, "YOU!"

"Oh, that was an easy answer," said Cavett. The music came up. Another intermission was on them.

CAVETT: I just wonder what the people at home think happened during the break. The four of us sat here in stony silence and —

VIDAL: No, somebody in the audience shouted, "Your argument is immature," to all four of us.

CAVETT: To all four of us. Oh. So we can each take as much —

FLANNER: We can each take a bow.

CAVETT: — as we feel we deserve. I'm sorry, Norman, I did interrupt you, and you were talking to the assembled audience.

MAILER: Yes, I was going to ask the audience what I was doing that was making them cheer every time the other side connected with a pass from one to the other of my three opponents.

MAN IN AUDIENCE: You're rude.

WOMAN IN AUDIENCE: You're a snot.

MAILER: That's fair. Someone said I'm rude and someone said I'm being a snot.

WOMAN IN AUDIENCE: You're a pig.

MAILER: Ohhh, the joint is loaded with libbies, ohhh. (*applause*) Gore, my God, it wasn't enough to trundle Janet Flanner along, the most formidable presence in the history of television, but you had to load the balcony with your libbies, your little libbies.

CAVETT: Well, now, wait a minute. There was only one lady's voice that rang out. Do you consider that loaded?

MAILER: It was the voice of legions. (*laughter*)

WOMAN IN AUDIENCE: Why do you have to argue so negatively and insulting to your guests?

MAILER: They're not my guests. They're not my guests any more than they're your guests.

CAVETT: It seems it's your show now.

WOMAN IN AUDIENCE: Why do you have to answer them with insults and nasty statements and they're answering you maturely and with dignity? (*applause*)

MAILER: That's because they're mature and full of dignity and they'd cut my throat in any alley and I answer rudely because I'm crude and a lout and a clod, that's why. (*applause*) Now have we progressed at all? Can I reach you, can I talk to any of you, or is it hopeless? I mean, if you care to listen, I do have a thing or two to say, believe it or not.

MAN IN AUDIENCE: Why are you bellyaching so much?

MAILER: Well, I'm bored with being misrepresented, you see. I've been misrepresented, by my own paranoid lights, for twenty-five years in this country, something like that, and to find an older litterateur like Gore Vidal, who knows his way around, you know . . . knows the ropes, and then suddenly, after all these years, he's suddenly developed a particularly dirty literary game. Well, it inflames me, you know. I've been so bold as to pretend to be the presumptive literary champ, you know, whether I deserve to be or not. The reason people always talk about me in relation to Hemingway is just that Hemingway at a certain point said to himself with his huge paranoia, "They're going to kill me for this but I'm going to be the champ, it's all I care about." And he shifted the course of American letters because up to that point people who wrote books were men of letters, they were gentlemen, they wrote books, and Hemingway said, in effect, "No, people who write books take as much punishment as prizefighters and one of them has to be a champion." Now, we've had a time that has not been interesting in terms of champions. In Hemingway's time there were great writers: there was Faulkner, there was Hemingway, and there were many other writers like Steinbeck and Farrell and Dos Passos and Thomas Wolfe, many, many really wonderful writers. Our time has been much more complicated and there hasn't been that many really extraordinary writers around, and I have presumed with all my extraordinary arrogance and loutishness and crudeness to step forth and say, "I'm going to be the champ until one of you knocks me off." Well, fine, but, you know, they don't knock you off because they're too damned simply yellow, and they kick me in the nuts, and I don't like it.

That was perhaps the most impassioned speech he had ever delivered on television. It said little but it was full of feeling, and it contained the cardinal virtue of television (for any ambitious performer) which is that it kept attention on himself. It suggested that his close-up in the scheme of things would demand more minutes than the others. The audience, obedient to these conditioned reflexes of television, actually gave him a hand, a powerful hand of applause. But, of course, he was hardly finished.

The time had now come to give his peroration on Women's Liberation. He was not opposed to it, he wished to tell the world, he even honored it. It would free the best of women to discover how brave they were; a world in which women were maintained systematically in cowardice had to be a bad world. But, look, he wanted to say, as in all revolutions, the worst are running with the best, and there is an evil loose in Women's Liberation. It is the idea that the male search for bravery is mean and ridiculous, and that it is easier to be a man than a woman. Destroy the difference in the sexes, he would tell this audience, and a world of asexual human units, ready to fit the computers of a future totalitarianism, would also be prepared; these were the questions Vidal was polluting with his use of M3.

It might have been worth giving, but the commercial came before he was half-launched, and what he had to say was unsaid.

During the intermission, they argued on how to proceed. Vidal now wanted time to reply. Cavett indicated that it was Cavett's place to decide; he decided Vidal was entitled to equal time. Mailer offered to accept if Vidal would at least read from his review. With nothing agreed, the music came up.

> CAVETT: Gore, the aim narrowed down to you and we have three and a half minutes left. I insist that you get them.
> VIDAL: Well, I'll begin to answer Norman's charge about what a bad person I am. The attack on him, really, if you want to know, Norman, is simply what I detest in you — and I like many things in you, as you know, I'm a constant friend despite this — but your violence, your love of murder, your celebration of rage, of hate ... "American Dream" — what was the dream? A man murders his wife and then buggers this woman

afterwards to celebrate an American man's dream. This violence, this knocking people down, this carrying on, is a terrible
thing. Now, it may make you a great artist —
MAILER: I demand one minute at the end —
VIDAL: It may make you a great artist —
MAILER: I'll listen, but I demand one minute at the end . . .
VIDAL: It may make you an interesting artist, I don't say that, but
to the extent that one is interested in the way the society is
going, there is quite enough of this stress, quite enough of this
violence, without what I think are your celebrations of it, your
attitude towards women in this thing, which I thought really
horrible, and you said I compared you to Charles Manson. I
said Henry Miller in his way, Norman in his, and Manson in
his far out mad way, are each reflecting a hatred of women and
a hatred of place.

One person was applauding loudly. At that moment, Norman got
up from his chair, took a few steps over to Vidal's chair, flipped the
review from *The New York Review of Books* out of his hand (for
Vidal had been waving it as he spoke) and then returned to his seat.
Vidal had been in the thick of saying, "And frankly if I may say so,"
when he saw Norman's bulk looming above, and he flinched. Vidal
flinched discernibly: a monumentally high number of electrons
were thereby shifted in millions of TV sets.
Back in his seat, Mailer began to read from Gore Vidal's review:

MAILER: "There has been from Henry Miller to Norman Mailer
to Charles Manson a logical progression." Period. "The
Miller–Mailer–Manson man, or M3 for short, has been conditioned to think of women as, at best, breeders of sons, at worst,
objects to be poked, humiliated, killed," and from there on in
the piece you speak of Miller, the great writer Henry Miller,
the greatest writer alive in America — if we're going to talk like
muckers, I'll talk too like a mucker — Henry Miller, the greatest writer alive in America, and myself, and Charles Manson, a
hugely complex and contradictory figure, are spoken of,
lumped together as M3, and if you call that good intellect
working, to lump together three people as curious as Henry
Miller, Norman Mailer and Charles Manson?
VIDAL: Well, you must read the piece. You can't —
MAILER: I read it.
VIDAL: You happened to read it but the audience has not. You are
selecting this one passage as representative of the whole. I made
my case very carefully. But I will say, giving you a few minutes

more on the program, you will prove my point. So, it is — I come back to what I said. I detest this violence in you. You have actually written that "murder is never nonsexual."

MAILER: Well, is it ever nonsexual?

VIDAL: Well, I'm —

MAILER: Don't you know, Gore?

VIDAL: Not having murdered anybody lately, no, I don't know.

MAILER: You bragged about what you did to Jack Kerouac, after all.

VIDAL: He didn't die.

MAILER: Well, he did.

VIDAL: Oh, come on.

MAILER: Don't you remember the stories you used to tell about him —

VIDAL: I'm going to give you a line that Degas said to Whistler — two celebrated painters — and Whistler was a great performer, like Norman, and Degas said, "You know, Whistler, you act as if you had no talent." You represent yourself as though you really had no talent at all and, of course, you are one of our best writers.

MAILER: I read it in the same place you read it, which is Edmund Wilson's answer to Vladimir Nabokov in last week's *Times*.

VIDAL: So what? What's that got to do with it?

MAILER: I thought it was marvelous.

VIDAL: Good. I'm happy that we both agree that the sentiment is correct.

MAILER: The difference is that I savor the remark and you throw it into the battle.

VIDAL: Oh, Norman.

MAILER: Now, may I have my one minute for rebuttal?

CAVETT: There is one minute remaining.

MAILER: There is one minute. All right. He speaks of a character in a book of mine murdering his wife and then buggering a woman as a celebration of American manhood. Now I throw myself upon your court, hanging judge. I say that's intellectual muckerism of the worst sort because the character I have there was a particularly complex character and, in fact, he did not simply bugger a woman, he entered her the other way as well and there was a particularly complicated —

FLANNER: Oh, goodness sake. (*laughter*)

MAILER: I know you've lived in France for many years, but believe me, Janet, it's possible to enter a woman another way as well.

FLANNER: So I've heard. (*laughter*)

CAVETT: On that classy note ... (*laughter*)

FLANNER: I don't think it's restricted to French information, dear.

CAVETT: She said she doesn't think that's restricted to the French.

FLANNER: Practically international.

MAILER: Are we quitting on that classy note?

CAVETT: On that classy note, we have a brief message from our local stations and we will be back.

Cavett and Mailer were not looking at each other. Vidal was looking off into space. Flanner was grinning at Mailer as if he were a most curious fellow. What a way to use his last minute!

The music came up.

CAVETT: Well, this has been an interesting evening around the old table and, Miss Flanner, I'm glad to see you got that box of cookies that you wanted. And you other two fellows —

FLANNER: It's the only solace.

CAVETT: Yeah. (*laughter*) Could you two come back New Year's Eve and maybe we can — (*laughter*)

MAILER: That's the night.

CAVETT: Christmas Eve. Well, let us know who you think won. That'll be interesting, and we'll see you next time we're on the air. If. (*laughter, applause*)

The goodbyes were short. Mailer turned around and Vidal was gone.

Channel 11

Afterward, long after the mail stopped coming (which took a time in itself) after the magazine accounts were finished, and he no longer heard students ask, "Were you really mad at Mr. Vidal?" every time he gave a lecture, long after he had lost every last bit of interest in the evening and remembered the program only because accounts kept coming back to him of Vidal saying on one network that Mailer-is-finished-as-a-writer, and Norman-is-bad-news on another, a string of claims that was now in its sixth year (and would never end since he knew he would never run into Vidal for an accounting — once when Norman was in Rome for a month to work on a movie script, Vidal managed to leave for New York) he finally had time to recognize that this Dick Cavett show, if it was one of the few occasions when television had come alive, had also been killing to the last of his hopes that television might be a forum for those curious ideas with which he lived.

Hundreds of letters came in, ten times more, or maybe it was fifty times more letters than he had ever received from any other show, and as many he was certain came to Vidal — all those lovers of Eleanor Roosevelt! His mail was favorable to him, even as Vidal's mail must in turn be favorable, but the letters, if they brought a sense of his real audience, were not in response to any triumph he had had over the medium, but more a note, even a chorus of outrage, at the restraints of television, the villainy of Cavett in choosing sides, the inanity of the audience, and much on Vidal's little flinch — hardly a letter did not pride itself on seeing that Vidal had flinched.

In turn he hardly had to speculate how other letters must be describing him: a boor, a drunk, an incoherent and unworthy opponent for Mr. Vidal.

It had been Bullshit Bisque when all was said. He had not only failed to dramatize his ideas, but had dramatized himself — it was himself rather than any idea that had come through the tube. He had succeeded at best in evoking sympathy for his own lack of taste and polish; yes, when it was all done, and psychic horizons could be glimpsed again, he knew that he had wasted another fierce piece of Time, and Limbo was by that measure more advanced on him, even knew at last from the vantage of Limbo, from the intimacy of this observation into the interstices of his past that it did not matter on how many TV shows he would yet appear, on Cavett again and Carson and Griffin and Douglas and Susskind and *Today* and *Tomorrow*, *Sixty Minutes*, no past and no future, no antipathy and no forgiveness, no, it did not matter, he had crossed over to the other side on this night of the Dick Cavett show, and now saw that television was an addiction whose pleasure (since every addiction has its pleasure) was to give a small sense of manners to the mannerless and pass a hint of style over to those who are hungry with some unfulfilled vision of themselves (even as he had once studied TV). Yet, as an addiction, it would exact, like any drug, its own cruel price. That took many a form, but for our purposes the price may be equal to the power to destroy the virility and fecundity of ideas. TV was not with us to make history but to leach the salts of history right out of our cells.

Since Mailer came to know this in his life, and yet continued to go on TV, he advanced from a wicked man to the beginnings of an evil figure, at least to his own eyes which here were unhappily congruent to the eyes of Limbo. If it was wicked to up the ante, it was evil to come to know the good and defy it, and the good in this case was to keep the hell off TV, which he did not. So he came to know his place in Limbo before he was even there. That is our story and we could be done if it were not demoralizing to cease at such a point, blanked in Limbo and empty of hope.

Since it is also the work of such a place, however, to cleanse the choked-up rivers of one's life and thereby enable us to voyage out to a more adventurous plane (where the walls are rough and the ascents are vertical) not every meditation in the mansion need brood over the hopelessness of the past. There is also the memory of odd and mysterious instants when hope is in the air, even if comprehension is dim. So Mailer, sentenced by Limbo to remember no experiences that were altogether separate from television, was nonetheless able to think fondly of two events he saw from the spectator's side of the tube and was agreeably overcome with the suspicion — suspicion being tonic to the dull recognitions of Limbo — that even in the middle of *something* there might be a force devoted to the extinction of *something*. If the Devil always appeared in the most splendid intentions of the Lord, the Devil being the most beautiful creature God ever made (in those days when the Lord was young and still vain in His vision and therefore wicked enough to create beauty before prudence) so, too, had God been obliged in His turn to enter all those baleful and Satanic mediums where the air is destroyed and electromagnetism chases its tail and shatters frequently, yes, maybe God was now as grim as the glimpse of defeat in the center of television when the set goes off, and yet was also ready if no longer young, to chase the Devil into every void, live in every static, and go to war on each bleak field. So there might be hope. Mailer did not know — Limbo gave no final purchase on the eschatological structure of things, but, still! Mailer remembered the night he invited friends to his house in Provincetown back in the summer of '66 because his great friend José Torres was defending the Light-Heavyweight Championship against Eddie Cotton in Las Vegas, and the fight was on TV. That was an occasion to remember in Limbo, and see again in Limbo, yes.

Torres was a strong favorite that night, but Cotton gave him trouble. Eddie Cotton was an old black fighter with a thousand tricks and more than a hundred fights, and being near the end of a distinguished and rugged career, he was ready to steal the championship if he could put it all together, and Cotton put it together. He fought the fight of his life. Before half of the fifteen rounds were gone, he was clearly ahead of José Torres.

There were eight guests in Mailer's living room and they were quietly drinking and commenting on the action. About this time, Norman began to go out of his mind. He did not really know a lot about boxing, not so much as he was reputed to know, but he knew Torres' style and had an insight into Torres' strengths, and on this night he felt as if he knew what Torres was not doing right. "Stick him," he began to shout at the set. "Get your jab working." Torres' vice, if he had one as a fighter, was vanity, and Torres was being beaten on combinations by Cotton. Since José's vanity was that nobody was better at combinations than Torres, he had been trading his best combinations against Cotton, and for one round after another, Cotton had been beating him by just a little. What a fight! One was seeing some of the finest combinations ever to come out of a war between Light-Heavyweights, fantastic combinations indeed for Light-Heavyweights, it was a great fight, but Torres was not using his jab, that jab off his long arm that had been finer even than the jab of Willie Pastrano on the night Torres took the championship from him, and so Norman began to scream at the set in a purple and apoplectic voice, "Stick him! Stick him! Get it going! Stick him!" And as if he had been in Torres' corner, and Torres was listening to him, so Torres began to pop Cotton with his jab, there in the middle of the fight, Torres shifted his pattern, and began to jab, and this threw Cotton off just a hair on his combinations, and the jab began to take the edge from Cotton and give it back to Torres, and Norman, watching the action, swallowed bourbon like gasoline, and screamed instructions, "Keep it up, keep it up. Keep the pressure!" to what must have been the *peculiar* horror of his guests; now more rounds were going to Torres than to Cotton, and Norman screamed him home, eight rounds to seven, and José kept his championship. Norman was never to get over the impression that somewhere in the depths of Torres' attention the message had come back through the tube. "Stick him!" A miracle in communication had occurred. A TV set, that malign corporate mechanism of valves that allow communication to pass in one direction only, had been transcended for half an hour, and managed to take messages back, or to say it real, the heart of Mailer's insanity that night was to think he had passed through the heart of *something* and was talking successfully to the tube.

Insanity has its rewards. Later that night, convinced he had broken through some encircling ring of the Devil, and was now out of his box, that is to say, alive in his life rather than sequestered in a psychic coffin, Norman began to run amok at a dress rehearsal of his play, *The Deer Park*, which would have its premiere the following night at the Art Association in Provincetown. He had kept his mouth shut at rehearsals when he wished to interfere, he had allowed, he thought, his director to take *The Deer Park* down lanes the play should not travel, and on this night, after the Torres–Cotton fight, having come to the rehearsal late, and lately filled with a sense of power few humans could know — he could talk back to the tube! — saw no reason why he should not talk back to his actors, and did. Sitting at the back of the hall, hardly able to hear their voices, he began to shout, "Louder!"

"Norman, will you please be quiet," said the director.

"I will not be quiet. I cannot hear the actors."

They had a quarrel in front of the cast. It grew worse, and the director, in a rage, called the rehearsal off. It was only on the next day that Mailer found out he had been witnessing not a dress rehearsal, but a walk-through for light cues, and that was why he could not hear the actors. They were saving their voices.

"When it comes to theater, you are an ignorant man," said the director, Leo Garen, next day, and since he was a young director and had no money at the time, and this play, if it went on to Off-Broadway, was his best prospect, Mailer knew the courage it required for Garen to tell him off, and shook his hand on the spot — it was somehow relaxing to hear in the middle of his fearsome hangover that he was ignorant; he had not been called ignorant in many a year; some insults come like a blow on the head the morning after, but a few are balm — and he later hired Garen to take *The Deer Park* to New York, and thus began a short career in theater and soon invested his own money in making and directing three films, and by way of them proceeded eventually to lose all his money and more, and so was obliged to keep writing fast for the rest of his life, a blessing to those who liked his stuff, a curse to those who didn't, but much change had certainly come to his life by daring to go up through the tube.

If this pale reminiscence of the rehearsal of *The Deer Park* was as far as he had been able to stray in Limbo away from grim recollections of television, still it cheered him, even if the new images were still of himself as a fool; at least they were recollections free of video. If such memories continued, he might even recall a happy copulation or two. Of course, he did not have the hope that Limbo would permit any rounded view of one's powers of compassion and detachment, fear and greed, strength and responsibility, as a good friend and a bad one, a lover and a monster of love, as egocentric and selfless, no, Limbo was strict, Limbo repaid you for dabbling in television by making you live in it; these walls like the inside of a TV tube were equal to the insomnia that got you up at two in the morning to peer into the box. He had never expected that the scale of payment would be as intimate as your worst enemy's judgment on your hopes.

Channel 12

Yet, as his mind went on, and he came to retrace every episode on this avenue of his sins, an itinerary for which he did not have to move a step, since the curved walls of Limbo served splendidly as a screen, he was at last entitled to move out of his most intolerable punishment (which here for the Narcissist, paradoxically, is constant and enforced contemplation of the self) and begin to consider the merits of others.

So he came at last to the one night on TV in many years that had given him real pleasure, and he thought often about it. In his partial comprehension of television, in his researches into the mystery of that hum in its void, he had always centered his hypotheses around the familiar certainty that Richard Nixon owned the human personality closest to the persona of the television set. Mailer had even built his distrust of TV and Nixon on their similarity to one another, their incorporation of baleful disregard for the finer possibilities of human attention.

Yet, when he replayed in his mind, that is on the curved walls of the mansion, Nixon's first appearance before David Frost, where the ex-President spoke of Watergate, Mailer was cheered by that ninety minutes. In later years, his detestation of TV close to complete, ninety minutes had become an immense dose of video, and left Mailer feeling like a canceroid (that is, like someone who could not justify why he should not bear the disease). Yet Nixon's ninety minutes were of another order; on the scale of video, they were alchemy itself: the American with the least charismatic personality of the twentieth century, the American most ready to be emitted from the tube and infiltrated into your pores had become for a few minutes a personality capable of moving multitudes, and had done it by the refractory art of the actor.

He had always believed Richard Nixon was the most untalented actor he had ever witnessed, and Mailer had often brooded on the first meeting decades ago of Richard and Pat Nixon in an amateur theatrical company, and wondered whether Nixon, if he had been somewhat better in those early years as an actor, would have become in later life a politician more like Ronald Reagan. Instead, his acting career had been given over to the practice of law, and Nixon had become one of the few politicians who was a consummately abominable actor on the American scene. His lack of conviction vibrated through the diodes, triodes, and later the transistors of every American set; the message he gave was profoundly depressing. Even as a district attorney who speaks in too-righteous tones to a jury will depress us on questions of law and order and their relation to justice (since the fact that a D.A. can prosper on such hypocritical terms has either to speak ill of the jury or of a system that encourages us to believe that phony voices carry the real tones of avenging authority) so Nixon's inability to act had always, by reflection, intimated that something in the American public must be atrocious if millions were ready to accept his transparent lack of sincerity, his push-button smile, and his simple lack of ability to offer even that resonance of the throat which is a ham actor's emotion.

Yet in the interview with Frost that Mailer witnessed, a miracle was visible — Richard Nixon had become not merely a good actor but a great actor, great by the measure of actors like Bogart, and Fonda and old Spencer Tracy, great — good God! — like Edward G. Robinson, like Edward G. Robinson playing Richard Nixon full of woe at what had come to him from Watergate, and after thirty or forty minutes of watching Nixon, it did not matter what the truth might be, any more than one would find fault with a great stage actor for bringing life and splendor and passion and the monumental echoes of tragic woe to lines that were not his own and that he could say in his sleep or while shaving, he had practiced them so well, yes, Nixon struck America with a miracle — a talentless actor had become a splendid actor — yes, Nixon now went to the root of good acting, where before he had lived in the center of bad acting. In his political years, Nixon used to comport himself as if acting were a set of semaphores and you frowned if you wished to look stern, and glanced heavenward to demonstrate that your motives were benign; now, face to face with Frost, he was an actor from the guts out, which is that he got his words out through every effort to control himself. The great actor does not play a drunk by staggering; rather, he plays a man whose stomach is raw and whose head is whirling, but a man who nonetheless believes he is sober and so will make every effort to convince others he is sober. The power of his drunkenness comes over the audience by his attempts to conceal it from us. That was Nixon's power on this night. What a mighty emotion he was seeking to hold like a man. It did not matter after a while that a part of one's brain could still remember many an intricacy of Watergate that Nixon was debauching once again; that was like saying of Olivier in *Marathon Man* that he might be playing an ex-Nazi, but actually was still Olivier and born British, what indeed did the truth of Nixon's guilt have to do with the higher truth that a talentless man had become a powerful actor? A fact such as this was kin to a miracle and warmed the heart. So as Richard came forth with those beautiful and unforgettable lines, beautiful, that is, and unforgettable, as examples of the actor's, not the playwright's, art, as he said: ". . . it was springtime. The tulips had just come out . . . it was one of those gorgeous days when, you know, no clouds were on the mountain. And" — his voice went husky here from the effort not to be husky — "I was pretty emotionally wrought-up, and I remember that I could just hardly bring myself to tell Ehrlichman that he had to go. . . . I said, 'I hoped, I almost prayed I wouldn't wake up this morning.' Well, it was an emotional moment. I think there were tears in our eyes, both of us. He said, 'Don't say that.' We went back in." Then he said goodbye to Haldeman and Ehrlichman, and took their resignation. ". . . It was late, but I did it." No actor alive, not Ralph Richardson, Jack Nicholson, or John Gielgud could have given a better reading than he gave on the next line. "I cut off one arm," Nixon said manfully, and in partial control of great pain, "and then cut off the other arm." He nodded. ". . . You could sum it all up," he said to Frost, "the way one of your British Prime Ministers summed it up, Gladstone, when he said that 'the first requirement for a Prime Minister is to be a good butcher.' Well,

I think . . . I did some of the big things rather well. But I . . . have to admit, I wasn't a good butcher."

It would come out later that Nixon's version of these events was not necessarily accurate; first Ehrlichman, then Haldeman, would dispute what he had said. He was not cutting off his own arms so quickly, it seemed, as he was cutting off their legs.

Yet with what a difference did he lie! In the past, a deadening actor and a lifeless politician, Nixon had lied with every dull light in his eye; now, his eye was bright, he had learned to act; his lies partook of art.

The impact upon Limbo was immense. Limbo had many mansions and took many shapes, but the rock on which Limbo was founded would state: men like Richard Nixon are not redeemable.

Nixon had shattered the rock. Reflecting on Nixon's Ode to the Prime Minister and the Art of Butchery, Mailer felt the breaking of the rock. Nixon had demonstrated that if one's suffering were great enough, even a hopeless actor could learn to act, and that meant millions of Americans dragged into the pit by Nixon and forced to believe that bad acting, and/or transparent hypocrisy, are the main road to success, would now be obliged to stare into the true pit: life demanded that one improve. Even a hypocrite was wise to sin with a light in his eye. So the fundament of Limbo cracked. It could not decide whether Richard Nixon was still the avatar of video, a TV set with a head and limbs, and video itself was altering into a higher form of the maligant; or, whether Nixon, having betrayed all other gods, had now betrayed the Devil as well, and would try to make a last career for himself good enough to bring Broadway back.

Mailer did not have time to care. He knew only that Limbo was looser now, and he was getting ready to move from the mansion; to go on — where to, he did not know, a curiosity or a horror could await him next. He hoped only that tomorrow — in the long tomorrow of Limbo — would lead to autumnal places where the record of his sins might reek of wood-smoke rather than the insulation of all those TV wires charring in the night.

It was on this note that he was allowed to think of a poem, but the irony was that it was by a poet named James Elroy Flecker he could hardly have read before, and only the last two lines would stay in mind. "O, is it," said Mailer to himself,

> *"Is it the mist or the dead leaves?*
> *"Or is it the dead men — November eves?"*

Two Letters
from Frank Crowther

⚘

May 13, 1976

Dear Norman,

I just wrote Joe Flaherty a note, and he'll probably call you.

But, at the last minute (and this is surely that), I couldn't check out without sending you a last note.

I've been reading Baudelaire's Last Poems (*1859–63*), and stopped after Le Voyage and Anywhere Out Of The World. They mean different things to different people (*especially the author*), but I saw some of myself in them. I sure as hell wish I'd written at least one or two things as good. . . .

Before checking out, I merely wanted to say a personal farewell and wish you all the best. If there's some way you can sneak the big novel over to the 'other side,' give it a try. It would be something fine to carry off into eternity.

So long, old man. Keep giving them hell.

Good luck and God bless,
Frank Crowther

P.S. One final thought. If you wouldn't mind, when you have a chance, I'd appreciate your dropping my father a note. I worry, as would any son, how he's going to take this. I had a good life, a good shot at things, and I leave with almost no regrets. It wasn't anything to do with my

82

parents. God knows. They were always loving and kind to me. I just had some bad luck, that's all, and chose this way of departure rather than lingering and getting worse by the day. It might help him through what will undoubtedly be a bad time. . . .

He wrote other letters that day to Wes Joyce, proprietor of the Lion's Head where he drank, and to Joe Flaherty, the writer who lived in the same house as himself. The letters were all postmarked at three in the afternoon. That evening he went to the Lion's Head, drank quietly, said little, and studied the faces of Joyce and Flaherty who were also at the bar and would receive his letters in the morning. Then he went home and took an overdose of pills and died in his tidy apartment, dead before he was forty-four. A number of us went to his funeral. Being asked to speak, I read aloud from his letter. I confess I had read the letter twice before I realized what it said, and so I tried to explain that Crowther lived, more than any friend I knew, by an idea of style. When style is a way of life rather than a literary act, it has only the modern fundament on which to base itself — grace under pressure. It is probable that Frank had more pressure in the last two years of his life than anyone I know, and he was not necessarily prepared for it; his early career had been an easy and attractive one. He had four years in the Marine Corps with two of them at the American Embassy in Paris, followed by a good campus career at the University of North Carolina, and then a stretch of nine years in the Kennedy and Johnson administrations and with Roger Stevens on the White House staff for the National Endowment for the Arts. He was that rarest of career men, a literary functionary on the national level, and it gave him a certain blandness. He was, in the years I first knew him — we would run into one another at Plimpton's parties — a well-built, pleasant-featured slightly round-faced acquaintance, with a half-agreeable, half-promiscuous heartiness, and a great knowledgeability of the activities of everyone in the literary world. I doubt if he missed reading a single issue of any magazine relevant to those times and those people. He was up on every bit of gossip. It was easy not to take him seriously, and I remember my surprise at discovering in 1971 when he came to visit in Provincetown, that Crowther was more of a literary man than I had realized, and had the passionate love of good writing you expect to find in people who have high literary ambitions but know agonies in trying to set it down.

After that, we were friends of a sort, and came closer when he managed my Fiftieth Birthday Party at the Four Seasons (where I announced the need for a Fifth Estate in a sixth-rate speech) and if the affair had any success at all, it was in Frank's skill at getting people to believe that my birthday party was the place you wanted to be seen on that night, a piece of social legerdemain when you consider the not wholly cordial reputation of the principal.

A year later, more or less, he was ill. Sick with a most mysterious and maddening disease. His skin turned red, peeled, and itched intolerably. He lived in the cauldron of a body that itched for twenty-four hours a day. The skin of his hands turned as red as the shell of a boiled lobster. His weight went down. His round face turned thin, and his gray eyes had the imploring light of a man who dwelt in unremitting torture. He was in and out of hospitals. They tested him for every cancer they could find — they found none; for every common and exotic disease of the skin — they found none. He managed to write during this period and did a screenplay which came close to a good sale and then fell through and he was living now on next to no money. It ought to have been unendurable to see a man with such misfortunes, but the suffering brought an expression close to beauty in what had been once an almost dough-shaped face. I think the first horror for him was that he did not know if his suffering was attached to the mystery of pain itself, or whether he was a sport, his illness a fluke, and himself a protagonist of the absurd.

That horror breaks through the reserve he usually managed to maintain in his letters. Let me quote from another written six and a half months before his death. He says it there better than I can, and I think he was enough of a literary man to be pleased that I would say so:

> *I came across the following in Kierkegaard's* Diary (*p. 19, Entry 18*): *"All of existence intimidates me, from the tiniest fly to the enigmas of incarnation; as a whole it is inexplicable, my own self most of all; all of existence is pestiferous, my own self most of all. . . ."*
>
> *I have no pleasure in these days, as well you know, I feel wasted and useless, although in clear moments, there is so much I wish to say, so much I would wish to write were I capable thereof. I remember your saying: "I'm a pro. I can work on a bad day." I'm not a pro, and therefore* must *try*

to work on both bad and *good days. But the raging of the flesh too often burns away all energy, all motivation. And God knows how terribly difficult it is even to sit down at the typewriter, much less write coherently and well. Ideas abound, but I am unable to capture them. . . .*

Finally, although I have both fear and disdain for death (the latter possibly being the greatest mistake of all), I smell its stench approaching, and hear the snicker of that jackal somewhere in the night. I feel useless and, worst of all, irrelevant. My strengths, whatever they were, have waned, and my weaknesses are beginning to overwhelm me. And I feel dirty (not only physically). My circle of 'friends' recedes, and I withdraw more and more. I drink more and more. Although before my illness I hardly ever took so much as an aspirin, I fall back on pills of all nature, knowing they are of no use other than a temporary sop. I loathe my body, and have little faith in whatever I might achieve were I not physically afflicted and mentally depressed. Life still has its light moments of frivolity, and I do have a well-developed sense of detachment, but the harsh realities have become a bad film. . . .

. . . I may soon disappear, or I well may hang about a while longer, but these are some things I wanted to say, sooner rather than later.

I send you my love and good wishes,
Frank Crowther

Miller and Hemingway

❧

Henry Miller, his work embraced, which is to say swallowed in four or five weeks, and then re-read over another month or two, can sit in one's mind with all the palpability of a huge elm lying in your back yard. The nobility of the trunk is on the ground for you to examine, not to speak of the rich nightmare of the roots and crawlers. To read Miller in that short a period reopens the old question which is always too large: What is a man? Just as our uprooted elm would take on constellations of meaning as it lay in the yard, until finally it could be reminiscent of a battleship, or a host of caverns in Hieronymus Bosch, so might you be forced to ask: What the devil is a tree? Just so does Miller return us to the first question of humanism. What, finally, is a Man? Nothing is settled after all. We have been given the illusion that we know Miller, know every one of his vices, peccadilloes, hustles, horrors, cadges, gifts, flaws, and transcendent generosities, are, yes, familiar with that man who is by his own description "confused, negligent, reckless, lusty, obscene, boisterous, thoughtful, scrupulous, lying, diabolically truthful ... filled with wisdom and nonsense." Nonetheless, when we are done reading, we wonder if we know anything. It is not that he bears no relation to the Henry Miller who is the protagonist of his books. (That Henry Miller is, indeed, the ultimate definition of the word protagonist.) No, the real Henry Miller, which is to say, the corporeal protean Miller a few writers knew intimately and wrote about well, Anaïs Nin being the first, is not very different from his work, but more like a transparency laid over a drawing, copied, and then skewed a degree. He is just a little different from his work. But in that difference is all the mystery of his own personality, and the paradoxes of a great artist. And the failure. For it is impossible to talk of a great artist without speaking of failure. The greater they are, the more they do not fulfill their own idea of themselves. Dostoyevsky failed to write The Life of a Great Sinner, and Tolstoy never brought a religious metamorphosis to man. Miller was never able to come to focus on the one subject which cried out to him: D. H. Lawrence's old subject — what is to be said of love between a man and a woman? Miller saw that Lawrence had come to grips with the poetry of sex but none of the sewer gas. Miller would strike matches to the sewer gas, and set off literary explosions, but he never blew himself over to the other side of the divide. While nobody can be more poetic than Miller about fornication itself — two hundred beer-hall accordions might as well be pumping away as he describes the more heavenly engagements he has played — the writing becomes an evocation of some disembodied but divine cunt and what it is doing to him — his appreciation equal to the enjoyment of a great symphony, yet he still cannot write about fucking with love. (Of course, it is fair to ask, who can?) Miller nonetheless pounds away on the subject like a giant phallus trying to enter a tiny vagina — in the pounding is one simple question: How the hell do you get in?

Miller has not lacked for adulation. A small but accountable part of the literary world has regarded him as the greatest living American writer for the last four decades and indeed, as other American writers died, and Hemingway was there no longer, nor Faulkner and Fitzgerald, not Wolfe, not Steinbeck, nor Dos Passos, and Sinclair Lewis long gone, Dreiser dead and Farrell in partial obscurity, who else could one speak of as the great American author? Moreover, Miller provided his considerable qualifications. One had to go back to Melville to find a rhetoric that could prove as noble under full sail. Miller at his best wrote a prose more overpowering than Faulkner's — the good reader is revolved in a farrago of light with words heavy as velvet, brilliant as gems; eruptions of thought cover the page. You could be in the vortex of one of Turner's oceanic holocausts where the sun shines in the very center of the storm. No, there is nothing like Henry Miller when he gets rolling. Men with literary styles as full as Hawthorne's appear by comparison stripped of their rich language; one has to take the English language back to

Marlowe and Shakespeare before encountering a wealth of imagery equal in intensity.

Yet it can hardly be said that the American Establishment walks around today thinking of Henry Miller as our literary genius, or one of the symbols of human wealth in America. Born in 1891, he will be eighty-five by December 26 of 1976, an artist of incomparably larger dimensions than Robert Frost, yet who can conceive of a President inviting him to read from his work on Inauguration Day, no, the irony is that a number of good and intelligent politicians might even have a slight hesitation over whether it is Arthur Miller or Henry Miller being talked about. "Oh, yes, *Henry* Miller," they might say at last, "the guy who writes the dirty books."

Even in the literary world, however, Miller's reputation survives in a vacuum. It is not that he lacks influence. It is not even excessive to say that Henry Miller had influenced the style of half the good American poets and writers alive today: Would books as different as *Naked Lunch, Portnoy's Complaint, Fear of Flying,* and *Why Are We in Vietnam?* have been as well received (or as free in language) without the irrigation Henry Miller gave to American prose? Even a writer so removed in purpose from Miller as Saul Bellow shows a debt in *Augie March.* Miller has had his effect. Thirty years ago, young writers learned to write by reading him along with Hemingway and Faulkner, Wolfe and Fitzgerald. With the exception of Hemingway, he has had perhaps the largest stylistic influence of them all. Yet there is still that critical space. Miller has only been written about in terms of adulation or dismissal. One does not pick up literary reviews with articles entitled "Ernest Hemingway and Henry Miller — Their Paris Years," or "The Social Worlds of F. Scott Fitzgerald and Henry Miller," no comments on "The Apocalyptic Vision of Henry Miller and Thomas Wolfe as Reflected in Their Rhetoric." Nor is there bound to be a work titled "Henry Miller and the Beat Generation," or "Henry Miller and the Revolution of the Sixties." Young men do not feel they are dying inside because they cannot live the way Henry Miller once lived. Yet no American writer, not even Hemingway, necessarily came closer to the crazy bliss of being alone in a strange city with no money in your pocket, not much food in your stomach, and a hard-on beginning to stir, a "personal" hard-on (as one of Miller's characters nicely describes it).

The paradox therefore persists. It is a wonder. To read *Tropic of*

Cancer today is to take in his dimension. He is a greater writer than one thought. It is one of the few great novels of our American century, a revolution in style and consciousness equal to *The Sun Also Rises.* You cannot pass through the first twenty pages without knowing that a literary wonder is taking place — nobody has ever written in just this way before, nobody may ever write by this style so well again. A time and a place have come to focus in a writer's voice. It is like encountering an archaeological relic. Given enough such novels, the history of our century could never be lost: there would be enough points of reference.

It is close therefore to incomprehensible that a man whose literary career has been with us over forty years, an author who wrote one novel that may yet be considered equal to the best of Hemingway, and probably produced more than Thomas Wolfe day by day, and was better word for word, and purple passage for purple passage, a writer finally like a phenomenon, has somehow, with every large acceptance, and every respect, been nonetheless ignored and near to discarded.

We must assume there was something indigestible about Miller which went beyond his ideas. His condemnations are virtually comfortable to us today, yet he is not an author whose complexities are in harmony with our own. Hemingway and Fitzgerald may each have been outrageous pieces of psychic work, yet their personalities haunt us. Faulkner inspires our reverence and Wolfe our tenderest thoughts for literary genius. They are good to the memories we keep of our reading of them — they live with the security of old films. But Miller does not. He is a force, a value, a literary sage, and yet in the most peculiar sense he does not become more compatible with time — he is no better beloved today than twenty, thirty, or forty years ago — it is as if he is almost not an American author; yet nobody could be more American. So he evades our sense of classification. He does not become a personality, rather he maintains himself as an enigma.

The authors who live best in legend offer personalities we can comprehend like movie stars. Hemingway and Fitzgerald impinge on our psyche with the clarity of Bogart and Cagney. We comprehend them at once. Faulkner bears the same privileged relation to a literary Southerner as Olivier to the London theatregoer. A grand and cultivated presence is enriching the marrow of your life. Nobody wishes to hear a bad story about Olivier or Faulkner.

Henry Miller, however, exists in the same relation to legend that anti-matter shows to matter. His life is antipathetic to the idea of legend itself. Where he is complex, he is too complex — we do not feel the resonance of slowly dissolving mystery but the madness of too many knots; where he is simple, he is not attractive — his air is harsh. If he had remained the protagonist by which he first presented himself in *Tropic of Cancer* — the man with iron in his phallus, acid in his mind, and some kind of incomparable relentless freedom in his heart, that paradox of tough misery and keen happiness, that connoisseur of the spectrum of odors between good sewers and bad sewers, a noble rat gnawing on existence and impossible to kill, then he could indeed have been a legend, a species of Parisian Bogart or American Belmondo. Everybody would have wanted to meet this post-gangster, barbarian-genius. He would have been the American and heterosexual equivalent of Jean Genet. But that was not his desire. Paradoxically, he was too separate from his work.

In fact, he could never have been too near to the character he made of himself in *Tropic of Cancer*. One part never fits. It is obvious he must have been more charming than he pretends — how else account for all the free dinners he was invited to, the people he lived on, the whores who loved him? There had to be something angelic about him. Anaïs Nin when describing the apartment in Clichy that Miller kept with Alfred Perles made the point that Miller was the one tidying the joint. "Henry keeps house like a Dutch housekeeper. He is very neat and clean. No dirty dishes about. It is all monastic, really, with no trimmings, no decoration."* Where in all of *Tropic of Cancer* is this neat and charming man?

The novel must be more a fiction than a fact. Which, of course, is not to take away a particle of its worth. Perhaps it becomes even more valuable. After all, we do not write to recapture an experience, we write to come as close to it as we can. Sometimes we are not very close, and yet, paradoxically, are nearer than if we had a photograph. Not nearer necessarily to the verisimilitude of what happened, but to the mysterious reality of what can happen on a page. Oil paints do not create clouds but the image of clouds; a page of manuscript can only evoke that special kind of reality which lives on the skin of the writing paper, a rainbow on a soap bubble. Miller is

---

* *The Diary of Anaïs Nin* (*Vol. 1*) (New York: The Swallow Press and Harcourt, Brace & World, Inc., 1966), p. 62.

forever accused of caricature by people who knew his characters, and any good reader knows enough about personality to sense how much he must be leaving out of his people. Yet, what a cumulative reality they give us. His characters make up a Paris more real than its paving stones until a reluctant wonder bursts upon us — no French writer, no matter how great, not Rabelais, nor Proust, not De Maupassant, Hugo, Huysmans, Zola or even Balzac, not even Céline, has made Paris more vivid to us. Whenever before has a foreigner described a country better than its native writers? For in *Tropic of Cancer* Miller succeeded in performing one high literary act: he created a tone in prose which caught the tone of a period and a place. If that main character in *Tropic of Cancer* named Henry Miller never existed in life, it hardly matters — he is the voice and spirit which existed at the time. The spirits of literature may be the nearest we come to historical truth.

For that matter, the great confessions of literature are apart from their authors. Augustine recollecting his sins is not the sinner but the pieties. Stendhal is not Julian Sorel, nor Kierkegaard the seducer. *On the Road* is close to Jack Kerouac, yet he gives a happier Kerouac than the one who died too soon. Proust was not his own narrator, even as homosexuality is not heterosexuality but another land, and if we take *The Sun Also Rises* as the purest example of a book whose protagonist created the precise air of a time and a place, even there we come to the realization that Hemingway at the time he wrote it could not have been equal to Jake Barnes — he had created a consciousness wiser, drier, purer, more classic, more sophisticated and more graceful than his own. He was still gauche in relation to his creation.

The difference between Hemingway and Miller is that Hemingway set out thereafter to grow into Jake Barnes and locked himself for better and worse, for enormous fame and eventual destruction, into that character who embodied the spirit of an age. Miller, following, had only to keep writing *Tropic of Cancer* over and over, refining his own personality to become less and less separate from his book, and he could have entered the American life of legend. But Henry, eight years older than Hemingway, yet arriving at publication eight years later, and so sixteen years older in 1934 than Hemingway was in 1926, chose to go in the opposite direction. He proceeded to move away from the first Henry Miller he had created. He did not wish to be a character but a soul — he would be various. He was.

The cruelest criticism ever delivered of Henry James is that he had a consciousness (and a style) so hermetic that his pen would have been paralyzed if one of his characters had ever entered a town house, removed his hat, and found a turd on his head (a matter we would hope of small moment to Tolstoy or to Dostoyevsky or to Stendhal). Hemingway would have been bothered more than he liked. Miller would have loved it. How did his host react to the shit? How did our host's wife? My God, the way she smacked her nostrils, you can be sure her thighs were in a lather.

In fact, Hemingway would have hated such a scene. He was trying to create a world where mood — which Hemingway saw as the staff of life — could be cultivated by the scrupulosity with which you kept mood aloft. Mood surviving through the excellence of your gravity, courage, and diction, that is to say, your manners.

Hemingway's dreams must have looked down the long vista of his future suicide. So he had a legitimate fear of chaos. He never wrote about the river — he contented himself with the quintessentially American aesthetic of writing about the camp he set up each night by the side of the river: That was the night we made camp at the foot of the cliffs just after the place where the rapids were bad.

Miller became the other half of literature, an *espontaneo* without fear of his end, a literary athlete at ease in air, earth, or water. I am the river, he was always ready to say, I am the rapids and the placids, I'm the froth and the scum and the twigs — what a roar as I go over the falls. Who gives a fart? Let others camp where they may. I am the river and there is nothing I can't swallow.

Hemingway's world was doomed to collapse so soon as the forces of the century pushed life into a technological tunnel; with Hemingway, mood could not survive grinding gears, surrealist manners — here's shit in your hat — static, but Miller took off at the place where Hemingway stopped. In *Tropic of Cancer* he was saying — and it is the force of the book — I am obliged to live where mood is in the meat grinder, so I know more about it. I know all of the spectrum that runs from good mood to bad mood, and can tell you — a stinking mood is better than no mood. Life has been designed to run in the stink.

Miller bounces in it. We read *Tropic of Cancer*, that book of horrors, and feel happy. It is because there is honor in the horror, and metaphor in the hideous. How, we cannot even begin to say. Maybe, mood is vastly more various, self-regenerative, hearty and sly than Hemingway ever guessed. Maybe mood is not a lavendar lady, but a barmaid. Without stoicism or good taste, or even a nose for the nicety of good guts under terrible pressure, Miller is still living closer to death than Hemingway, certainly he is closer if the sewer is nearer to our end than the wound.

History proved to be on Miller's side. Twentieth-century life was leaving the world of individual effort, liquor, and tragic wounds, for the big-city garbage can of bruises, migraines, static, mood chemicals, amnesia, absurd relations, and cancer. Down in the sewers of existence where the cancer was being cooked, Miller was cavorting. Look, he was forever saying, you do not have to die of this crud. You can breathe it, eat it, suck it, fuck it, and still bounce up for the next day. There is something inestimable in us if we can stand the smell. Considering where the world was going — right into the world wide sewer of the concentration camps — Miller may have had a message that gave more life than Hemingway.

Papa & Son

ॐ

What characterizes every book about Hemingway I have read is the way his character remains out of focus. Even a writer with an edge as hard as Lillian Ross did not seem able to catch him properly in her famous *New Yorker* piece. Hemingway was there, but much too precise in his portrait, as if he had sat for one of those neo-realistic paintings where the pride of the artist is to make the subject look as if he has been photographed, not painted.

For contrast, there is Carlos Baker's monumental biography and it gives us an immense amount of day-to-day material somewhat modestly undigested. It is nonetheless an invaluable book which every ambitious biography to come will evaluate detail by detail, a necessary task, for Baker's book was written with a determinedly soft focus as if the author felt his literary mission was not so much to present the man as to cover every year of Hemingway's existence in the recollections of his friends.

There is also A. E. Hotchner's book which gives a portrait, and most readable it is, but askew. Hotchner is using a wide-angle lens; the very nostrils of the great man are distorted. Sadly we learn there is reason to believe the materials are transposed. A long and marvelously articulated speech which Hemingway makes once to Hotchner turns out in fact to have been taken from a letter. It is a minor literary peccadillo of the sort professional magazine writers

94

commit often, since their skills mature in a school that demands you tell your story fast and make it track (and a quotation from a letter comes off slower than a man talking), but such methods breed distortion with their speed.

Now, we have here a book* written by a son about his father, written by a son who is not a professional writer as he is quick to tell you (although he can write interestingly enough — it may even be a book which will be read at one sitting by more than half the readers who pick it up). That is because it is unlike most books written by sons about great fathers. There is nothing slavish here. The son lies to the father, and the father pays him back, meanly; the son loves the father and the father loves him back, but in his own style, and it is remote enough for the son to hate him a little as well. If it is a portrait written in love, it is with all the sweets and sours of love. What characterizes love when not wholly blissful is how damnably sweet and sour it gets. It kills any man or woman if they have the bad luck to be deeply in love with a veritable son of a bitch, and every bad thing we have ever heard about Hemingway can find its echo in this book. You do not have to wonder when you are done why any number of men and women could know Hemingway well and hate him. Yet everything fine, noble, attractive, and splendid in the man comes in with its echo as well. For once, you can read a book about Hemingway and not have to decide whether you like him or not. He is there. By God, he exists. He is a father, good and bad by turns, even sensational and godawful on different days of the year, and his contradictions are now his unity, his dirty fighting and his love of craft come out of the same blood. We can feel the man present before us, and his complexes have now become no more than his moods. His pride and his evasions have become one man, his innocence and sophistication, his honesty and outsize snobbery, his romantic madness and inconceivably practical sense of how to be outrageously romantic, it all comes through as in no other book about Hemingway, and for the simplest reason — the father was real to the son. Whereas those of us who approach Hemingway from without have been in the position of trying to find the reality behind the legend, and that is an especially contemporary form of analysis which tends to come out wrong. Hemingway, when all is said, was a Midwestern boy seized by success and ripped out of every root, and

---

* *Papa* by Gregory H. Hemingway, M.D.

he spent the rest of his life in trying to relocate some of his old sense of terra firma by following each movement of the wind (and there were many) through his talent and his dread. What a remarkable achievement, that the sense of that talent and dread, while hardly ever referred to in these pages, is nonetheless in every paragraph of this unassuming and affective memoir.

My Friend,
Jean Malaquais

✨

I did not like this book* twenty years ago, and thought it disappointing. Since I had learned as much about writing from the author as from anyone alive, large demands were put upon the manuscript. Jean Malaquais was not only my good friend, perhaps even my best friend, but my mentor, more — he had had more influence upon my mind than anyone I ever knew from the time we had gotten well acquainted while he was translating *The Naked and the Dead* into French. Part of the friendship rested on his candor. He is hardly rich now, and he was poor then, as only a French intellectual who teaches an evening course at the New School can be bread-crust poor in New York, and he made no pretense — he was not in love with *The Naked and the Dead*. No, he was doing the translation because he needed the work. It proved a munificent sum. The publisher was giving him $2,000, and in the course of the year, I added another $1,000 out of shame. I had never seen a man work so hard at a job for which he did not have respect. In the year it took him to make that translation, he must have worked eight hours a day, five or six days a week; he was a perfectionist and a French stylist, and hated my prose in that book with much detailed justice: he would draw vectors across the pages to show how sloppily I had repeated words, or worse, *ideas* — how he detested anything slovenly in literature! He had, after all, fashioned the style of his own French prose out of the hungriest inner disciplines. Like Conrad, he was Polish, and also began to learn the language in which he would write

---

* (From an introduction to *The Joker*.)

only after he was out of his adolescence. Conceive of such hungry disciplines when he was a young emigrant from Warsaw who worked in French mines and came to clarify the literature of his new tongue by spending fourteen hours a day in the Bibliothèque Nationale in order to keep warm — it was cold on the winter streets of Paris in the years of the Depression — yes, learned his French by reading and writing in that library with all his imagination, ambitions and privations going into it, and took a post-graduate course in the hierarchical elegance of the tongue by being secretary to André Gide for a period, indeed met his future employer by composing a furious letter on the spur of reading a casual piece the author had done for a literary review.[1]

In those pages, Gide had written that he sometimes wondered if poverty might not have deepened his art. We can imagine the irony with which he would surround so direct a sentimentality. Malaquais, however, pulled up the barbarism and shook it in the air. *You ought to get down on your knees and pray to that God you occasionally pretend to believe in that He has let you be a comfortable bourgeois so you can make your art.* Such was the note of the letter, a howl of ferocity torn right out of the bitterness of trying to write at the maximum of one's possible talents when there was no money in the pocket and no food in the belly. Gide wrote back to apologize. He confessed he had not been thinking of the situation of young writers like Malaquais for whom such words had to be naturally and justifiably intolerable, no, he feared he had been playing too inconsiderately with a conceit; he had wished to startle a number of his confreres who were overconcerned with their sensibility and so had been cushioning themselves against too much shock. He hoped to pose the possible stimulations of shock. But it had been unfeeling to ignore the situation of penniless young men like Malaquais and their sentiments on reading his words.[2] To the letter, Gide pinned a bill,

---

[1] I think it is worth printing Malaquais' corrections (by way of a recent letter) to a few of my biographical facts.

"The library was la bibliothèque Sainte-Genevieve, the only one in Paris that stayed open till 10 P.M. I'd remain there all day long (10–12 hours), often without a meal. At closing time I'd go to Les Halles where, with some luck, I'd be unloading crates of cackling poultry or frozen cabbage. Still, job or no job, I could always grab there an apple or a couple of carrots to keep the man alive."

[2] *From Malaquais' letter:* "Gide's piece, an excerpt from his *Journal* dated March 1935, appeared in the October issue of la Nouvelle Revue Française. I think it was December when I happened to read it. Had you a chance to look it up (cf. Justin O'Brien's transl., Knopf), I am sure you'd agree it was plain sentimental gibberish, and not in the least ironic. Idiocy was the price one had to pay for going along — even for a while — with the Stalinists."

something like ten pre–World War II francs. Let us say the sum might bring back twenty dollars' worth of groceries today. Malaquais tore up the money and mailed the scraps back to Gide. "Do not think," he wrote, "that you can buy a postage stamp for your soul. If you wish to do something for me, do something real, give me a job! Do not throw me crumbs!"

Now came another letter. Would Malaquais come and visit?[3]

"C'est toi, Malaquais?" asked Gide on the day he appeared.

"Oui, c'est moi. C'est toi, Gide?"

Could fifty years have gone by since a younger man had said "toi" to him? Still, it was the period of Gide's growing sympathy for the USSR. How characteristic to be intrigued, therefore, with a young Pole who was both an intellectual and a worker, not only a Marxist, but — perverse prize to esteem — a species of rare Marxist from some rarefied splinter group, the absolute antithesis, therefore, of all those Soviet bureaucrats with whom Gide was now trying to find tillable intellectual ground. All the more intoxicating to listen then to the concentrated polemic of a Marxist who was altogether anti-Soviet — that was in the grain for Gide. He could hardly move toward atheism without encouraging the friendship of every cleric he knew.

So began an intellectual relationship which would continue intermittently for years. If Gide was to absorb little of Marx from Malaquais (which may have been Gide's fault!) the new secretary was to learn a great deal about writing from the master.[4] A decade and a half later during the winter and spring of 1949 while Malaquais was translating *The Naked and the Dead* and we became friends despite his aforesaid abomination of my writing (with which I secretly

---

[3] *From Malaquais' letter:* "G. pinned to his letter a postal order for 100.00 francs (20.00 doll. is about right). I mailed it back, telling him he couldn't buy himself a piece of real estate in paradise at my expense. Not that I was beyond bribery. Had he sent 1.000.00 francs, I might have considered. But for 100.00 francs I'd rather have him stay in hell. That's when he wrote, would I come and visit."

[4] *From Malaquais' letter:* "I was not G's secretary or otherwise in his pay. He did ask me from time to time to do this or that for him — read and comment upon the hundreds of letters (mostly insulting) he had received as a sequel to his two books on Russia; or he'd want me to put some order in his voluminous archives; or call on me at any odd hour for a game of chess; or drag me along the streets through lengthy aimless errands; or drop in my lap a manuscript of his and out of the corners of his eyes watch me as I sniffed over it, and so on. But there was never a question of employment or salary. Yet, it is true that he gave me a helping hand. He had me examined by his doctor, saw to it that I put on a few badly needed pounds of flesh, that I was taken care of when in the hospital, in short possibly kept me from spitting my lungs. And he supported me intermittently when I was writing my first book, and it was he who secured for Galy and myself the Mexican visa which saved our hides."

agreed — was I the first to think that *The Naked and the Dead* was a good novel in spite of its style?) I would be obliged in my turn to pick up Malaquais' literary precepts, live with them, wrestle with their intent, and even absorb one or two while hearing Gide's example cited so repeatedly during debates on style that I came to feel at last as if I knew him, or at least knew something of his taste and how his strictures were formed.

There was nothing slavish about Malaquais, least of all his mind. He was an intellectual sultan, still is, and so my ongoing education in the niceties of good writing was not a simple concert of homage to Gide — Malaquais had for his old employer the comfortable respect we offer a writer whose virtues are prominent but whose lacks are clear in our estimate. After any harangue by Malaquais designed to reduce my truculence toward elegance, severity, and restraint (which virtues were elevated through all of my friend's dialectic in order to purify the quality of *surprise* in one's work — a traditional Gallic presentation under the very shadow of the great literary chef, André G., himself) my mentor was also perfectly capable of saying in an aside, "Of course when it comes to an analysis of history, Gide is like a schoolboy. He has every gift for seizing the paradox of character — he is virtually the first to comprehend that character *is* paradox — but give him a social context and he will lose all instinct for the dialectic."

On reflection, it was true. Gide did not live with dialectic. His mind was singularly particular just where Malaquais' was marvelously abstract. Malaquais had the most powerful ability to move from any particular offered him into the Leviathan of his general theory — he was not a Marxist for nothing! — and trying to argue in his presence was analogous to being drawn with one's brain along a magnetic field of the intellect. Willy-nilly was one's mind reoriented along one Polish Frenchman's poles. Nothing vulgar or bullying about it. Malaquais loathed formula, propaganda, or any variety of thinking which deprived a situation of its nuance. So he was capable of advancing a new thesis, anticipating your objections, stating them with clarity (like Freud disarming his critics) and then would overtake his own verification of your position in the return swing of the dialectic. He would do this with such power that when he argued, the veins in his forehead would throb as though to demonstrate that the human head was obliged to be the natural site if not the very phallus of Mind. Malaquais would have at such times a remarkable resemblance to Picasso — the same noble vault of forehead and workingman's knob of a nose, same characterological determination of chin, same cleft. (Of course, Malaquais might detest the comparison. "What a stinker!" I heard him say once of Picasso.)[5] Still, speaking of genius, I heard Malaquais give a lecture once at the New School. I never heard a better one. For fifty minutes he spoke (without a note) exploring into the recesses of a novelist's unique relation to his time — memory across the years suggests the lecture may have been on Stendhal, or was it Proust? — I only remember the sensation of feeling my intelligence conducted through exercises I might not ordinarily have been able to follow. He had the same intense application of energy upon a given point that one finds only in those few great athletes who bring absolute concentration to every instant of a contest and so reveal to you by their body movement some meanings of the sport. When Malaquais lectured, it was inconceivable that his mind and tongue could separate. To cerebrate was to speak. Once at a party, he went on for hours, dominated the conversation. When his wife later remonstrated, "Jean, you talked nine-tenths of the time," he grunted and said, "I had ten times as much to say." It was not arrogance. Merely his grim estimate of the proportions, grim because this small French Pole with his rugged face and mighty brow, his virile purchase on any question to come his way, this prodigy of debate, this behemoth of orality — he spoke out of the same gusto with which a good appetite devours steak — was a man locked in chains when it came to writing. No author ever had more to be grim about.

With no belief in karma, one might still have to postulate a phenomenon like reincarnation to explain the enormity of Malaquais' woes when he tried to write — only a soul paying in this life for outrages it had performed in another could pass through such suffering. So Malaquais may once have been Gilles de Rais. In the late Forties and the early Fifties when Jean was writing *The Joker*, just those years when I first came to know him well, he would sit at his desk for ten or twelve or fourteen hours a day, every day. It was his boast that he would not get up, not pace around, not break for a meal, no, he would sit, contemplate his page, and would write . . . to the tune of two or three hundred words a day. Two hundred words in ten hours! It is twenty words an hour, or a new word every three minutes. Can any torture be more horrifically designed for a man who

---

[5] *From Malaquais' letter:* "Did I ever say of Picasso, 'What a stinker!'? If so, it must have been in relation to some concrete occasion, perhaps his drawing a 'dove of peace' in Stalin's honor."

could deliver an extempore lecture complete in thought, example, and syntax, a work of seven or eight thousand words in less than an hour, to be reduced now, down now, with a pen in his hand, to twenty words in sixty minutes? The culture of the past must have sat on his mind like Gibraltar. How could he dare to write about anything? Given his profound contempt for authors who rushed to place their shoddy artifacts into that small temple where only a few perfect works ought to be installed, how presume to add to the excrementa? So this flame-thrower of a mind (when free at its own unrecorded speech) was now confined to one burning wire which sought to drill a tiny hole into the rock of his weighty regard for the value of literature. A man who sat twelve hours at his desk in meditation might have enjoyed such a life even with no more than two hundred words a day, but Malaquais, like many an author before him, labored in depression and whole fatigue. "Yes," he said once, "if you want to do good work, you must *pisser le sang,*" and he must have pissed the blood of every disappearing ambition into the hours he chained himself to that desk. What an effort! Over two years, then three years of just such work, slowly *The Joker* bored its little hole into the great rock of his resistance to himself, and Malaquais emerged at last with this novel.

2.

I was aghast when I read it. So much had happened in his life. He had escaped from the Germans after being a prisoner of war, then as a man without a passport had slipped out of Occupied France, only to become metamorphosized into a Jew again, obliged still to hide from the Nazis in Cadiz, while haunting visa factories like a character in *The Consul,* then a penniless émigré living by his wits in Venezuela and Mexico for the rest of the war. He had also been a movie-script writer with respectable credits and an award winner of a major literary prize, the Prix Renaudot, as well as the post-war author of a major novel, *Planete Sans Visa,* and a much-lauded war diary, an ideologist, a romantic, a Marxist, a man with a charmingly demonic wife as well as a critic with every elevated instinct for the kill. He had now written a book so empty of the novelistic riches of his life, that I was in a fury as I read. I had wanted something I was not receiving. *The Joker* seemed bizarre and unlovable — a tract on the bureaucratic horrors of the future written in a nineteenth-century style, an inconglomerate, an *incondominium* of Kafka, *Alice in Wonderland,* some TV afternoon laugh-snort, and *Mission Impossible.* I thought it indigestible; worse, some of the dialogue was guaranteed to grate your teeth. Perhaps it was the fault of the translation I suggested in desperation. No, it was a fine translation, Malaquais insisted. He had worked closely with the translator, a most intelligent woman.

What was one to do with passages like this?

> "I'm called Bomba," he said, "and she's called Kouka. What's your name?"
> I took his hand absent-mindedly and said nothing. He had a grip of iron.
> "You're a oner," he said.
> A radio was blasting away on the mantel of a dummy fireplace. Mistress Kouka unstoppered one of my jars and plunged her nose into it with delight.
> "Oner, punner," she said.

No, Malaquais liked it fine. Nothing wrong with, "You're a oner."

It was obvious this intellectual conquistador had no feeling for the little rhapsodies of the English tongue. I told him what I thought of his book — he had hardly been gentle in his earlier turn on *The Naked and the Dead* and *Barbary Shore* whose imperfections were left forever mortal to me by his critique. What unconscious anger must have been stored in my own reactions; with what an unwitting hostility I must have gone through his pages. The recognition that Malaquais was not one of the world's greatest living writers exploded in me a critical response akin in judgment to a slave rebellion. I was obviously trying to forge my escape from all influence; Malaquais took it like a master. Indeed, it was his turn; if I had been one attentive student through every severity he visited on my work, so he absorbed everything I had to say on the faults of *The Joker,* listened with a half-smile on his face, that painful touch of merriment we feel when good friends are an abyss of agreement apart, and shook his head gloomily from time to time as if it were all too possible that what I had to say might even be true.

Still, he always recovered the private heat of that private and indispensable arrogance which had enabled him to drill the wire into the rock. No, he would always finish by saying, it was a modest book and doubtless had its serious flaws; *quand même*, it had its irreducible little value — he thought finally there was something to it. That was to prove a small consolation in the face of his ongoing poverty, and the modest reception when it came out, its even more modest sale, hardcover for a couple of thousand and no paperback, its quick disappearance. Even in France, where the reviews were good, the book did little.

None of that could have offered him much, and in fact he has not published another novel over all these twenty years — perhaps we keep writing fiction until the pressure of everything in the scheme of things which does not desire novels squeezes us back. It could be said that civilization will enter hell when no more good novels are written and the hum of the TV set is the only resonance in our ear — certain enough, at any rate, a novelist feels that void of substance in his soul (which saints refer to as hell) about the time all urge to write a novel has deserted him. Just as it is the human fate to die, so it may be the novelist's fate to stop writing novels — it comes finally out of the baggage of disappointment in one's life, a species of cumulative nothingness, and Malaquais' fictional talents have indeed been silent.*

Still, it was also part of the character, part of the dignity of a master, that my intense dislike of *The Joker* never affected our friendship, in fact may have improved it, for in coming to revere him less and comprehend him a little more, I came also to understand that he was made of the noble material from which the best friendships are formed.

For he was utterly without rancor at my dislike of his work, and it was a soup of good marrow for any friendship to know that the intensity of the critical standard he imposed on others was applicable to himself. Literary criticism had to exist for itself. This is what this good Marxist, full of his own paradox, proceeded to teach me: that there were more important things than vanity or self-expression. One of them was art. Critical standards were the praetorian guard of that most perishable majesty, art. It is, as an original insight, equal to the claim that one has discovered the wheel, but then every artist

---

* He has published a book: "Kierkegaard: Faith and Paradox" which must surely be one of the most extraordinary studies ever done on the Dane. Unfortunately it has not been translated from French to English.

may have to discover this wheel for himself, and I never knew another writer who was as impersonal about his own work and the work of others, friends or enemies, than Malaquais. If we are buddies we must naturally be ready to die for one another on the barricade, was his unspoken premise, but do not ever ask me to approve of a literary performance I cannot respect. Could anything be less American than to be ready to die for friends if they do not agree with you?

It is the last of my debts to Malaquais and far from the smallest. For whenever I cannot write with ease, whenever the weight of the stone I drag up the ramp of my own pyramid becomes onerous, and I wish for any other occupation than the heavy hours of a writer, the example of my good friend Jean is before me, and I bow my head and go to work again. "Start to pity yourself," says the little voice within, "and you will end up working as hard as Malaquais." How many friends can one count on to set examples for a life?

Narcissism

⚘

June Edith Smith, Henry Miller's second wife, became a figure of obsessive importance in his work. Seen first as Mara in *Tropic of Cancer*, she is called Mona in his trilogy, *The Rosy Crucifixion*, and that novel covers exhaustively (through sixteen hundred pages) the day-to-day movement of their five years together in New York. If the first book, *Sexus*, was begun in 1940 it was not finished until 1945, and *Plexus* took from 1947 to 1949. *Nexus*, the final volume, was not even started until 1952 nor done before 1959. Close to twenty years is spent on this magnum opus! Of course, he has written other books in the same time, *The Air-Conditioned Nightmare*, *The Time of the Assassins*, *The Books in My Life*, *Big Sur and the Oranges of Hieronymus Bosch*, but he is not far from seventy when he is done. The mysteries of his relation with June-Mara-Mona have so beguiled him that he has spent thirty-six obsessive years first living with her, then writing about her, and he never succeeds, never quite, in making her real to us, that is, novelistically real, like Anna Karenina or Emma Bovary. Instead, she hovers in that tricky space between the actual and the fictional where everything is just out of focus. Indeed, Anaïs Nin in one page of her diary succeeds in making the lady as vivid as Miller ever can. (Yet, no more real.)

> Henry came to Louveciennes with June. As June walked toward me from the darkness of the garden into the light of the door, I saw for the first time the most beautiful woman on earth. A startlingly white face, burning black eyes, a face so alive I felt it would consume itself before my eyes. Years ago I tried to imagine

a true beauty; I created in my mind an image of just such a woman. I had never seen her until last night. Yet I knew long ago the phosphorescent color of her skin, her huntress profile, the evenness of her teeth. She is bizarre, fantastic, nervous, like someone in a high fever. Her beauty drowned me. As I sat before her, I felt I would do anything she asked of me. Henry suddenly faded. She was color and brilliance and strangeness. By the end of the evening I had extricated myself from her power. She killed my admiration by her talk. Her talk. The enormous ego, false, weak, posturing. She lacks the courage of her personality, which is sensual, heavy with experience. Her role alone preoccupies her. She invents drama in which she always stars. I am sure she creates genuine dramas, genuine chaos and whirlpools of feelings, but I feel that her share in it is a pose. That night, in spite of my response to her, she sought to be whatever she felt I wanted her to be. She is an actress every moment. I cannot grasp the core of June.

By the end of the evening I felt as Henry did, fascinated with the face and body which promises so much, but hating her invented self which hides the true one.

Curious! If we fix on Miller's mind rather than June's beauty, Nin could be giving a description of Henry's talent: *startling, burning, phosphorescent, bizarre, fantastic, nervous, in a high fever,* full of *color, brilliance,* and *strangeness,* but possessed of an *enormous ego, false, weak, posturing,* and finally *lacking the courage of (its) personality,* leaving behind *chaos* and *whirlpools of feelings.* Yet it may be all a *pose.* One *cannot grasp* the core of Henry Miller, and one can come near to *hating* (his) *invented self which hides the true one.*

It works. If one is to judge Miller's talent by the vices of his mind, the result is not unequal to the flaws in June's beauty. No wonder they spend seven years together. It is a relation which proves compulsive yet is stripped of roots; as emotional as blood but as insecure as emotion itself. She will take him a long way in seven years from the hard-nosed Brooklyn hard-on he pictured himself to be when they met. More enterprising than he, wiser about the world, a better hustler, she convinces him to quit work and try to write while she makes their living. If ever there is an inner movement in his life, it is here. We are witness to his first metamorphosis. He changes from a promoter of bad debts and riotous Brooklyn nights, to a faithful and tortured young writer helplessly in love with a voluptuous woman whose maddening lack of center leads him into an awareness of his own lack of identity. He comes to discover all those modern themes that revolve around the difficulty of discovering oneself. Soon he will dive into the pit of recognizing that there may not be any geological fundament in the psyche that we can call identity. Like June, he will have to re-create himself each morning. Soon, he realizes he has been doing it all his life. He has never had to look back in moral guilt because whatever act he committed yesterday could be looked in the eye today. The man who did it was no longer himself. In the act of doing it, he had become another man, free to go in a new direction. It could be 180 degrees away from yesterday's attempt. Tomorrow he may be close again to the man he was day before yesterday, but it will never be the same. Since he has a life full of adventure, mishaps, and constant lack of funds, since June brings in their living as irregularly as changes in the weather, so there is no nicety to his liberation. Miller's new psychic life is more like a scatback scampering upfield on a punt return. He can lose ten yards as easily as gain them. And his head is forever ringing from the last concussion.

His confusion, however, is great; his passivity feels pervasive. He has changed from a stand-up hallway-fucker to an indolent husband-pimp. His wife is having the adventures. He is home doing the writing, sometimes the cooking. The wife is a consummate liar, and makes money off men to the tune of hundred-dollar bills dropped in from the sky, never tells him how, a woman even more changeable than himself, and vastly more bisexual — their love will crash finally when she brings home a girl to live with them, and becomes hooked on the girl. Sixteen hundred pages of *The Rosy Crucifixion* will founder on Miller's inability to penetrate these bisexual depths, or even come near them. He was brought up by a moral code that taught love was attached to the living room; one's family was one's house. The living room carpet was one's rock. Now he floats in a fluid as limitless as amniotic fluid. He has no limbs and his feet are over his head, his eyes smell sounds and his nose feels colors, he is in the confusion of living with a woman even more unpredictable than himself. He will not use the word, it is not in the vein of his literary blood, but our present temperament can have less difficulty in seeing him as a narcissist awash in the uncategorizability of such experience.

Let us look at the word with fresh interest, however. It is too simple to think of the narcissist as someone in love with himself. One can detest oneself intimately and still be a narcissist. What characterizes narcissism best is that the fundamental relationship is with oneself. That same to-and-fro of love and hate which mates feel for one another is experienced within the self. A special kind of insanity always underwrites the narcissist, therefore. The inner dialogue almost never ceases. Each half of oneself is forever scrutinizing the other. Two narcissists in love are not like two lovers who may feel a visceral need holding them together. Narcissists, rather, are linked up into themselves. They do not attach to each other so much as they approach like crystals brought into communication. They have a passionate affair to the degree that each makes it possible for the other to resonate more fully than when alone. Two narcissists might live together for fifty years in every appearance of matrimonial solidity (although it probably helps if money is present) but essentially, no matter how considerate they may be to one another, the mutual courtesies come more from the decision to be *loving* rather than issuing forth from a love which will express itself whether one wishes it or not. The narcissistic relation insists that the mate be good for one's own resonance. In the profoundest sense, one narcissist is never ready to die for the other. It is not love we encounter so much as fine tuning. Small wonder that the coming together of narcissists is the natural matrimony of the Stereo Century. Small wonder that Henry Miller, the last great American pioneer, is first to boff and bang his way across this last psychological frontier, there first with the most. No love in literature is so long recounted as his sixteen-hundred-page affair and marriage and separation from Mona. *The Rosy Crucifixion* becomes a literary cake as large as the Himalayas. Across half at least of its sixteen hundred pages are peaks and avenues and haunches and battlements and aretes and basins and summits and valleys of writing so good one shakes one's head. Pity the poor aspiring mediocrity of a writer who reads Miller without protection — he will never write another word if he has any decency left. Pity for that matter the good writer. At times Miller is too good.

Yet *The Rosy Crucifixion* is one of the monumental failures in the history of the novel. For those sixteen hundred pages, Miller knocks on the door of ultimate meaning, and it never opens a crack. By the end he is where he was at the beginning, at least so far as sexual satori is concerned. I-got-laid-and-it-was-wondrous is the opening theme of the book. By the end not one new philosophical connection has been laid onto that first lay. Miller and the reader know no more of the wonders beneath the first wonder.

An obvious critical impulse is to decide the work is too long. But on examination it cannot be cut. Rather, as it stands, it is too fragmentary. Perhaps it should be a novel of four thousand pages. What Miller has bogged into (precisely because he is the first American to make the attempt) is the uncharted negotiations of the psyche when two narcissists take the vow of love. Yet it is finally his own true novelistic terrain. He has always eschewed politics as a literary subject (he merely issues calumnies against it). He has also been indifferent to the finicky if invaluable literary task of trying to place people in society, indeed, he never really writes about society except through metaphor. Since he is a great writer, however, his metaphors can occasionally draw the whole of society over one's brain like an incubus. He does this with his vision of the Cosmodemonic Telegraph Company and the unforgettable metaphor in *Tropic of Cancer* when Miller and Van Norden are exhaustedly fucking a worn-out whore like men standing up in the trenches.

His preference, however, is to create his literary world through the dreams and myths that are appropriate to his use. That has to be a perfumed and farty literary game unless there is real novelistic meat on each mythic tendon. So Miller naturally goes to sex for his meat. He is not a social writer, but a sexual writer. Even Lawrence never let go of the idea that through sex he could delineate society; Miller, however, went further. Sex, he assumed, was a natural literary field for the novel, as clear and free and open to a landgrab as any social panorama. One could capture the sex-life of two people in all its profundity and have quite as much to say about the cosmos as any literary plot laid out the other way with its bankers and beggars, ladies and whores, clerks and killers. The real novel, went Miller's assumption, could short-circuit society. Give it to us by way of a cunt impaled on a cock.

That is a herculean assumption. Because you need the phallus of Hercules to bring it off (and conceivably the brain of Einstein). A writer works with what he is given, and in Miller's case, for cosmic blast-off, he had a narcissistic cunt on a narcissistic cock and thirty-six years of bewilderment from the day of meeting his love to the hour he finished writing of her. She was so *changeable* went his everlasting lament.

It is hard enough for a man twisting a pencil through the traps and loops of his handwriting to get a character onto an empty page, but to create someone who shifts all the time! As soon teach one's spine to wind like a snake. The narcissist is always playing roles. If there is any character more difficult for an author to create than a writer more talented than himself, it must be a great actor. We do not even begin to comprehend the psychology of actors. Yet the narcissist not being obliged to conform to the severe discipline of the stage or the camera, is, in effect, on the measure of complexity, a great actor without a stage, a Hamlet without a sea of faces to listen to what is nobler.

The narcissist suffers from too much inner dialogue. The eye of one's consciousness is forever looking at one's own action. Yet — let us try to keep the notion clear — a narcissist is not self-absorbed so much as one self is immersed in studying the other. The narcissist is the scientist and the experiment in one. Other people exist, have value to the narcissist because of their particular ability to arouse one role or another in oneself. And are valued for that. May even be loved for that. Of course, they are loved as an actor loves his audience.

Since the amount of stimulation we can offer ourselves is obviously limited, the underlying problem of the narcissist is boredom. So there are feverish, even violent, attempts to shift the given. One must alter that drear context in which one half of the self is forever examining the stale presence of the other. That is one reason why narcissists are forever falling in and out of love, jobs, places, and addictions. Promiscuity is the opportunity to try a new role. The vanity gained from a one-night stand is an antidote to claustrophobia. That is, if the gamble of the one-night stand turns out well! Miller complains bitterly of June's lack of center, her incapacity to tell the truth or even recognize it. "I want the key," he says once to Anaïs Nin, "the key to the lies." Blind to himself — does not every artist have to live in partial and self-induced blindness, or he could never find a foundation for his effort? — Miller does not want to recognize that the key may be simple. Every day is a scenario for June. On the best of days she creates a life into which she can fit for a few hours. She can feel real love and real hate for strangers, and thereby leave the circle of her self-absorption. Through scenarios, she can arrive in an hour at depths of emotion other people voyage toward for years. Of course, the scenario once concluded, so, too, is the love for the day. The passing actor she played with is again a stranger. It is useless to speak of whether she loves or does not love Miller. It depends on whether he is in her scenario that day. So it is also useless to speak of her lies. They are no more real to her than yesterday's role. It is today's scenario that is her truth and her life. That is her liberty from the prison cell of the narcissist.

Of course, it is not all that bad. Part of Miller's continuing literary obsession with June is due to the variety of her roles. Each, after all, offers its new role for Miller. He does play opposite the leading lady. If one day he is a detective, and the next, a criminal, that keeps interest in one's personality alive.

Narcissists, after all, induce emotion in one another through their minds. It is not their flesh which is aroused so much as the vibrancy of the role. Their relations are at once more electric and more empty, more perfect and more hollow. But the hollow seems never to fill, experience is poured into no vessels of the psyche, but seems to drain away. So, narcissism may be a true disease, a biological displacement of the natural impulse to develop oneself by the lessons of one's experience, which could bear the same relation to love that onanism does to copulation, or cancer to the natural growth of tissue. Can we come a little nearer to the recognition that there may be a base beneath all disease, an ultimate disease, a psychosomatic doom, so to speak, against which all the other illnesses, colds, fevers, infections, and deteriorations are bulwarks to protect us against a worse fate? Which is none other than that irreversible revolt of the flesh or the mind into cancer or insanity. That is psychosomatic doom — to follow the growth of the flesh or the mind into hideous anomaly. But if that is the case, how can we not suppose that for the narcissist — always so aware that something is wrong within — there is a constant unconscious terror: his or her isolation, if unrelieved, will end in one arm or the other of the ultimate disease.

The paradox is that no love can prove so intense, therefore, as the love of two narcissists for each other. So much depends on it. Each — the paradox turns upon itself — is capable of offering deliverance to the other. To the degree that they tune each other superbly well, they begin to create what before had been impossible — they begin to acquire the skills that enable them to enter the world. (For it is not love of the self, but dread of the world outside the self, which is the seed of narcissism.) Narcissists can end, therefore, by having a real need of each other. That is, of course, hardly the characteristic relation. The love of most narcissists tends to become comic. Seen from the outside, their suffering manages to be equaled only by the rapidity with which they recover from suffering.

The reality, of course, is considerably more painful. Given the delicacy of every narcissist, and the timidity which created their detachment, we can see again that the intensity of their relations is for good cause with themselves. For their own self-protection, they need an excess of control over external events. (Not too removed in analogy is that excess of control which technology is forever trying to exact from nature.)

To the degree, however, that narcissism is an affliction of the talented, the stakes are not small, and the victims are playing a serious game right in the midst of their scenarios. For if one can break out of the penitentiary of self-absorption, then there may be artistic wonders to achieve.

Miller could have been playing, therefore, for the highest stakes. He had the energy, the vision, the talent, and the outrageous individuality to have some chance of becoming the greatest writer in America's history, a figure equal to Shakespeare. (For Americans.) Of course, to invoke such contrasts is to mock them. A writer cannot live too seriously with the idea that he will or will not beat Tolstoy — he has rather some sense of a huge and not impossible literary destiny in the reverberations of his own ambition; he feels his talent, perhaps, as a trust; so he sees his loves as evil when they balk him. He is living, after all, with his own secret plot. He knows that a writer of the largest dimension can alter the nerves and marrow of a nation; no one, in fact, can measure what collective loss would have come to English people if Shakespeare had failed to write. (Or, for that matter, conceive how the South would be subtly less interesting without Faulkner.)

In those seven years with June, Miller was shaping the talent with which he would go out into the world. It is part of the total ambiguity of narcissism (despite the ten thousand intimate details he offers of his life) that we do not know by the end of *The Rosy Crucifixion* whether she breathed a greater life into his talent or exploited him. We do not know whether Miller if he had never met Mona could have become something like equal to Shakespeare and capable of writing about tyrants and tycoons (instead, repetitively, of his own liberation) or — we are left wide open — the contrary is the true possibility and he might never have written at all if he had not met her. All we know is that after seven years of living with her, he went off to Paris alone and learned to live by himself, having come into that confluence of his life where he could extract a clean and unforgettable aesthetic from ogres and sewers. It is kin to the nightmare of narcissism that we are left with this question and no answer.

Tango, Last Tango

❧

To pay one's $5.00 and join the full house at the Translux for the evening show of *Last Tango in Paris* is to be reminded once again that the planet is in a state of pullulation. The seasons accelerate. The snow which was falling in November had left by the first of March. Would our summer arrive at Easter and end with July? It is all that nuclear radiation, says every aficionado of the occult. And we pullulate. Like an ant-hive beginning to feel the heat.

We know that Spengler's thousand-year metamorphosis from Culture to Civilization is gone, way gone, and the century required for a minor art to move from commencement to decadence is off the board. Whole fashions in film are born, thrive, and die in twenty-four months. Still! It is only a half year since Pauline Kael declared to the readers of *The New Yorker* that the presentation of *Last Tango in Paris* at the New York Film Festival on October 14, 1972, was a date that "should become a landmark in movie history — comparable to May 29, 1913 — the night *Le Sacre du Printemps* was first performed — in music history," and then went on to explain that the newer work had "the same kind of hypnotic excitement as the *Sacre*, the same primitive force, and the same jabbing, thrusting eroticism. . . . Bertolucci and Brando have altered the face of an art form." Whatever could have been shown on screen to make Kael pop open for a film? "This must be the most powerfully erotic movie ever made, and it may turn out to be the most liberating movie ever made. . . ." Could this be our own Lady Vinegar, our quintessential cruet? The first frigid of the film critics was treating

115

us to her first public reception. Prophets of Baal, praise Kael! We had obviously no ordinary hour of cinema to contemplate.

Now, a half year later, the movie is history, has all the palpability of the historic. Something just discernible has already happened to humankind as a result of it, or at least to that audience who are coming in to the Translux to see it. They are a crew. They have unexpected homogeneity for a movie audience, compose, indeed, so thin a sociological slice of the New York and suburban sausage that you cannot be sure your own ticket isn't what was left for the toothpick, while the rest of the house has been bought at a bite. At the least, there is the same sense of aesthetic oppression one feels at a play when the house is filled with a theater party. So, too, is the audience at *Tango* an infarct of middle-class anal majesties — if Freud hadn't given us the clue, a reader of faces could decide all on his own that there had to be some social connection between sex, shit, power, violence, and money. But these middle-class faces have advanced their historical inch from the last time one has seen them. They are this much closer now to late Romans.

Whether matrons or young matrons, men or boys, they are *swingers*. The males have wife-swapper mustaches, the women are department-store boutique. It is as if everything recently and incongruously idealistic in the middle class has been used up in the years of resistance to the Vietnamese War — now, bring on the Caribbean. Amazing! In America, even the Jews have come to look like the French middle class, which is to say that the egocentricity of the Fascist mouth is on the national face. Perhaps it is the five-dollar admission, but this audience has an obvious obsession with sex as the confirmed core of a wealthy life. It is enough to make one ashamed of one's own obsession (although where would one delineate the difference?). Maybe it is that this audience, still in March, is suntanned, or at the least made up to look suntanned. The red and orange of their skins will match the famous "all uterine" colors — so termed by the set designer — of the interiors in *Last Tango*.

In the minute before the theater lights are down, what a tension is in the house. One might as well be in the crowd just before an important fight commences. It is years since one has watched a movie begin with such anticipation. And the tension holds as the projection starts. We see Brando and Schneider pass each other in the street. Since we have all been informed — by *Time* no less — we know they are going to take carnal occupation of each other, and very soon. The audience watches with anxiety as if it is also going to be in the act with someone new, and the heart (and for some, the bowels) shows a tremor between earthquake and expectation. Maria Schneider is so sexual a presence. None of the photographs has prepared anybody for this. Rare actresses, just a few, have flesh appeal. You feel as if you can touch them on the screen. Schneider has nose appeal — you can smell her. She is every eighteen-year-old in a mini-skirt and a maxi-coat who ever promenaded down Fifth Avenue in the inner arrogance that proclaims, "My cunt is my chariot."

We have no more than a few minutes to wait. She goes to look at an apartment for rent, Brando is already there. They have passed in the street, and by a telephone booth; now they are in an empty room. Abruptly Brando cashes the check Stanley Kowalski wrote for us twenty-five years ago — he fucks the heroine standing up. It solves the old snicker of how do you do it in a telephone booth? — he rips her panties open. In our new line of *New Yorker*–approved superlatives, it can be said that the cry of the fabric is the most thrilling sound to be heard in World Culture since the four opening notes of Beethoven's Fifth.[1] It is, in fact, a hell of a sound, small, but as precise as the flash of a match above a pile of combustibles, a way for the director to say, "As you may already have guessed from the way I established my opening, I am very good at movie making, and I have a superb pair, Brando and Schneider — they are sexual heavyweights. Now I place my director's promise upon the material: you are going to be in for a grave and wondrous experience. We are going to get to the bottom of a man and a woman."

So intimates Bertolucci across the silence of that room, as Brando and Schneider, fully dressed, lurch, grab, connect, hump, scream, and are done in less than a minute, their orgasms coming on top of one another like trash cans tumbling down a hill. They fall to the floor, and fall apart. It is as if a hand grenade has gone off in their entrails. A marvelous scene, good as a passionate kiss in real life, then not so good because there has been no shot of Brando going up Schneider, and since the audience has been watching in all the som-

---

[1] John Simon, as predictable in his critical reactions as a headwaiter, naturally thought *Last Tango* was part of the riff-raff. Since it is Simon's temper to ignore details, he not only does not hear the panties tearing (some ears reside in the music of the spheres) but announces that Schneider, beasty abomination, is wearing none.

ber awe one would bring to the first row of a medical theater, it is like seeing an operation without the entrance of the surgeon's knife.

One can go to any hard-core film and see fifty phalluses going in and out of as many vaginas in four hours (if anyone can be found who stayed four hours). There is a monumental abstractedness about hard core. It is as if the more a player can function sexually before a camera, the less he is capable of offering any other expression. Finally, the sexual organs show more character than the actors' faces. One can read something of the working conditions of a life in some young girl's old and irritated cunt, one can even see triumphs of the human spirit — old and badly burned labia which still come to glisten with new life, capital! There are phalluses in porno whose distended veins speak of the integrity of the hardworking heart, but there is so little specific content in the faces! Hard core lulls after it excites, and finally it puts the brain to sleep.

But Brando's real cock up Schneider's real vagina would have brought the history of film one huge march closer to the ultimate experience it has promised since its inception (which is to re-embody life). One can even see how on opening night at the Film Festival, it did not matter so much. Not fully prepared for what was to come, the simulated sex must have quivered like real sex the first time out. Since then we have been told the movie is great, so we are prepared to resist greatness, and have read in *Time* that Schneider said, " 'We were never screwing on stage. I never felt any sexual attraction for him . . . he's almost fifty you know, and' — she runs her hand from her torso to her midriff, 'he's only beautiful to here!' "

So one watches differently. Yes, they *are* simulating. Yes, there is something slightly unnatural in the way they come and fall apart. It is too stylized, as if paying a few subtle respects to Kabuki. The real need for the real cock of Brando into the depths of the real actress might have been for those less exceptional times which would follow the film long after it opened and the reaction had set in.

Since *Tango* is, however, the first major film with a respectable budget, a superbly skilled young director, an altogether accomplished cameraman, and a great actor who is ready to do more than dabble in improvisation, indeed will enter heavily into such near to untried movie science, so the laws of improvisation are before us, and the first law to recognize is that it is next to impossible to build on too false a base. The real problem in movie improvisation is to find some ending that is true to what has gone before and yet is sufficiently untrue to enable the actors to get out alive.

We will come back to that. It is, however, hardly time to let go of our synopsis. Real or simulated, opening night or months later, we know after five minutes that, at the least, we are in for a thoroughgoing study of a man and a woman, and the examination will be close. Brando rents the empty apartment; they will visit each other there every day. His name is Paul, hers is Jeanne, but they are not to learn each other's names yet. They are not to tell one another such things, he informs her. "We don't need names here . . . we're going to forget everything we knew. . . . Everything outside this place is bullshit."

They are going to search for pleasure. We are back in the existential confrontation of the century. Two people are going to fuck in a room until they arrive at a transcendent recognition or some death of themselves. We are dealing not with a plot but with a theme that is open range for a hundred films. Indeed we are face to face with the fundamental structure of porno — the difference is that we have a director who by the measure of porno is Eisenstein, and actors who are as gods. So the film takes up the simplest and richest of structures. To make love in an empty apartment, then return to a separate life. It is like every clandestine affair the audience has ever had, only more so — no names! Every personal demon will be scourged in the sex — one will obliterate the past! That is the huge sanction of anonymity. It is equal to a new life.

What powerful biographical details we learn, however, on the instant they part. Paul's wife is a suicide. Just the night before, she has killed herself with a razor in a bathtub; the bathroom is before us, red as an abattoir. A sobbing chambermaid cleans it while she speaks in fear to Paul. It is not even certain whether the wife is a suicide or he has killed her — that is almost not the point. It is the bloody death suspended above his life like a bleeding amputated existence — it is with that crimson torso before his eyes that he will make love on the following days.

Jeanne, in her turn, is about to be married to a young TV director. She is the star in a videofilm he is making about French youth. She pouts, torments her fiancé, delights in herself, delights in the special idiocy of men. She can cuckold her young director to the roots of his eyes. She also delights in the violation she will make of her own bourgeois roots. In this TV film she makes within the movie she presents her biography to her fiancé's camera: she is the daughter of a dead Army officer who was sufficiently racist to teach his dog to detect Arabs by smell. So she is well brought up — there are glimpses of a suburban villa on a small walled estate — it is nothing less than the concentrated family honor of the French Army she will surrender when Brando proceeds a little later to bugger her.

These separate backgrounds divide the film as neatly between biography and fornication as those trick highball glasses which present a drawing of a man or a woman wearing clothes on the outside of the tumbler and nude on the inside. Each time Brando and Schneider leave the room we learn more of their lives beyond the room; each time they come together, we are ready to go further. In addition, as if to enrich his theme for students of film, Bertolucci offers touches from the history of French cinema. The life preserver in *Atalante* appears by way of homage to Vigo, and Jean-Pierre Léaud of *The 400 Blows* is the TV director, the boy now fully grown. Something of the brooding echo of *Le Jour Se Lève* and Arletty is also with us, that somber memory of Jean Gabin wandering along the wet docks in the dawn, waiting for the police to pick him up after he has murdered his beloved. It is as if we are to think not only of this film but of other sexual tragedies French cinema has brought us, until the sight of each gray and silent Paris street is ready to evoke the lost sound of the *Bal musette* and the sad near-silent wash of the Seine. Nowhere as in Paris can doomed lovers succeed in passing sorrow, drop by drop, through the blood of the audience's heart.

Yet as the film progresses with every skill in evidence, while Brando gives a performance that is unforgettable (and Schneider shows every promise of becoming a major star), as the historic buggeries and reamings are delivered, and the language breaks through barriers not even yet erected — no general of censorship could know the armies of obscenity were so near! — as these shocks multiply, and lust goes up the steps to love, something bizarre happens to the film. It fails to explode. It is a warehouse of dynamite and yet something goes wrong with the blow-up.

One leaves the theater bewildered. A fuse was never ignited. But where was it set? One looks to retrace the line of the story.

So we return to Paul trying to rise out of the bloody horizon of his wife's death. We even have some instinctive comprehension of how he must degrade his beautiful closet-fuck, indeed we are even given the precise detail that he will grease her ass with butter before he buggers her family pride. A scene or two later, he tricks forth her fear of him by dangling a dead rat which he offers to eat. "I'll save the asshole for you," he tells her. "Rat's asshole with mayonnaise."[2] (The audience roars — Brando knows audiences.) She is standing before him in a white wedding gown — she has run away from a TV camera crew that was getting ready to film her pop wedding. She has rushed to the apartment in the rain. Now shivering, but recovered from her fear, she tells him she has fallen in love with somebody. He tells her to take a hot bath, or she'll catch pneumonia, die, and all he'll get is "to fuck the dead rat."

No, she protests, she's in love.

"In ten years," says Brando looking at her big breasts, "you're going to be playing soccer with your tits." But the thought of the other lover is grinding away at him. "Is he a good fucker?"

"Magnificent."

"You know, you're a jerk. 'Cause the best fucking you're going to get is right here in this apartment."

No, no, she tells him, the lover is wonderful, a mystery . . . different.

"A local pimp?"

"He could be. He looks it."

She will never, he tells her, be able to find love until she goes "right up into the ass of death." He is one lover who is not afraid of metaphor. "Right up his ass — till you find a womb of fear. And then maybe you'll be able to find him."

"But I've found this man," says Jeanne. Metaphor has continued long enough for her. "He's you. You're that man."

In the old scripted films, such a phrase was plucked with a movie composer's chord. But this is improvisation. Brando's instant response is to tell her to get a scissors and cut the fingernails on her right hand. Two fingers will do. Put those fingers up his ass.

"*Quoi?*"

"Put your fingers up my ass, are you deaf? Go on."

No, he is not too sentimental. Love is never flowers, but farts and flowers. Plus every superlative test. So we see Brando's face before us — it is that tragic angelic mask of incommunicable anguish

---

[2] Dialogue from *Last Tango in Paris* was not entirely written in advance, but was in part an improvisation. In other words, a small but important part of the screenplay has in effect been written by Brando.

which has spoken to us across the years of his uncharted heroic depths. Now he is entering that gladiator's fundament again, and before us and before millions of faces yet to come she will be his surrogate bugger, real or simulated. What an entrance into the final images of history! He speaks to us with her body behind him, and her fingers just conceivably up him. "I'm going to get a pig," are the words which come out of his tragic face, "and I'm going to have a pig fuck you," — yes, the touch on his hole has broken open one gorgon of a fantasy — "and I want the pig to vomit in your face. And I want you to swallow the vomit. You going to do that for me?"

"Yeah."

"Huh?"

"Yeah!"

"And I want the pig to die while," — a profound pause — "while you're fucking him. And then you have to go behind, and I want you to smell the dying farts of the pig. Are you going to do that for me?"

"Yes, and more than that. And worse than before."

He has plighted a troth. In our year of the twentieth century how could we ever contract for love with less than five hundred pounds of pig shit? With his courage to give himself away, we finally can recognize the tragedy of his expression across these twenty-five years. That expression has been locked into the impossibility of ever communicating such a set of private thoughts through his beggar's art as an actor. Yet he has just done it. He is probably the only actor in the world who could have done it. He is taking the shit that is in him and leaving it on us. How the audience loves it. They have come to be covered. The world is not polluted for nothing. There is some profound twentieth-century malfunction in the elimination of waste. And Brando is on to it. A stroke of genius to have made a speech like that. Over and over, he is saying in this film that one only arrives at love by springing out of the shit in oneself.

So he seeks to void his eternal waste over the wife's suicide. He sits by her laid-out corpse in a grim hotel room, curses her, weeps, proceeds to wipe off the undertaker's lipstick, broods on her lover (who lives upstairs in the hotel), and goes through some bend of the obscure, for now, off-stage, he proceeds to remove his furniture from the new apartment. We realize this as we see Jeanne in the empty rooms. Paul has disappeared. He has ordered her to march into the farts of the pig for nothing. So she calls her TV director to look at the empty apartment — should they rent it? The profound practicality of the French bourgeoisie is squatting upon us. She appreciates the value of a few memories to offer sauce for her lean marriage. But the TV director must smell this old cooking for he takes off abruptly after telling her he will look for a better apartment.

Suddenly Brando is before her again on the street. Has he been waiting for her to appear? He looks rejuvenated. "It's over," she tells him. "It's over," he replies. "Then it begins again." He is in love with her. He reveals his biography, his dead wife, his unromantic details. "I've got a prostate like an Idaho potato but I'm still a good stick man. . . . I suppose if I hadn't met you I'd probably settle for a hard chair and a hemorrhoid." They move on to a hall, some near mythical species of tango palace where a dance contest is taking place. They get drunk and go on the floor. Brando goes in for a squalid parody of the tango. When they're removed by the judges, he flashes his bare ass.

Now they sit down again and abruptly the love affair is terminated. Like that! She is bored with him. Something has happened. We do not know what. Is she a bourgeoise repelled by his flophouse? Or did his defacement of the tango injure some final nerve of upper French deportment? Too small a motive. Must we decide that sex without a mask is no longer love, or conclude upon reflection that no mask is more congenial to passion than to be without a name in the bed of a strange lover?

There are ten reasons why her love could end, but we know none of them. She merely wants to be rid of him. Deliver me from a fifty-year-old, may even be her only cry.

She tries to flee. He follows. He follows her on the Métro and all the way to her home. He climbs the spiraling stairs as she mounts in the slow elevator, he rams into her mother's apartment with her, breathless, chewing gum, leering. Now he is all cock. He is the memory of every good fuck he has given her. "This is the title shot, baby. We're going all the way."

She takes out her father's army pistol and shoots him. He murmurs, "Our children, our children, our children will remember . . ." and staggers out to the balcony, looks at the Paris morning, takes out his chewing gum, fixes it carefully to the underside of the iron railing in a move that is pure broth of Brando — culture is a goat turd on the bust of Goethe — and dies. The angel with the tragic face slips off the screen. And proud Maria Schneider is suddenly and most unbelievably reduced to a twat copping a plea. "I don't know who he is," she mutters in her mind to the oncoming *flics*, "he followed me in the street, he tried to rape me, he is insane. I do not know his name. I do not know who he is. He wanted to rape me."

The film ends. The questions begin. We have been treated to more cinematic breakthrough than any film — at the least — since *I Am Curious, Yellow*. In fact we have gone much further. It is hard to think of any film that has taken a larger step. Yet if this is "the most powerful erotic film ever made" then sex is as Ex-Lax to the lady. For we have been given a bath in shit with no reward. The film, for all its power, has turned inside out by the end. We have been asked to follow two serious and more or less desperate lovers as they go through the locks of lust and defecation, through some modern species of homegrown cancer cure, if you will, and have put up with their modern depths — shit on the face of the beloved and find love! — only to discover a peculiar extortion in the aesthetic. We have been taken on this tour down to the prostate big as an Idaho potato only to recognize that we never did get into an exploration of the catacombs of love, passion, infancy, sodomy, tenderness, and the breaking of emotional ice, instead only wandered from one onanist's oasis to another.

It is, however, a movie that has declared itself, by the power of its opening, as equal in experience to a great fuck, and so the measure of its success or failure is by the same sexual aesthetic. Rarely has a film's value depended so much on the power or lack of power of its ending, even as a fuck that is full of promise is ready to be pinched by a poor end. So, in *Tango*, there is no gathering of forces for the conclusion, no whirling of sexual destinies (in this case, the audience and the actors) into the same funnel of becoming, no flying out of the senses in pursuit of a new vision, no, just the full charge into a blank wall, a masturbator's spasm — came for the wrong reason and on the wrong thought — and one is thrown back, shattered, too ubiquitously electrified, and full of criticism for the immediate past. Now the recollected flaws of the film eat at the pleasure, even as the failed orgasm of a passionate act will call the character of the passion into question.

So the walk out of the theater is with anger. The film has been in reach of the greatness Kael has been talking about, but the achievement has only been partial. Like all executions less divine than their conception *Tango* will give rise to mutations that are obliged to explore into dead ends. More aesthetic pollution to come! The performance by Brando has been unique, historic, without compare — it is just possible, however, that it has gone entirely in the wrong direction. He has been like a lover who keeps telling consummate dirty jokes until the ravaged dawn when the girl will say, "Did you come to sing or to screw?" He has come with great honor and dignity and exceptional courage to bare his soul. But in a solo. We are being given a fuck film without the fuck. It is like a Western without the horses.

Now the subtle sense of displacement that has hung over the movie is clear. There has been no particular high passion loose. Brando is so magnetic an actor, Schneider is so attractive, and the scenes are so intimate that we assume there is sexual glue between their parts, but it is our libido which has been boiling that glue and not the holy vibration of the actors on the screen. If Kael has had a sexual liberation with *Tango,* her libido is not alone — the audience is also getting their kicks — by digging the snots of the celebrated. (Liberation for the Silent Majority may be not to attend a fuck but hear dirty jokes.) So the real thrill of *Tango* for $5.00 audiences becomes the peephole Brando offers us on Brando. They are there to hear a world-famous actor say in reply to "What strong arms you have,"
"The better to squeeze a fart out of you."
"What long nails you have."
"The better to scratch your ass with."
"Oh, what a lot of fur you have."
"The better to let your crabs hide in."
"Oh, what a long tongue you have."
"The better to stick in your rear, my dear."
"What's this for?"
"That's your happiness and my ha-penis."
Pandemonium of pleasure in the house. Who wants to watch an act of love when the ghost of Lenny Bruce is back? The crowd's joy is that a national celebrity is being obscene on screen. To measure the media magnetism of such an act, ask yourself how many hundreds of miles you might drive to hear Richard Nixon speak a line like: "We're just taking a flying fuck at a rolling doughnut," or "I went to the University of the Congo; studied whale fucking." Only liberal unregenerates would be so progressive as to say they would

ot drive a mile. No, one could start mass migrations if Nixon were to give Brando's pig-and-vomit address to the test of love.

Let us recognize the phenomenon. It would be so surrealistic an act, we could not pass Nixon by. Surrealism has become our objective correlative. A private glimpse of the great becomes the alchemy of the media, the fool's gold of the century of communication. In the age of television we know everything about the great but how they fart — the ass wind is, ergo, our trade wind. It is part of Brando's genius to recognize that the real interest of audiences is not in having him portray the tender passages and murderous storms of an unruly passion between a man and a woman, it is rather to be given a glimpse of his kinks. His kinks offer sympathetic vibration to their kinks. The affirmation of passion is that we rise from the swamps of our diapers — by whatever torturous route — to the cock and the cunt; it is the acme of the decadent to go from the first explosive bout of love in *Tango* down to the trimmed fingernails up his rectum.

Then follows the murder. Except it does not follow. It has been placed there from the beginning as the required ending in Bertolucci's mind, it has already been written into the screenplay first prepared with Trintignant and Dominique Sanda in mind. But complications and cast changes occurred. Sanda was pregnant, et cetera. Brando appeared, and Schneider was found. Yet the old ending is still there. Since it did not grow convincingly out of the material in the original script, it appears, after Brando's improvisation, to be fortuitous altogether.

In the original screenplay, the dialogue is so general and the characters so vague that one has to assume Trintignant, Sanda, and Bertolucci planned to give us something extraordinary precisely by overcoming their pedestrian script. It is as if Bertolucci purposely left out whole trunklines of plot in order to discover them in the film. Only it was Brando who came along rather than Trintignant to make a particular character out of a general role, to "superimpose" — in accordance with Bertolucci's desire — his own character as Marlon Brando, as well as something of his life, and a good bit of his private obsessions. As he did that, however, the film moved away from whatever logic the script had originally possessed. For example, in the pre-Brando treatment, we would have been obliged to listen to the following:

LEON (alias Paul): I make you die, you make me die, we're two
murderers, each other's. But who succeeds in realizing this is
twice the murderer. And that's the biggest pleasure: watching you die, watching you come out of yourself, white-eyed,
writhing, gasping, screaming so loud that it seems like the
last time.

Oo la la! We are listening to a French intellectual. It is for good
cause that Bertolucci wants to superimpose Brando's personality.
Anything is preferable to Leon. And Brando most certainly obliter-
ates this mouthy analysis, creates instead a character who is half
noble and half a lout, an overlay drawn on transparent paper over
his own image. Paul is an American, ex-boxer, ex-actor, ex-foreign
correspondent, ex-adventurer, and now with the death of his wife,
ex-gigolo. He is that character and yet he is Brando even more. He is
indeed so much like Brando that he does not quite fit the part of
Paul — he talks just a little too much, and is a hint too distinguished
to be the proprietor of a cheap flophouse at the age of fifty — let us
say that at the least Paul is close enough to the magnetic field of
Marlon for an audience to be unable to comprehend why Jeanne
would be repelled if he has a flophouse. Who cares, if it is Marlon
who invites you to live in a flophouse? On the other hand, he is also
being Marlon the Difficult, Marlon the Indian from the Underworld, Marlon the shade of the alienated, Marlon the young star
who when asked on his first trip to Hollywood what he would like
in the way of personal attention and private creature comfort, points
to the nerve-jangled pet he has brought with him and says, "Get my
monkey fucked."

Yes, he is studying whale-pronging in the Congo. He is the rau-
cous out-of-phase voice of the prairie. Afterwards, contemplating
the failure, we realize he has been shutting Schneider off. Like a
master boxer with a hundred tricks, he has been out-acting her
(with all his miser's hoard of actor's lore), has been stealing scenes
from her while she is nude and he is fully dressed, what virtuosity!
But it is unfair. She is brimming to let go. She wants to give the
young performance of her life and he is tapping her out of position
here, tricking her there — long after it is over we realize he does not
want the fight of the century, but a home town decision. He did not
come to fuck but to shit. To defecate into the open-mouthed wonders of his audience and take his cancer cure in public. It is the fast-
est way! Grease up the kinks and bring in the pigs. We'd take a

stockyard of pigs if he would get into what the movie is about, but he is off on the greatest solo of his life and artists as young as Schneider and Bertolucci are hardly going to be able to stop him.

So he is our greatest actor, our noblest actor, and he is also our national lout. Could it be otherwise in America? Yet a huge rage stirs. He is so great. Can he not be even greater and go to the bottom of every fine actor's terror — which is to let go of the tricks that ring the person and enter the true arena of improvisation? It is there that the future of the film may exist, but we won't find out until a great actor makes the all-out effort.

But now we are back to the core of the failure in *Last Tango*. It is down in the difficulty of improvisation, in the recognition that improvisation which is anything less than the whole of a film is next to no improvisation. It has diminished from the dish to a spice that has been added to the dish (usually incorrectly). Bertolucci is a superb young director, adventurous, steeped in film culture, blessed with cinematic grace. He gives us a movie with high ambition, considerable risk, and a sense of the past. Yet he plows into the worst trap of improvisation — it is the simple refusal of film makers to come to grips with the implacable logic of the problem. One does not add improvisation to a script that is already written and with an ending that is locked up. No matter how agreeable the particular results may be, it is still the entrance of tokenism into aesthetics: "You blacks may work in this corporation, and are free to express yourselves provided you don't do anything a responsible white employee won't do." Stay true to the script. It reduces improvisation to a free play period in the middle of a strict curriculum.

The fundamental demand upon improvisation is that it begin with the film itself, which is to say that the idea for the film and the style of improvisation ought to come out of the same thought. From the beginning, improvisation must live in the premise rather than be added to it. The notion is not easy to grasp, and in fact is elusive. It may even be helpful to step away from *Tango* long enough to look at another example of possible improvisation. An indulgence is asked of the reader — to think about another kind of film altogether, a distracting hitch to the argument, but it may not be possible to bring focus to improvisation until we have other models before us.

So the following and imaginary film is offered: Orson Welles to play Churchill while Burton or Olivier does Beaverbrook in the week of Dunkirk. Let us assume we have the great good fortune to find these actors at the height of their powers, and have for *auteur* a film maker who is also a brilliant historian. To these beginnings, he adds a company of intelligent English actors and gives them the same historical material to study in order to provide a common denominator to everyone's knowledge. At this point the *auteur* and the company agree upon a few premises of plot. The *auteur* will offer specific situations. It will help if the episodes are sufficiently charged for the actors to lose their fear first of improvisation — which is that they must make up their lines.

Then a narrative action can begin to emerge out of the interplay of the characters, in much the way a good party turns out differently from the expectations of the hostess, and yet will develop out of her original conception. With a script, actors try to convince the writer, if he is present, to improve their lines — with improvisation they must work upon their wits. Why assume that the wits of this company of intelligent English actors will have less knowledge of manner and history than an overextended script writer trying to work up his remote conception of what Churchill and Beaverbrook might have been alike? Why not assume Welles and Burton have a better idea? Are they not more likely to contain instinctive knowledge in their ambulating meat? Isn't the company, in its steeping as good British actors into their own history, able to reveal to us more of what such a week might have been like than any but the most inspired effort by a screenwriter?

We all contain the culture of our country in our unused acting skills. While Clark Gable could probably not have done an improvisation to save himself, since he had no working habits for that whatsoever, the suspicion still exists that Gable, if he had been able to permit himself, could have offered a few revelations on the life of Dwight D. Eisenhower, especially since Ike seems to have spent a good part of his life imitating Gable's voice. If violence can release love, improvisation can loose the unused culture of a film artist.

The argument is conceivably splendid, but we are talking about *historical* improvisation where the end is still known, and it is the details that are paramount. How simple (and intense) by comparison become the problems of doing a full improvisation for *Tango*. There we are given a fundamental situation, a spoiled girl about to be married, a distraught man whose wife is a suicide. The man and the girl are in the room to make love. We are back at the same beginning. But we can no longer project ahead! If the actors feel nothing for one another sexually, as Schneider has indicated in several interviews was the case for Brando and herself — she may even have been telling the truth — then no exciting improvisation is possible on sexual lines. (The improvisation would have to work on the consequences of a lack of attraction.) Actors do not have to feel great passion for one another in order to give a *frisson* to the audience, but enough attraction must exist to provide a live coal for improvisation to blow upon. Without some kernel of reality to an improvisation only a monster can continue to offer interesting lines. Once some little attraction is present, there is nothing exceptional about the continuation of the process. Most of us, given the umbilical relation of sex and drama, pump our psychic bellows on many a sensual spark, but then most affairs are, to one degree or another, improvisations, which is to say genuine in some part of their feeling and nicely acted for the rest. What separates professional actors from all of us amateur masses with our animal instinct for dissembling, our everyday acting, is the ability of the professional to take a small emotion in improvisation and go a long distance with it. In a scripted piece of work, some professionals need no relation to the other actor at all, they can, as Monroe once said, "wipe them out" and substitute another face. But improvisation depends on a continuing life since it exists in the no-man's-land between acting and uncalculated response, it is a *special* psychic state, at its best more real than the life to which one afterward returns, and so a special form of insanity. All acting is a corollary of insanity, but working from a script offers a highly controlled means of departing from one's own personality in order to enter another. (As well as the formal power to return.)

What makes improvisation fertile, luminous, frightening, and finally *wiggy* enough for a professional like Gable to shun its practice is that the actor is doing two things at once — playing at a fictitious role, while using real feelings, which then begin to serve (rather than the safety of the script) to stimulate him into successive new feelings and responses, until he is in danger of pushing into emotional terrain that is too far out of his control.

If we now examine *Tango* against this perspective, the risks (once there is real sexual attraction between the man and the woman) have to multiply. They are after all not simply playing themselves, but have rather inserted themselves into highly charged creatures, a violent man with a blood-filled horizon and a spoiled middle-class girl with buried tyrannies. How, as they continue this improvisation, can they avoid falling in love, or coming to hate one another? With good film actors, there is even every real danger that the presence of the camera crew will inflame them further since in every thespian is an orgiast screaming to get out.

So murder is the first dramatic reality between two such lovers in a continuing film of improvisation. They progress toward an end that is frighteningly open. The man may kill the woman, or the woman the man. For, as actors, they have also to face the shame of walking quietly away from one another, a small disaster when one is trying to build intensity, for such a quiet ending is equal to a lack of inspiration, a cowardice before the potential violence of the other. Improvisation is profoundly wicked when it works, it ups the ante, charges all dramatic potential, looks for collision. Yet what a dimension of dramatic exploration is also offered. For the actors can even fall in love, can truly fall in love, can go through a rite of passage together and so reach some locked crypt of the heart precisely because they have been photographed fucking together from every angle, and still — perhaps it is thereby — have found some private reserve of intimacy no one else can touch. Let the world watch. It is not near.

So the true improvisation that *Tango* called for should have moved forward each day on the actors' experience of the day before; it would thereby have offered more aesthetic excitement. Because of its danger! There is a very small line in the last recognitions of the psyche between real bullets in a gun, and blanks. The madness of improvisation is such, the intensities of the will become such, that one hardly dares to fire a blank at the other actor. What if he or she is so carried away by excitement that they will refuse to fall? Bring on the real bullet, then. Bite on it.

Of course, literal murder is hardly the inevitable denouement in improvisation. But it is in the private design of each actor's paranoia. Pushed further together in improvisation than actors have gone before, who knows what literal risks might finally have been taken. That is probably why Brando chose to play a buffoon at a very high level and thereby also chose to put Schneider down. Finally we laugh at those full and lovely tits which will be good only for playing soccer (and she will choose to lose thirty pounds after the film is done — a whole loss of thirty pounds of pulchritude). Brando with his immense paranoia (it is hardly unjustified) may have concluded like many an adventurous artist before him that he was adventuring far enough. No need for more.

Still he lost an opportunity for his immense talent. If he has been our first actor for decades, it is because he has given us, from the season he arrived in *Streetcar*, a greater sense of improvisation out of the lines of a script than any other professional actor. Sometimes he seemed the only player alive who knew how to suggest that he was about to say something more valuable than what he did say. It gave him force. The lines other people had written for him came out of his mouth like the final compromise life had offered for five better thoughts. He seemed to have a charged subtext. It was as if, whenever requested in other films to say script lines so bad as, "I make you die, you make me die, we're two murderers, each other's," the subtext — the emotion of the words he was using behind the words — became, "I want the pig to vomit in your face." That was what gave an unruly, all but uncontrolled, and smoldering air of menace to all he did.

Now, in *Tango*, he had nothing beneath the script, for his previous subtext was the script. So he appeared to us as a man orating, not improvising. But then a long speech can hardly be an improvisation if its line of action is able to go nowhere but back into the prearranged structures of the plot. It is like the aside of a politician before he returns to that prepared text the press already has in their hands. So our interest moved away from the possibilities of the film and was spent on the man himself, his nobility and his loutishness. But his nature was finally a less interesting question than it should have been, and weeks would go by before one could forgive Bertolucci for the aesthetic cacophony of the end.

Still, one could forgive. For, finally, Bertolucci has given us a failure worth a hundred films like *The Godfather*. Regardless of all its solos, failed majesties, and off-the-mark horrors, even as a highly imperfect adventure, it is still the best adventure in film to be seen in this pullulating year. And it will open an abyss for Bertolucci. The rest of his life must now be an improvisation. Doubtless he is bold enough to live with that. For he begins *Last Tango* with Brando muttering two words one can hardly hear. They are: Fuck God.

The unmanageable in oneself must now offer advice. If Bertolucci is going to fuck God, let him really give the fuck. Then we may all know a little more of what God is willing or unwilling to forgive. That is, unless God is old and has indeed forgot, and we are merely out on a sea of human anality, a collective Faust deprived of Mephisto and turning to shit. The choice, of course, is small. Willy-nilly, we push on in every art and every technology toward the re-embodiment of the creation. It is doubtless a venture more demented than coupling with the pig, but it is our venture, our white whale, and by it or with it shall we be seduced. On to the Congo with sex, technology, and the inflamed lividities of human will.

The
Faith of Graffiti

❧

1.

Journalism is chores. Journalism is bondage unless you can see
yourself as a private eye inquiring into the mysteries of a new phenomenon. Then you may even become an Aesthetic Investigator
ready to take up your role in the twentieth-century mystery play.
Aesthetic Investigator! Make the name A-I for this is about graffiti.

A-I is talking to CAY 161. That is the famous Cay from 161st
Street, there at the beginning with TAKI 183 and JUNIOR 161, as
famous in the world of wall and subway graffiti as Giotto may have
been when his name first circulated through the circuits of those
workshops that led from Masaccio through Piero della Francesca to
Botticelli, Michelangelo, Leonardo and Raphael. Whew! In such
company Cay loses his name, although he will not necessarily see it
that way. He has the power of his own belief. If the modern mind
has moved from Giotto who could find beatitude in a beheading as
well as the beginnings of perspective in the flight of angels across
the bowl of a golden sky, if we have mounted the high road of the
Renaissance into Raphael's celebration of the True, the Good and
the Beautiful in each succulent three-dimensionality of the gluteus
maximus on out to our own vales and washes in Rothko and Ells-
worth Kelly, why so, too, have we also moved from the celebration
to the name, traveled from men and women who wrested a degree of
independence from Church and God down now to the twentieth-
century certainty that life is an image.

A couple of stories:

134

The first is a Jewish joke. Perhaps it is *the* Jewish joke. Two grandmothers meet. One is pushing a baby carriage. "Oh," says the other, "what a beautiful grandchild you have." "That's nothing," says the first, reaching for her pocketbook. "Wait'll I show you her picture!"

The second seems apocryphal. Willem de Kooning gives a pastel to Robert Rauschenberg who takes it home and promptly erases it. Next he signs his name to the erasure. Then he sells it. Can it be that Rauschenberg is saying, "The artist has as much right to print money as the financier?" Yes, Rauschenberg is giving us small art right here and much instruction. Authority imprinted upon emptiness is money. And the ego is capital convertible to currency by the use of the name. Ah, the undiscovered links of production and distribution in the psychic economy of the ego! For six and a half centuries we have been moving from the discovery of humanity into the circulation of the name, advancing out of some primitive obeisance to dread so complete that painting once lay inert on the field of two dimensions (as if the medieval eye was not ready to wander). Then art dared to rise into that Renaissance liberation from anxiety. The painterly capacity entered the space-perspective of volume and depth. Now, with graffiti we are back in the prison of two dimensions once more. Or is it the one dimension of the name — the artform screaming through space on a unilinear subway line?

Something of all this is in the mind of our Aesthetic Investigator as he sits in a bedroom on West 161st Street in Washington Heights and talks to CAY 161 and JUNIOR 161 and LI'L FLAME and LURK. They talk about the name. He has agreed to do a centerpiece for a book of photographs on graffiti by Jon Naar, has agreed to do it on the instant (in a Los Angeles hotel room) that he has seen it. The splendid pictures and his undiscovered thoughts on the subject leap together. There is something to find in these pictures, thinks A-I, some process he can all but name. The intellectual hedonism of an elusive theme is laid out before him. So, yes, he accepts. And discovers weeks later that his book has already been given a title. It is *Watching My Name Go By*. He explains to the pained but sympathetic ears of his collaborators that an author needs his own title.

Besides, there is a practical reason. Certain literary men cannot afford titles like *Watching My Name Go By*. Norman Mailer may be first in such a category. One should not be able to conceive of one's bad reviews before writing a word.

But then he also does not like *Watching My Name Go By* for its own forthright meaning. These young graffiti writers do not use their own name. They adopt one. It is like a logo. Moxie or Socono, Tang, Whirlpool, Duz. The kids bear a not quite definable relation to their product. It is not MY NAME but THE NAME. Watching The Name Go By. He still does not like it. Yet every graffiti writer refers to the word. Even in newspaper accounts, it is the term heard most often. "I have put my name," says Super Kool to David Shirey of the *Times*, "all over the place. There ain't nowhere I go I can't see it. I sometimes go on Sunday to Seventh Avenue 86th Street and just spend the whole day" — yes, he literally says it — "watching my name go by." But then they all use it. JAPAN I, being interviewed by Jon Naar and A-I in a subway, grins as a station cop passes and scrutinizes him. He is clean. There is no spray can on him today. Otherwise he would run, not grin. Japan says, with full evaluation of his work, "You have to put in the hours to add up the names. You have to get your name around." Since he is small and could hardly oppose too many who might choose to borrow his own immortal JAPAN I, he merely snorts in answer to the question of what he would do if someone else took up his name and used it. "I would still get the class," he remarks.

Whether it is one's own interviews or others, the word which prevails is always the name. MIKE 171 informs *New York Magazine*, "There are kids all over town with bags of paint waiting to *hit* their names." A bona-fide clue. An object is hit with your name, yes, and in the ghetto, a hit equals a kill. "You must kill a thing," said D. H. Lawrence once, "to know it satisfactorily." (But then who else could have said it?) You hit your name and maybe something in the whole scheme of the system gives a death rattle. For now your name is over their name, over the subway manufacturer, the Transit Authority, the city administration. Your presence is on their presence, your alias hangs over their scene. There is a pleasurable sense of depth to the elusiveness of the meaning.

So he sits with Cay and Junior and the others in the bedroom of Junior's parents and asks them about the name. It is a sweet meeting. He has been traveling for all of a wet and icy snowbound Sunday afternoon through the monumental drabs of South Bronx and Washington Heights, so much like the old gray apartment house ranks of Eastern Parkway in Brooklyn near where he grew up, a trip back across three generations. The Puerto Ricans in this apartment may not be so different from the poor ambitious families of relatives his mother would speak of visiting on the Lower East Side when she came as a child up from the Jersey shore to visit. So little has changed. Still the-smell-of-cooking-in-the-walls, a single word, and the black-pocked green stucco of the halls, those dark pits in the plaster speaking of the very acne of apartment house poverty. In the apartment, entering by the kitchen, down through the small living room and past the dark bedrooms in a file off the hall, all the shades drawn, a glimpse has been had of the television working like a votive light in some poor slum church chapel (one damp fire in the rain-forest) while the father in shorts sleeps on the sofa, and the women congregate — the kitchen is near. The windows are stained glass, sheets of red and yellow plastic pasted to the glass — the view must be on an air shaft. No light in this gray and late winter day. It is all the darkness of that gloom which sits in the very center of slum existence, that amalgam of worry and dread, heavy as buckets of oil, the true wages of the working class, with all that attendant fever for the attractions of crime, the grinding entrapments of having lost to the law — lawyers' fees, bondsmen, probation officers, all of it.

Yet now there is also a sense of protection in the air. The mood is not without its reverence: CAY 161 has the face of a martyr. He looks as if he has been flung face first against a wall, as if indeed a mighty hand has picked him up and hurled him through the side of a stone house. He is big, seventeen, and almost six feet tall, once good-looking and may yet be good-looking again, but now it is as if he has been drawn by a comic strip artist, for his features express the stars, comets, exclamation points, and straight-out dislocation of eyes and nose and mouth that accompanies any hero in a comic strip when he runs into a collision. SOCK! ZAM! POW! CAY 161, driving a stolen van, fleeing the cops in an old-fashioned New York street chase, has gone off the road on a turn, "and right on 161st Street where he was born and raised, he hit a hydrant, turned over a few times, and wound up inside a furniture store. . . . When the police looked inside the car," — description by José Torres in the N.Y. *Post* — "Cay lay motionless in the driver's seat, and another youth, a passenger, sprawled unconscious outside, hurled from the car by the impact." The friend had a broken leg, and Cay had part of his brain taken out in a seven-hour operation. The doctor gave warning. He might survive. As a vegetable. For two months he did not make a move. Now, six months later, Cay is able to talk, he can move. His lips are controlled on one side of his face but slack on the other — he speaks as if he has had a stroke. He moves in the same fashion. Certain gestures are agile, others come up half-paralyzed and top-heavy, as if he will fall on his face at the first false step. So his friends are his witness. They surround him, offer the whole reverence of their whole alertness to every move he makes. There is all the elegance of good manners in the way they try to conceal that he is different from the others.

But Cay is happy now. He is in Junior's house, JUNIOR 161, his best friend. They used to go out writing together for years, both tall, a twin legend — when one stands on the other's shoulders, the name goes up higher on the wall than for anyone else. True bond of friendship: they will each write the other's name, a sacramental interchange. Junior has a lean body, that indolent ghetto languor which speaks of presence. "I move slow, man," says the body, "and that is why you watch me. Because when I move fast, you got to watch out." He is well dressed, ghetto style — a white turtleneck sweater, white pants, a white felt hat, white sneakers, nothing more. Later he will step out like this into the winter streets. You got to meet the eye of the beholder with class. Freezing is for plants.

A-I interviews them. Yes, they started three years ago and would hit four or five names a day. Junior liked to work at least an hour a day. So go the questions: Cay liked to use red marker, Junior blue. Hundreds of masterpieces to their credit. Yes, Junior's greatest masterpiece is in the tunnel where the track descends from 125th Street to 116th Street. There, high on the wall, is JUNIOR 161 in letters six feet high. "You want to get your name in a place where people don't know how you could do it, how you could get up to there. You got to make them think." It is the peril of the position which calls. Junior frowns on the later artists who have come after Cay and himself. The talk these days is of SLY and STAY HIGH, PHASE 2, BAMA, SNAKE, and STITCH. The article by Richard Goldstein in *New York* (March 26, 1973) has offered a nomenclature for the styles, Broadway, Brooklyn and Bronx, disquisitions on bubble and platform letters. Perhaps his source is BAMA, who has said to another reporter in his full articulate speaking style, "Bronx style is bubble letters, and Brooklyn style is script with lots of flourishes and arrows. It's a style all by itself. Broadway style, these long slim letters, was brought here from Philadelphia by a guy named Topcat. Queens style is very difficult, very hard to read."

Junior is contemptuous of this. The new forms have wiped out respect for the old utilitarian lettering. If Cay likes the work of STAY HIGH, Junior is impressed by none. "That's just fanciness," he says of the new. "How're you going to get your name around doing all that fancy stuff?"

Cay speaks into this with his deep, strangled, and wholly existential voice — he cannot be certain any sound he utters will come out as he thinks. "Everybody tries to catch up to us," he says.

"You have to put in the hours?"

A profound nod.

Of course, he is not doing it any longer. Nor is Junior. Even before the accident, both had lost interest. On the one hand, the police were getting tough, the beatings when you were caught were worse, the legal penalties higher, the supplies of paint getting to be monitored, and on the other hand something had happened to the process itself. Too many names had grown — a jungle of ego creepers.

A-I queries them about the prominence of the name. He hesitates how to pose the question — he fears confidence will be lost if he asks straight-out. "What is the meaning of the name?" but, indeed, he does not have to — Cay speaks up on what it means to watch the name go by. "The name," says Cay, in a full voice, Delphic in its unexpected resonance — as if the idol of a temple had just chosen to break into sound — "The name," says Cay, "is the *faith* of graffiti."

It is quite a remark. He wonders if Cay knows what he has said. "The name," repeats Cay, "is the *faith*." He is in no doubt of the depth of what he has said. His eyes fix on A-I, his look is severe. Abruptly, he declares that the proper title is "The Faith of Graffiti." So it is.

A Sunday afternoon has come to its end. A-I walks downstairs with Junior, Cay, Lurk and Li'l Flame, and is shown modest examples of their writing on the apartment house walls. Cay has also used another name. At times he has called himself THE PRAYER 161. They say goodbye in the hall. Cay shows A-I the latest 161st Street sequence of thumb-up finger-curled handshakes. The pistol-pointed forefinger and upraised thumb of one man touch the thumb and forefinger of the other in a quick little cat's cradle. Cay's fingers are surprisingly deft. Then he and Junior spar a bit, half-comic for he lurches, but with the incisive tenderness of the ghetto, as if his moves also say, "Size don't come in packages. A cripple keeps the menace." It is agreeable to watch. As he attempts to spar, Cay is actually moving better than he has all day.

The name is the faith of graffiti. Was it true that the only writing which did not gut one's health lay in those questions whose answers were not known from the start? A-I still had no more than a clue to graffiti. Were the answers to be found in the long war of the will against the power of taboo? Who could know when one of the gods would turn in sleep as images were drawn? Was that a thought in the head of the first savage to put the silhouette of an animal on the wall of a cave? If so, the earliest painting had been not two dimensions but one — one, like graffiti — the hand pushing forward into the terror of future punishment. Only later would come an easier faith that the Lord might be on the side of the artist.

2.

No, size doesn't come in packages, and the graffiti writers had been all heights and all shapes, even all the ages from twelve to twenty-four. They had written masterpieces in letters six feet high on the side of walls and subway cars, and had scribbled furtive little toys, which is to say small names without style, sometimes just initials. There was panic in the act for you wrote with an eye over your shoulder for oncoming authority. The Transit Authority cops would beat you if they caught you, or drag you to court, or both. The judge, donning the robes of Solomon, would condemn the early prisoners to clean the cars and subway stations of the names. HITLER 2 (reputed to be so innocent of his predecessor that he only knew Hitler 1 had a very big rep!) was caught, and passed on the word of his humiliation. Cleaning the cars, he had been obliged to erase the work of others. All proportions kept, it may in simple pain of heart have been not altogether unequal to condemning Cézanne to wipe out the works of Van Gogh.

So there was real fear of being caught. Pain and humilation were implacable dues, and not all graffiti artists showed equal grace under such pressure. Some wrote like cowards, timidly, furtively, jerkily. "Man," was the condemnation of the peers, "you got a messed-up handwriting." Others laid one cool flowering of paint upon another, and this was only after having passed through all the existential stations of the criminal act, even to first *inventing* the paint, which was of course the word for stealing the stuff from the stores. But then, an invention is the creation of something which did not exist before — like a working spray can in your hand. (Indeed, if Plato's Ideal exists, and the universe is first a set of forms, then what is any invention but a theft from the given universal Ideal?)

There was always art in a criminal act — no crime could ever be as automatic as a production process — but graffiti writers were opposite to criminals since they were living through the stages of the crime in order to commit an artistic act — what a doubling of intensity when the artist not only steals the cans but tries for the colors he wants, not only the marker and the color, but steal them in double amounts so you don't run out in the middle of a masterpiece. What a knowledge of cops' habits is called for when any Black or Puerto Rican adolescent with a big paper bag is bound to be examined by a Transit cop if he goes into the wrong station. So after his paint has been invented a writer has to decide by which subway entrance it is to be transported, and once his trip is completed back to the station which is the capital of his turf, he still has to find the nook where he can warehouse his goods for a few hours. To attempt to take the paint out of the station is to get caught. To try to bring it back to the station is worse. Six or seven kids entering a subway in Harlem, Washington Heights, or the South Bronx are going to be searched by Transit cops for cans. So they stash it, mill around the station for a time painting nothing, they are, after all, often in the subways — to the degree they are not chased, it is a natural clubhouse, virtually a country club for the sociability of it all — and when the cops are out of sight, and a train is coming in, they whip out their stash of paint from its hiding place, conceal it on their bodies, and in all the wrappings of oversize ragamuffin fatigues, get on the cars to ride to the end of the line where in some deserted midnight yard they will find their natural canvas which is of course that metal wall of a subway car ready to reverberate into all the egos on all the metal of New York, what an echo that New York metal will give into the slapped-silly senses of every child-psyche who grew up in New York, yes, metal as a surface on which to paint is even better than stone.

But it is hardly so quick or automatic as that. If they are to leave the station at the end of the line, there is foreign turf to traverse which guarantees no safe passage, and always the problem of finding your way into the yards.

In the A-train yard at 207th Street, the unofficial entrance was around a fence that projected out over a cliff and dropped into the water of the Harlem River. You went out one side of that fence on a narrow ledge, out over the water, and back the other side of the fence into the yards "where the wagons," writes Richard Goldstein, "are sitting like silent whales."

We may pick our behemoth — whales and dinosaurs, elephants folded in sleep. At night, the walls of cars sit there possessed of soul — you are not just writing your name but trafficking with the iron spirit of the vehicle now resting. What a presence. What a consecutive set of iron sleeping beasts down all the corrals of the yard, and the graffiti writers stealthy as the near-to-silent sound of their movements working up and down the line of cars, some darting in to squiggle a little toy of a name on twenty cars — their nerve has no larger surge — others embarking on their first or their hundred-and-first masterpiece, daring the full enterprise of an hour of living with this tension after all the other hours of waiting (once they had come into the yard) for the telepathic disturbance of their entrance to settle, waiting for the guards patrolling the lines of track to grow somnolent and descend into the early morning pall of the watchman. Sometimes the graffiti writers would set out from their own turf at dark, yet not begin to paint until two in the morning, hiding for hours in the surest corners of the yard or in and under the trains. What a quintessential marriage of cool and style to write your name in giant separate living letters, large as animals, lithe as snakes, mysterious as Arabic and Chinese curls of alphabet, and to do it in the heart of a winter night when the hands are frozen and only the heart is hot with fear. No wonder the best of the graffiti writers, those mountains of heavy masterpiece production, STAY HIGH, PHASE 2, STAR III, get the respect, call it the glory, that they are known, famous and luminous as a rock star. It is their year. Nothing automatic about writing a masterpiece on a subway car. "I was scared," said Japan, "all the time I did it." And sitting in the station at 158th and St. Nicholas Avenue, watching the trains go by, talking between each wave of subway sound, he is tiny in size, his dark eyes as alert as any small and hungry animal who eats in a garden at night and does not know where the householder with his varmint gun may be waiting.

Now, as Japan speaks, his eyes never failing to miss the collection of names, hieroglyphs, symbols, stars, crowns, ribbons, masterpieces and toys on every passing car, there is a sadness in his mood. The city has mounted a massive campaign. There was a period in the middle when it looked as if graffiti would take over the world, when a movement that began as the expression of tropical peoples living in a monotonous iron-gray and dull brown brick environment, surrounded by asphalt, concrete, and clangor, had erupted to save the sensuous flesh of their inheritance from a macadamization of the psyche, save the blank city wall of their unfed brain by painting the wall over with the giant trees and petty plants of a tropical rain-forest. Like such a jungle, every plant, large and small, spoke to one another, lived in the profusion *and* harmony of a forest. No one wrote over another name, no one was obscene — for that would have smashed the harmony. A communion took place over the city in this plant growth of names until every institutional wall, fixed or moving, every modern new school which looked like a brand-new factory, every old slum warehouse, every standing billboard, every huckstering poster, and the halls of every high-rise low-rent housing projects which looked like a prison (and all did) were covered by a foliage of graffiti that grew seven or eight feet tall, even twelve feet high in those choice places worth the effort for one to stand on another, ah, if it had gone on, this entire city of blank architectural high-rise horrors would have been covered with paint. Graffiti writers might have become mountaineers with pitons for the ascent of high-rise high-cost swinger-single apartments in the East Sixties and Seventies. The look of New York, and then the world, might have been transformed, and the interlapping of names and colors, those wavelets of ego forever reverberating upon one another, could have risen like a flood to cover the monstrosities of abstract empty techno-architectural twentieth-century walls where no design ever predominated over the most profitable (and ergo most monotonous) construction ratio implicit in a twenty-million-dollar bill.

The kids painted with less than this in view, no doubt. Sufficient in the graffiti-proliferating years of the early Seventies to paint the front door of every subway car they could find. The ecstasy of the roller coaster would dive down their chest if they were ever waiting in a station when a twelve-car train came stampeding in and their name, HONDO, WILDCAT, SABU or LOLLIPOP, was on the *front!* Yes, the graffiti had not only the feel and all the super-powered whoosh and impact of all the bubble letters in all the mad comic strips, but the *zoom*, the *aghr*, and the *ahhr* of screeching rails, the fast motion of subways roaring into stations, the comic strips come to life. So it was probably not a movement designed to cover the world so much as the excrescence of an excrescence. Slum populations chilled on one side by the bleakness of modern design, and brain-cooked on the other by comic strips and TV ads with zooming letters, even brain-cooked by politicians whose ego is a vir-

tue — I am here to help my nation — brained by the big beautiful
numbers on the yard markers on football fields, by the whip of the
capital letters in the names of the products, and gut-picked by the
sound of rock and soul screaming up into the voodoo of the firma-
ment with the shriek of the performer's insides coiling like neon letters in the blue satanic light, yes, all the excrescence of the highways
and the fluorescent wonderlands of every Las Vegas sign frying
through the Iowa and New Jersey night, all the stomach-tightening
nitty-gritty of trying to learn how to spell was in the writing, every
assault on the psyche as the trains came slamming in. Maybe it was
no more than a movement which looked to take some of the excrescence left within and paint it out upon the world, no more than a
species of collective therapy of grace exhibited under pressure in
which they never dreamed of painting over the blank and empty
modern world, but the authority of the city reacted as if the city itself might be in greater peril from graffiti than from drugs, and a
war had gone on, more and more implacable on the side of the authority with every legal and psychological weedkiller on full employ
until the graffiti of New York was defoliated, cicatrized, Vietnam-
ized. Now, as A-I sat in the station with Jon Naar and Japan and
they watched the trains go by, aesthetic blight was on the cars. Few
masterpieces remained. The windows were gray and smeared. The
cars looked dull red or tarnished aluminum — their recent coat of
paint remover having also stripped all polish from the manufacturer's surface. New subway cars looked like old cars. Only the
ghost-outline of former masterpieces still remained. The kids were
broken. The movement seemed over. Even the paint could no longer
be invented. Now the cans set out for display were empty, the mis-
demeanors were being upped to felony, the fines were severe, the
mood was vindictive. Two hideous accidents had occurred. One boy
had been killed beneath a subway car, and another had been close to
fatally burned by an inflammable spray can catching a spark, yes, a
horror was on the movement and transit patrols moved through the
yards and plugged the entrances. The white monoliths of the high-
rise were safe. And the subways were dingier than they had ever
been. The impulse of the jungle to cover the walled tombs of technology had been broken. Was there a clue to graffiti in the opposite
passion to look upon monotony and call it health? As A-I walked the
streets with Jon Naar, they passed a sign: DON'T POLLUTE —
KEEP THE CITY CLEAN. "That sign," the photographer mur-
mured, "is a form of pollution itself."

3.

Since the metaphor of plant life had climbed all over his discussion of graffiti he went with profit to the Museum of Modern Art for it confirmed the botanical notion with which he began: that if subway graffiti had not come into existence, some artist might have found it necessary to invent, for it was in the chain of such evolution. Art had been rolling down the fall-line from Cézanne to Frank Stella, from Gauguin to Mathieu. On such a map, subway graffiti was an alluvial delta, the mud-caked mouth of a hundred painterly streams. If the obvious objection was that you might interview a thousand Black and Puerto Rican kids who rushed to write their name without having ever seen a modern painting, the answer, not quite as obvious, was that plants spoke to plants.

Famous plant-man Backster, attaching the electrodes of his polygraph to a philodendron one night, wonders in the wake of this passing impulse how to test the plant for some emotional reaction. Abruptly, a current courses through the philodendron at the horror of this thought. (When Backster cuts or burns the leaf, however, the polygraph registers little: now, the plant is numb. Its sensitivity seems to be its life, its suffering an abstention from life.) By the new logic of the experiment, plants must be a natural species of wireless. (What, indeed, did Picasso teach us if not that every form offers up its own scream when it is torn?) Radio is then no more than a prosthetic leg of communication, whereas plants speak to plants, and are aware of the death of animals on the other side of the hill. Some artists might even swear they have known this from the beginning, for they would see themselves as stimulants who inject perception into the blind vision of the century. (And like a junkie, does the century move into apathy from the superbrilliance of its injections?)

Still, when it comes to a matter of who might influence the writers of graffiti, one is not obliged to speak only of neon signs, comic strips and TV products, one has the other right to think the kids are enriched by all art which offers the eye a resemblance to graffiti. Which might enable us then to talk of Jackson Pollock and the abstract graffiti of his confluences and meanderings, of Stuart Davis' dramatization of print as a presence that grows in swollen proportion to its size, even include Hans Hofmann's *Memoria in Aeter-*

num where those red and yellow rectangles float like statements of a name over indistinct washes beneath, or Matisse's blue and green *Dance*. (Matisse's limbs wind onto one another like the ivy-creeper calligraphies of New York graffiti.) So might one refer to work which speaks of ghetto emotion in any place, of Siqueiros' *Echo of a Scream*, or Van Gogh's *Starry Night*. If the family histories of the most messed-up families have all the garbage-can chaos of de Kooning's *Woman*, no wonder the subway writers prided themselves on style and eclat — "you got a messed-up handwriting" being the final term of critical kill.

But on reflection, was A-I trying to slip in some old piety on the distribution of art down from the museums through media to the masses? — these subway children may never have seen *Memoria in Aeternum* at the head of the stairs at MOMA, but it filtered through to them by way of advertising artists. Fell crap! Rather say art begot art, and the migrations were no one's business. For if plants were telepathic, then humans lived in a psychic sea where all the forms of art also passed through the marketplace of the dreamer in his sleep, and every part of society spoke to every other part, if only with a curse.

So he had the happy thought during his visit to the Modern Art to decide that some paintings might be, by whatever measure, *on the air* — leave it to the engineers of some future techno-coven to try to determine the precise migrations of Miró's *Plate 8 from Series One, 1953, "The Family"* into the head of an espontaneo with a spray can looking over his shoulder for the black mother in a uniform who will beat his own black blue.

4.

Like a good reporter he goes to see the Mayor. It is ten days to Christmas and the last two weeks of the Lindsay administration on that Saturday morning he has his appointment to visit, nearly a week from the previous Sunday when he talked to Junior and Cay. Again the weather is iron-gray and cold. At Gracie Mansion, the wind is driving in from the East River, and the front porch looks across its modest private lawn to the Triboro Bridge in the north. (To the west apartment houses rise like the sheer face of Yosemite.)

It is not a large lawn in front of the Mayor's residence nor even a large house. Old white Gracie Mansion might be no exceptional residence on any wealthy road in Portland, Oregon or Portland, Maine — there is even a basketball hoop on a backboard not far from the front door, a political touch dating from recent years when the Knicks became the most consistently successful team in New York — yet with all its limited grandeur, Gracie Mansion is still one fine Federalist of a house (built in 1799) and if the spirit of an age could have been captured by a radio, then where better to measure this magic mean if not in the proportions of the Mansion's living room and dining room? They speak in their harmony of some perfect period of Arcadian balance between the early frontier being settled to the West and the new sense of democratic government forging itself in the state capitals of the East. How better to characterize the decorum, substance, grace, and calm center of such architecture if not to think that the spirit and style of the *prose* of the American Constitution is also in it (even to the hint of boredom in prose and buildings both), yet, why not precisely these high ceilings, paucity of curves, and all the implicit checks and balances of the right angle? Lindsay, it may be said, is at home in such surroundings. They seem built to his frame. Only a tall lean man could look well-proportioned in so *enlightened* a set of rooms. Nothing like a Gothic arch is present to suggest any mad irreconcilable opposites of God and man, no Corinthian columns to resonate with praetorian tyrannies (and orgies at the top), nor any small and slanted ceilings to speak of craft and husbandry, just government here in Federal style without the intervention of Satan or Jehovah (and next to nothing of Christ), just a fundament of Wasp genius, a building style to state that man could live without faith if things were calm enough. Perhaps the economy of balance is the true god of the Wasp.

His appointment is at eleven, but it is an unusual morning for the Lindsay family since they have been up until five the night before at a farewell party given the Mayor to honor the eight years of his administration. Lindsay has worked as hard as any man in New York for eight years, and can afford the luxury of being hungover before a reporter this Saturday morning. What a nice relaxation. Lindsay chuckles at the memory of each unexpected rejoinder of party dialogue and laughs at the expression on Tom Morgan's face, press secretary to the Mayor, a tall man with a dark brush mustache who recapitulates in the sardonic gloom of his hungover eyes the incandescence of all those good drinks at that good party. Watching them all, studying Lindsay's face with its patrician features so endowed with every purchase on the meaning of handsome that he could be not only a movie star but there at the front, right ahead of Burt Lancaster and Steve McQueen, on a par with Robert Redford, and hardly a millimeter of profile behind Paul Newman, it occurs indeed that no movie star could be more convincing than Lindsay if it came to playing some very important American politician in the quiet American years from 1800 to 1825. Even his eroded teeth — Lindsay's one failing feature — speak with authenticity of the bad teeth of those English ruling classes who became the American ruling classes in that Federalist era one hundred and seventy years ago. So sitting in such a dining room, and a little later adjourned to a living room with Lindsay and Morgan to bring up the subject of his interview, he is thinking that Gracie Mansion never had a Mayor nearly so perfectly suited to itself; if there were some divine renting agency in the halls of karma, then come soon or late the post of Mayor of New York would have had to be found for John Vliet Lindsay or the house would feel unfulfilled.

For Lindsay, however, the question may have been whether an ambitious man had ever come to power at a time less promising for himself. He had labored in his two terms, innovated and negotiated, explored, tinkered, tampered, and shifted the base of every municipal machine of government upon which he could work his cadres. He had built a constituency in the ghetto. Mailer-Breslin running for the mayoralty in '69 also ran into one argument over and over in Bedford-Stuyvesant, Harlem and the South Bronx. It was, "What do we want with you? Lindsay's our man." Lindsay had walked the streets in summer riots, and held some kind of line for decontrol, which is to say, local control, in the ghetto schools. That had taken political courage. Yet make him no saint! He had also worked with the most powerful real estate interests in the city. No question that in his eight years, the ugliest architecture in the history of New York had also gone up. The new flat tops of the skyline now left New York as undistinguished in much of its appearance as Cleveland or Dallas. It is possible Lindsay had bought ghetto relief at the price of aesthetic stultification. Call it desecration. The view of New York's offices and high-rise apartments proved sacrilegious to the mood of any living eye — Wasp balance had done it again.

Still, with all this effort, New Yorkers hated him. For every intolerable reason, first of which was his defense of the ghettos. "If I wanted a nigger for Mayor, I'd have voted for a nigger," said every archetype of a cab driver to any tourist who would listen. And yet this Federalist movie star, this hard-working mayor for ghetto rights, had been the first and most implacable enemy of subway graffiti. So there was a feather falling through the mood when he told Lindsay and Morgan why he had come.

But A-I had his speech. If he thought the Mayor had done an honorable job, and was prepared to say so, he still could not comprehend how a man who worked so hard to enter the spirit of ghetto conditions had been nonetheless so implacable in his reaction to graffiti. "Insecure cowards," Lindsay had called the kids. "A dirty shame." Others in his administration offered civic blasts: "graffiti pigs," "thoughtless and irresponsible behavior." It was surprising. While the management of a city required you to keep it clean — where would a mayor hide if he could not get the garbage out? — there was a difference between political necessity and the fury of this reaction. How could he call the kids cowards? Why the venom? It seemed personal.

Lindsay grinned. He had heard enough preambles from reporters to know when an interview was manageable. "Well, yes," he said, "I did get hot under the collar, and I suppose if we had to go through it again, I would hope to lose my temper a little less, but you have no idea what a blow that graffiti was to us." He shook his head at the memory. "You see, we had gone to such work, such ends, to get those new subway cars in. It meant so much to people here in the city to get a ride for instance in one of the new air-conditioned cars. On a hot summer day their mood would pick up when they had the luck to catch one. And you know, that was work. It's hard to get anything done here. You stretch budgets, and try to reason people into activities they don't necessarily want to take up on their own. We were proud of those subway cars. It took a lot of talking to a lot of committees to get that accomplished."

Morgan nodded. "And then," Lindsay said, "the kids started to deface them."

A-I put his demurrer. "Deface," after all, was the core of the argument. Some people might think subway graffiti was art. He suggested in passing Claes Oldenburg's classic remark, ". . . You're standing there in the station, everything is gray and gloomy and all of a sudden one of those graffiti trains slides in and brightens the place like a big bouquet from Latin America."

Lindsay smiled as if recalling the screams, moans, epithets, and agonized squawks of every bright college intellectual on his staff when Oldenburg's quote first came riding in. Grand division in the Establishment! Aesthetic schism! "Yes, we remember that quote," Lindsay's grin seemed to say. He had the most curious quality of personality. One did not know if he were secretly more or less decent than his personality. While the personality itself was decent enough, it was also patently not the man, nor, unhappily for him, characteristic at all of New York. He seemed now like a Westerner, full of probity, rawhide and something buried in the personality, a man you might not get to know at all even after a night of drinking together. He wasn't in the least like Richard Nixon except to share one quality. Lindsay was out of focus. He had always been out of focus. Part of his political trouble.

Well, Lindsay suggested, they had never really wondered whether it was anything but defacement. "People would come into new cars and suddenly they'd see them all marked up, covered inside and out, and it depressed people terribly. You know, we have to be a kind of nerve center to the city. Reports came in from everywhere. This graffiti was profoundly depressing — it truly hurt people's moods. The life would go out of everybody when they saw the cars defaced, they felt it was defacement, no question of that. And we kept hearing one request over and over, 'Can't you do something about it?' Then, too, we had our own pride in these matters. You know, you get to feel after you've put through a new municipal building that it's yours in some way. As Mayor I'd get as angry when a city building got marked up as if I owned it personally. Oh, it's easier to talk about it now, but I must say it was hard at times not to blow up."

"Actually," Morgan observed, "the Mayor would go around calming some of us down. 'Remember,' he would tell us, 'they're only kids.' "

Yes, in the framework of that time in the Summer of '71 and the Winter and Spring of '72 when Lindsay was looking to get the Democratic nomination for President, what an upset to his fortunes, what a vermin of catastrophe that these writings had sprouted like weeds all over the misery of Fun City, a new monkey of unmanageables to sit on Lindsay's overloaded political back. He must have sensed the presidency draining away from him as the months went by, the graffiti grew, and the millions of tourists who passed through the city brought the word out to the rest of the nation: "Filth is sprouting on the walls."

Of course, where was the tourist who could distinguish between men's-room and subway graffiti? Who was going to dare to look long enough to see that it was a name and not an obscene thought in the writing. Today, just before he had come to Gracie Mansion, he had stopped in the lavatory of a York Avenue bar for a minute, and there on the john wall was drawn a pure old-fashioned piece of smut graffiti. A balloon of dialogue issued out of a girl's mouth. No art in the lettering, no style. "Did you know," said her balloon, "that your clit is in your ass?" Some lost shred of fecal communion now nailed to the wall. Was there a public comfort station in America which did not have a dozen such insights, "Suck me," "Fuck you"? That was what people expected to see on the subways. They assumed the full mad explosive shithouse of America was now erupting in their faces. So they did not look but rode in the cars with their heads down, and brought the news out to the rest of America that Lindsay could not keep the city clean. No wonder he called it a dirty shame. And labeled the aplomb of the graffiti writers cowardice. That was his attempt to soothe the terror in the heart of every subway citizen who looked at the graffiti and put his head down so his eye would not meet any eye that might be connected to a hand which held a knife, yes, that was one side of the fear, and the other was fear of the insane graffiti writer in the self. For what filth would burst out of every civilized office worker in New York if ever *they* started to write on moving public walls, my god, the feces to spread and the blood to spray, yes, the good voting citizen of New York would know that the violent ward at Bellevue was opening its door to him on the day he would take a spray can to a subway. So, New York citizenry saw all the children as mad — and therefore saw madness, instability, and horror in the New York Transit. No wonder Lindsay had gone to war against graffiti. The city would tolerate junk, graft, insanities of traffic, mugging, every petty crime of the street, and every major pollution, but it could not accept a towering rainforest of graffiti on all the forty-story walls. Yes, build a wall and balance a disease. For the blank wall of the new architecture was a deadening agent to balance the growing violence beneath. (Could it be said that the monotony of modern architecture increased all over the world in direct relation to the volcanic disturbances of each society it would contain?) Plastic above, dynamite below.

In the face of such questions the interview was effectively over. They chatted for a while, and got up to say goodbye. On the way out, A-I noticed there was a Rauschenberg on the wall.

Lindsay, in his courtesy, walked with him to the gate. Wearing a blue windbreaker he looked in the gray outdoor light like a veteran big league ballplayer, tall, weathered, knowledgeable. They took leave not uncordially, and he complimented the Mayor on eight good years, even meant it.

"I wish I had the talent to write," Lindsay said in parting. Was that a politician's gift? A-I pulled back the reply that he wished he could have been Mayor.

Outside the fence, a policeman was standing with a drawn gun. It was a simple measure of the times: be forever ready at the Gracie gate.

And indeed a ten-year-old boy on roller skates cried aloud, "That's him, that's him, that's the Mayor," and promptly took out a cap pistol and fired a number of bang-bangs at the back of John Lindsay going back into his house.

For a while, A-I walked, and had a little fantasy of how impossible it would have proved if the miracle worked and he had been elected in the campaign of 1969. What would he have done about graffiti? Would he have tried to explain its virtues to the people of New York — and laughed in all the pain of absolute political failure. The answer was simple — nobody like himself would ever be elected Mayor until the people agreed bad architecture was as poisonous as bad food. No, graffiti as a political phenomenon had small hope for life. His faith in the value of the question would have to explore in another place. Did the final difficulty lie in the meaning of graffiti as art? There the inquiry might become as incomprehensible as the motives of the most advanced artists. On then to the rim of the enigma, to the Sea of Vortices where the meanings whirl with no meaning.

5.

Years ago, so much as twenty years ago, A-I had conceived of a story he was finally not to write, for he lost his comprehension of it. A rich young artist in New York in the early Fifties, bursting to go beyond Abstract Expressionism, began to rent billboards on which he sketched huge, ill-defined (never say they were sloppy) works in paint chosen to run easily and flake quickly. The rains distorted the lines, made gullies of the forms, automobile exhausts laid down a patina, and comets of flying birds crusted the disappearing surface with their impasto. By the time fifty such billboards had been finished — a prodigious year for the painter — the vogue was on. His show was an event. They transported the billboards by trailer-truck and broke the front wall of the gallery to get the art objects inside. It was the biggest one-man exhibition in New York that year. At its conclusion, two art critics were arguing whether such species of work still belonged to art.

"You're mad," cried one, "it is not art, it is never art."

"No," said the other, "I think it's valid."

So would the story end. Its title, Validity. But before he had written a word he made the mistake of telling it to a young Abstract Expressionist whose work he liked. "Of course it's valid," said the painter, eyes shining with the project. "I'd do it myself if I could afford the billboards."

The story was never written. He had assumed he was proposing a satire, but it was evident he had no insight into how painters were ready to think. Some process had entered art and he could not discern it out.

Let us go back to the pastel by de Kooning which Rauschenberg erased. The details, when further inquiry is made, are less impromptu. Rauschenberg first informed de Kooning of what he would do, and de Kooning agreed. The work, when sold, bore the inscription "A drawing from Willem de Kooning erased by Robert Rauschenberg." Both artists are now proposing something more than that the artist has the same right as the financier to print money, they may even be saying that the meat and marrow of art, the painterly core, the life of the pigment, and the world of technique with which hands lay on that pigment are convertible to something other. The ambiguity of meaning in the twentieth century, the hollow in the heart of faith, has become such an obsessional hole that art may have to be converted into intellectual transactions. It is as if we are looking for stuff, any stuff with which to stuff the hole, and will convert every value into packing for this purpose. For there is no doubt that in erasing the pastel and selling it, art has been diminished but our knowledge of society is certainly enriched. An aesthetic artifact has been converted into a sociological artifact. It is not the painting that intrigues us now but the lividities of art fashion which made the transaction possible in the first place. Something rabid is loose in the century. Maybe we are not converting art into some comprehension of social process, but rather are using art to choke the hole, as if society has become so hopeless, which is to say so twisted in knots of faithless ideological spaghetti, that the glee is in strangling the victims.

But take the example further. Let us imagine a show at the Guggenheim. It will be like many we have seen. Let us make it a plausible modern one-man show. Nothing will be exhibited but computer read-out sheets from a statistical operation. Hundreds of such sheets tacked to the wall. Somewhat irregularly. Attempts at neatness will be contradicted by a confusion in the style of placing them on the wall of the Guggenheim as it spirals up the ramp. Checkerboards alternate with ascending bands, then cul-de-sacs, paper stapled up every way.

We try to digest the aesthetic experience. Of what do the computer read-out sheets consist? What is the subject of their inquiry? we ask. And what is the motive of the artist? Is he telling us something about the order and disorder of the mind in relation to a technological world? Has he presented us with an ongoing composition of exceptional cunning? Is it possible he even has set the problem for the computer himself? Maybe the endless numbers on these computer sheets reflect some analogue to the tension of major themes in his brain. Do we then have here an arithmetical display whose relation to art is as complex as *Finnegans Wake* to literature?

Bullshit, responds the painter. The computer sheets were selected at random. Because the artist did not even wish to bear an unconscious responsibility for the selection, he chose an acquaintance with whom he shared no great psychic identity to pick up the computer sheets for him. Neither he nor the acquaintance ever inquired into the subject of the statistical problem, and he never took a look at what was brought back. Rather, he spoke to the janitor at the Guggenheim by telephone and told him to tack up the pages any way at all. The checkerboards and bands and cul-de-sacs of stapled paper were merely a reflection of the personnel: the janitor worked with two assistants. One was neat, the other drunk. And the painter never came to see the show. The show was the fact that people came, studied the walls, lived for an uncertain hour in the Guggenheim and went out again, their minds exercised by a question that not only had no answer, but may not even have been a question. The artist had done his best to have no intent. Not unless his intent was to demonstrate that most of the experience of viewing a painting is the context of the museum itself. We are next to one of John

Cage's compositions in silence. Art has been saying with more and more intensity: The nature of the painting has become less interesting than the relation of painting to society — we can even erase Rauschenberg's erasure. Get the artist out of it altogether, and it is still art. The world is turning inside out.

What step is left to take? Only one. A show that offers no object at all. The last reference to painting or sculpture is the wall on which something can be hung, or the floor on which a piece can sit. That must now disappear. The art-piece enters the artist: the work can only be experienced within his psyche.

From the New York *Times*, September 2, 1973, by Peter Plagens:

> a marksman-friend shot Chris Burden in the upper left arm with a .22 long-jacket before an audience of 12 intimates. He (Burden) figured on a graze wound with a Band-Aid slapped on afterward, but it "felt like a truck hit my arm at 80 miles per hour"; he went to the hospital, nauseous, and filed the requisite police report ("accident").

Plagens goes on to describe other "pieces." Burden chooses situations for their possibility of danger, pain, humiliation, or boredom. There is:

> "Movie on the Way Down," in which Burden, hanging by his heels, nude, six feet off a gym floor with a movie camera in his hands, is summarily chopped loose.

The movie is presumably taken on the way down (is it filmed in slow motion?) and he ends with a cut lip. There are other pieces where he rockets flaming matches "at his nude supine wife" or sets ablaze two 16-foot wooden crosses on Laguna Canyon Road at 2 A.M. — "the intended audience for that piece," says Burden, "was the one guy driving down the road who saw it first." Ah, Los Angeles! For "Endurance/real time," he 1) stays in a locker for five days, 2) does 1600 tours of a gallery on his bicycle and 3) remains in bed for three weeks and a day. He also pretends to be a dead man lying under a tarpaulin on the street and is arrested by the police for creating a traffic hazard. He gets a hung jury at his trial and the case is dismissed but "one of the nine votes for conviction, a stewardess, told Burden if she ever saw him under a tarp again, she'd run over him herself." He even does a study in the shift of identity. For "I Became a Secret Hippie," Burden cuts his hair short and dresses in

FBI clothes. "If you want to be a heavy artist nowadays," Plagens, reporting on Burden, concludes, "you have to do something unpleasant to your body, because everything *else* has been done. . . . [Burden] may be a product of art-world art history — backed into some untenable masochistic corner because all the other novelty territory has been claimed."

At the least, Burden is fulfilling the dictum of Jean Malaquais that once there are enough artists in the world, the work of art will become the artist himself. Burden is refining his personality. Through existential tests. Burden is not exploring his technique, but his vibrations. The situations he chooses are, as Plagens describes, "edgy." They have nothing remotely resembling a boundary until they are done. In "Movie on the Way Down," Burden can hardly know if he will cut his lip or break his neck, feel a live instant on the descent or some dull anxiety. When he shoots lighted matches at his nude wife the areas defined are empty before the action begins. Given every variable from Women's Liberation to the sadomasochistic tales of Wilhelm Stekel, Burden can know in advance only that a psycho-dramatic enterprise will be commenced. But where it may end, and what everybody might feel — will the matches burn her skin? — will the marriage be fortified or scorched? — no, there is no confidence which question is going to offer an answer. Perhaps he is not refining his personality so much as attempting to clear a space in his psyche free of dread. But isn't that the fundamental operation of the primitive at the dawn of civilization, the establishment of the ego? For what is the human ego but a clearing in the forest of the psyche free of dread? Money, held in one's hand, is free of time. Cash has no past; its future is assignable. It is powerful and empty. So, too, is the ego. It bears the same relation to the psyche as cash bears to the security or comfort of the body. The ego is virtually separate from the psyche even as money is still separate from every organic communicating logic of nature.

We are back to the cave man and his cave painting. His hand draws the outline of the animal in defiance of those gods who watch him. Burden is smashing his nose on the floor or displaying his wife in defiance of the last gods of conventional art. They are that audience remnant of a once-leviathan bourgeois culture. They still trickle out to see Happenings, the desire of the middle class to preserve its last religion: the world of the artist, palette, museum and gallery wall. Middle-class passion is to appreciate the work of art.

But art may be the little ball rolling off the table. Perhaps art now signifies some unheard reverberation from the subterranean obsession of us all: Is civilization coming to an end? Is society burning? Is the day of the cave man returning? Has our search for ego which was once so routine — a useful (somewhat heartless) ego to be fashioned for a useful (if heartless) society — now gone past the measure of our experience so that we no longer try to construct a control center at the core of the mind, but plunge instead into absurdities which offer us that curious calm we find in the art of the absurd, even as the cave man, defying his gods, discovered he was not always dead on the next day.

But we are at the possible end of civilization, and tribal impulses start up across the world. The descending line of the isolated artist goes down from Michelangelo all the way to Shoot. But Chris Burden is finally more comfortable to us than the writers of graffiti. For Burden is the last insult from the hippie children of the middle class to the bourgeois art-patron who is their spiritual parent, but graffiti speaks of a new civilization where barbarism is stirring at the roots.

If at the beginning of Western painting, man was small and God was large; if, in the Renaissance, man was mysteriously large in his relation to God; now, in our times man has disappeared into God. He is mass-man without identity, and he is God. He is all the schizophrenia of the powerless and all-powerful in one psyche.

As we lose our senses in the static of the oncoming universal machine, so does our need to exercise the ego take on elephantiasistical proportions. Graffiti is the expression of a ghetto that is near to the plague, for civilization is now closed off from the ghetto. Too huge are the obstacles to any natural development of a civilized man. In the ghetto it is almost impossible to find some quiet identity. No, in the environment of the slum, the courage to display yourself is your only capital, and in the streets crime is the only productive process that converts such capital to the modern powers of the world, ego and money. Art is not peace but war, and form is the record of that war.

Yet there is a mystery still. From which combat came these curious letters of graffiti, with their Chinese and Arabic calligraphies? Out of what connection to the past did these lights and touches of flame become so much like the Hebrew alphabet where the form of the letter itself was worshipped as a manifest of the Lord? No, it is not enough to think of the childlike desire to see one's name ride by in letters large enough to scream your ego across the city, no, it is almost as if we must go back into some more primeval sense of existence. If our name is enormous to us, it is also not real — as if we have come from other places than the name, and lived in other lives.

Perhaps that is the unheard echo of graffiti, the vibration of that profound discomfort it arouses. Can the unheard music of its proclamation and/or its mess, the rapt intent seething of its foliage, be the herald of some oncoming apocalypse less and less far away, and so graffiti lingers on our subway door as a memento of all the lives ever lived, sounding now like the bugles of gathering armies across the unseen ridge.

A Harlot
High and Low

There are no answers. There are only questions.
— Jean Malaquais

A Harlot High and Low was the English title given to *Splendeurs et misères des courtisanes,* one of Balzac's best novels. The book was concerned as much with secret police as with the prostitutes who passed through its pages, but then whores and political agents made a fair association for Balzac. The harlot, after all, inhabited the world of *as if.* You paid your money and the harlot acted for a little while — when she was a good harlot — *as if* she loved you, and that was a more mysterious proposition than one would think, for it is always mysterious to play a role. It is equal in a sense to living under cover. At her best, the harlot was a different embodiment of a fantasy for each client, and at those moments of existence most intense for herself, the role she assumed became more real than the reality of her profession.

A harlot high and low. The pores of society breathe a new metaphor — the enigma of Intelligence itself. For we do not know if the people who make our history are more intelligent than we think, or whether stupidity rules the process of thought at its highest level. Is America governed by accident more than we are ready to suppose, or by design? And if by design, is the design sinister? Are the actors playing roles more intricate than we expect? Trying to understand whether our real history is public or secret, exposed or — at the highest level — underground, is equal to exploring the opposite theaters of our cynicism and our paranoia.

For instance, we may be getting ready to decide that the CIA was the real producer of Watergate (that avant-garde show!) but where is the proof? We have come to a circular place. The CIA occupies a region in the modern mind where every truth is obliged to live in its denial; facts are wiped out by artifacts; proof enters the logic of counterproof and we are in the dream; matter breathes next to antimatter.

There are Americans whose careers are composed of fact. One does not begin to comprehend certain men without their collections of fact. It would probably be crucial to know if Harry S. Truman had been happy or angry on a given day since that would enter the event of the day. He lives on an elementary level of biography. There are personalities, however, like Marilyn Monroe, for whom there are no emotional facts. It does not matter on any particular occasion if she was pleased or annoyed, timid or bold, even successful or unsuccessful. Her mood did not matter on a given day since she would as easily be feeling the opposite five minutes later. Moreover, she was an actress. She was able to simulate the opposite of what she felt. Since she was surrounded by people in show business who felt no need to be accurate if that interfered with a good story, one could not begin to discover the facts about such a woman, only the paradoxes. It may be that the difficulties in coming to know Marilyn Monroe offer a modest model for our penetration of Central Intelligence.

1.
A Skew in Sociology

Questions of social class and snobbery have always been very important in the CIA. With its roots in the wartime Office of Strategic Services (the letters OSS were said, only half-jokingly, to stand for "Oh So Social"), the agency has long been known for its concentration of Eastern Establishment, Ivy League types. Allen Dulles, a former American diplomat and Wall Street lawyer with impeccable connections and credentials, set the tone for an agency full of Roosevelts, Bundys, Cleveland Amory's brother Robert, and other scions of America's leading families. There

have been exceptions, to be sure, but most of the CIA's top leaders have been white, Anglo-Saxon, Protestant, and graduates of
the right Eastern schools. While changing times and ideas have
diffused the influence of the Eastern elite throughout the government as a whole, the CIA remains perhaps the last bastion in official Washington of WASP power, or at least the slowest to
adopt the principle of equal opportunity.

— Victor Marchetti and John D. Marks,
The CIA and the Cult of Intelligence

What a baby! Known affectionately as the Company, it was delivered to America by the Central Intelligence Agency Act of 1949,
and grew from 5,000 employees in 1950 to 15,000 by 1955. Because
the old OSS was not nearly large enough to make up its cadres, the
CIA raided the FBI to obtain some of its first agents (thereby com-
mencing an immense feud with J. Edgar Hoover) and also did its
best to strip the army, the navy, the air force, the State Department,
and virtually every other government bureau of good personnel.
There was, after all, a vision. The potential functions of the CIA
were calculated to become immense. They became immense. All intelligence was the purview. There was no reason, for instance, why
the best long-term weather forecasts in America should not derive
from CIA weather experts — knowledge of the weather helped
crops; large crops were an instrument of foreign policy. No vein,
therefore, of American business or culture was independent of Intelligence — not finance, media, economic production, labor-man-
agement relations, cinema, statistical theory, fringe groups, Olym-
pic teams. There was no natural end to topics the CIA could
legitimately interest itself in.

Since we live in an age of general systems, where all knowledge is
assumed to live ultimately in the same field as other knowledge, so,
from its inception, the CIA looked to draw its experts from every
field: bankers, journalists, lobbyists, colonels, professors, commo-
dores, soil-erosion specialists, diplomats, business consultants, students, lawyers, doctors, poison specialists, art experts, public-relations men, magazine editors, movie technicians. Out of every
occupation in American life, men and women were drawn to make
up the first cadres of the CIA, and they were often the best in their
field.

Because the CIA, like other government bureaus, had a table of
organization which limited the rank and salary of its employees, the
Company had from the beginning an army of officers serving as pri-
vates. There was not room for the amount of ambition in its ranks.

People moved out of the CIA almost as quickly as they went in and returned to universities, businesses, other government departments, and major foundations, or back to their previous occupations in American life. Of course, a banker who had been a CIA man and was now in finance again was hardly the same banker. Nor had he necessarily left the CIA. If it had been the most exciting experience of his life and/or the most patriotic, he had sentimental loyalties to the Company. He was out of the CIA but still an effective member of it. Sometimes he might even be on call for special jobs or be asked for privileged information on the movements of his financial community.

Like the breaking out of a virus from the host cell, the metastasis of a cancer colony, or the leavening of yeast in bread — depending on one's point of view — the CIA offered a suffusion into the joints and pores of American life so complete that no master list of its active and reserve members (not to speak of its devoted sympathizers) was ever available. One CIA man could never know for certain whether a CIA man who had left the CIA did not still belong to it, and if he did, there were often excellent reasons no record should exist, particularly if he belonged to the Company as to a club, and took no salary. Some agents who left the CIA but were still in it, or of it, might have given reports every week of their life. Others may never have reported once. Like "moles" — it is the CIA word — they waited underground through the seasons working at their private career in order to be of eventual use. Some old agents might still be reliable, some might not — some might report only to one old friend in the Agency. No one would be certain finally who belonged and who did not. In places like the State Department, one could begin to guess, but never know, whether the first allegiance of many a foreign-service officer was to the State desk or to the Company's cover. Since the leaders of the CIA came from a social, financial, and corporate elite, it could be said that the Agency was the militant arm of the Establishment, an order of potential martyrs to Henry Luce's American Century.

The CIA is currently the owner of one of the biggest — if not *the* biggest — fleets of "commercial" airplanes in the world. Agency proprietaries include Air America, Air Asia, Civil Air Transport, Intermountain Aviation, Southern Air Transport, and several other air charter companies around the world ... [but] CIA headquarters ... has never been able to compute ex-

actly the number of planes flown by the airlines it owns, and personnel figures for the proprietaries are similarly imprecise. An agency holding company, the Pacific Corporation, including Air America and Air Asia, alone accounts for almost 20,000 people, more than the entire work force of the parent CIA. For years this vast activity was dominated and controlled by one contract agent, George Doole, who later was elevated to the rank of a career officer. Even then his operation was supervised, part time, by only a single senior officer who lamented that he did not know "what the hell was going on."
— *The CIA and the Cult of Intelligence*

One cannot follow the CIA's use of funds: Nobody is meant to know where all the Company's sources of money originate nor how they begin to end. At the core of many a CIA operation is the need for secrecy in the use of money. Some foreign official has to be bought, or expensive military equipment must be left as a gift in another country. If spies are to be paid, and foreign companies infiltrated, if Central American troops are to be trained for invasion forces, and drug traffics infiltrated for the information they will supply on Indochinese troop movements, if a hundred semilegal or near-to-criminal patriotic activities need to be lubricated without congressional grit in the bearings, then money has to pass down to active operative levels in the middle regions of the Company without scrupulous bookkeeping. It was better for the Director of the CIA not to know what his agents were up to, not if he had to testify on oath before congressional committees. What one did not know, one could not tell. It was therefore the essence of policy for no one to be in command of more information than he needed — a cellular society has to have waterproof compartments, enclaves. Money, therefore, did not always have to be accounted for; indeed, it often was put into an activity on no more than the word of the good character (and/or good family) of the agent who requisitioned it. No word needed to come back on what had been done with the bread, who was bought, who was killed, who made a profit.[1]

Since inside information on foreign currencies, or the domestic commodities market and gold market, or advance warning of a de-

---

[1] The Pike committee in Congress had a withheld report (published in the *Village Voice*, February 16, 1976) which decided that the real intelligence budget is not $3 billion, the estimate given to Congress, but is "closer to $10 billion," the missing $7 billion being buried in the appropriations of other departments. Ten billion dollars is roughly equal to the annual budget of New York City.

valuation in the dollar, was as available on occasion as money, it is unthinkable that some of the Wall Street men in the CIA did not make secret investments for the Agency (that is, for their enclave in the Agency) which soon brought back huge profits by virtue of the secret information which had first encouraged the investment. That kind of surplus could now be used for ultrasecret operations or for even more resplendent financial investments. It is novelistically intoxicating to contemplate the pyramiding of wealth which must have gone on in some enclaves of the CIA. What a congeries of friendly and competitive financial empires may have begun to exist within the agency! For all we know, and we will not soon know, half the Swiss banks are now controlled by agents, facets, wings, arms, committees, councils, operators, and officers of the CIA. Contemplating the mix of real names and false names, actual companies and fronts, declared and secret investment, legal and illegal accounting, fair and flawed computers, it is doubtful that we will ever be able to measure the wealth manipulated by the CIA. Add to this the inevitable intimacies and financial interrelations of such prime possibilities as Hughes, Vesco, and J. Paul Getty, plus the covert investments of the Agency in any number of multinational corporations (with the Mafia and without) — lo, it is not so difficult to think that the economic history of the Arab nations may yet be seen to shine by the secret light of the Company's resources. One cannot, of course, know. It is just that it is easier to believe in such a scenario than to assume that all those proud, powerful Company patriots with their comprehensive information and financial skills never used CIA money to make money that did not have to be accounted for.

Besides, it would be interesting to guess the magnitude of the CIA's secret funds. Out of the real $10-billion Intelligence budget would come the seed money for concealed investments; if the process has been going on for twenty-five years with continuous reinvestment, then these secret investments could total by now anywhere from $25 billion to $100 billion, not an impossible sum for the twenty-five years it has been burgeoning if we compare it to the income of the CIA's senior partner, the Mafia — but we anticipate.

I have worked on projects with many CIA men so unaware of the entire operation that they had no realization and awareness of the roles of other CIA men working on the same project. I would know of this because inevitably somewhere along the line both

groups would come to the Department of Defense for support. I actually designed a special office in the Pentagon with but one door off the corridor. Inside, it had a single room with one secretary. However, off her office there was one more door that led to two more offices with a third doorway leading to yet another office, which was hidden by the door from the secretary's room. I had to do this because at times we had CIA groups with us who were not allowed to meet each other, and who most certainly would not have been there had they known that the others were there. (For the record, the office was 4D1000 — it may have been changed by now; but it stayed that way for many years.)
— L. Fletcher Prouty,
The Secret Team

It is inevitable that there should be a loss to CIA agents of a clear boundary to their identity. A man may work in the CIA for twenty years and never perform the role his title suggests he is performing. Two men may work side by side in the same office for ten years and never learn the other's real work, or to the contrary may know the work intimately but not have a clue on what it is designed to cover. A man's wife may only guess at his real activities. Old moles who have been working at a separate career for years might find themselves suddenly activated as agents and have to deal with CIA men who are present under a new cover themselves.

After years of such work, one may no longer be certain of one's own function, loyalty, or sanity — one can hardly be certain of the identity of one's friends, and one can never be sure the CIA has or has not made a new piece of history. It is impossible, for example, for anyone in the Company ever to be positive the Agency had absolutely nothing to do with the assassinations of the sixties. In such a medium of existence, paranoia is equal to logic itself, and an infinite number of scenarios may dance on the head of a pin. There is always the unforgettable paradigm of the double agent Azev, who, in the years before the Russian Revolution, spied on the Bolsheviks for the czarist police, but in the course of his false Bolshevik duties murdered czarist police with such daring that Azev rose high in Bolshevik circles and became one of Lenin's most trusted men. Indeed, Lenin could not at first believe the captured files of the czarist police although they gave unimpeachable evidence that Azev was a double agent. Where is the root of identity in that kind of man?

The human brain is divided: into a right lobe and a left lobe; a bold side and a cautious one; a moralist and a sinner; a radical and a conservative; a live lover and a dead one; a wit and an idiot; a hard worker and a sloth. We are all ourselves, and to some degree we are the opposite of ourselves. Consider the overlays of personality which accompany these shifts of identity when a cover story is added — there must be an actual need to function as double agents now that the psyche has been already once divided! Then contemplate the variety of political activities which take place within the Company: from the right-wingers of the John Birch Society to the social engineers who brood in private over *The New York Review of Books;* consider the ideological wars which go on between cold warriors and lovers of détente, between those who would presumably die for more government and those who wouldn't mind killing for less. If we take into account the functional need of the agency to have its enclaves cut off from responsibility or accountability, and in turn the national propensity of these enclaves to become — in compensation for the dirtiness of the work — political, that is, to fight for political ends within the CIA and maneuver for power at the top, as well as engage in capers *on their own* to affect the internal history of the United States, how then can they not use every tool ranging from straight financial manipulation to Syndicate involvement to assassination? Yes, try to keep up (if you are the Director) with the movements of agents in the CIA attempting to infiltrate rival enclaves. The mind reels. The scenarios do a dervish. To live with a role is to live as an actor — so soon as the role is more satisfying than the life, all clear boundaries of identity are lost. All the more reason, then, for the CIA man to try to find an identity within his false identity by way of some enclave that satisfies his political needs. It is a way of saying he looks for a secret political action which will seem authentic to him — an action that can cut through the confusion of enigmatic projects and multiple identities in order to give the country what it really needs, that is, what he believes America secretly desires.

It is against the background of this mammoth of shuffled identities, concealed fortunes, fever-hot enclaves, secret killers, paranoid visions, osmotic bureaucratic walls, pervasive unaccountability, double agents, infiltrated capers, and cross capers that we attempt to look at Watergate. If what has been proposed already is valid at all, then we can be certain no clear picture will come to us soon. It is better to recognize that we are blind and can only try, through the distorted reverberation of the echo, to improve our knowledge of the mood. Of course, that is the true perception of the blind.

2.
A Hitch in Historiography

Haldeman ordered an exhaustive investigation into O'Brien's relationship with billionaire Howard Hughes. Caulfield reported back in a Jan. 25, 1971, memo that the investigation could bubblegum in Nixon's face.

The Hughes organization's "tentacles touch many extremely sensitive areas of government," cautioned Caulfield, "each of which is fraught with potential for Jack Anderson type exposures."[2]

— Jack Anderson, the Washington *Post*,
June 6, 1974

The phantom billionaire repeatedly insisted upon total secrecy. He didn't want "the most microscopic chance of the slightest hint being accidentally dropped to *anyone*," stressed a typical memo. Another time, he declared that his informants "put their very lives in jeopardy with some of the disclosures they make to me, and if they thought this information went to anybody — no matter whom — they would not continue to inform me."

— Jack Anderson, May 23, 1974

Howard Hughes has not been interviewed or photographed by any pressman since 1958.

— Stephen Fay, et al., *Hoax*

By the end of his life, Hughes satisfies some idea in us of the giant amoeba or master spider. If he first appeared on the screen of the American media as a rich and prodigiously eccentric young man, reminiscent of Orson Welles at the beginning of *Citizen Kane*, he ended as one of the wealthiest recluses and most mysterious right-wingers of history (that is, assuming it was Hughes who just died and not one of his — more than one — legendary doubles). He is at once the principle of total invisibility in public life and a gargoyle out of *The Day of the Locust*. We think fondly of young Hughes, his racing planes, and his movies: *Scarface*, *The Front Page*, and

---

[2] The memo actually said "Maheu's tentacles. . . ." We will meet Maheu before long.

Hell's Angels; his stars: George Raft, Jean Harlow, Bob Mitchum, Jane Russell; and then we read of the old gink who abhors bacteria as Dracula fears the cross.

> Hughes kept his last wife, movie actress Jean Peters, on a yo-yo string. He would disappear for long stretches and send her endearing but false messages. . . .
> In 1965, he promised to have Thanksgiving dinner with her. But because of his fear of germs, he told her to sit across the room from him. She walked out in a huff.
> The following year, he persuaded her to join him in Boston where he promised they would settle down. But again, he kept her at across-the-room distance. She put up with it for three days.
> — Jack Anderson, May 23, 1974

Since secrecy was his antiseptic, the media are often tempted to portray his ventures as absurd. The story of the $350-million CIA contract for the Glomar Explorer came out in the press as a huge and peculiar sum for the CIA to pay Hughes to design a boat that could "retrieve military codes and nuclear warheads from a Soviet submarine sunk three miles deep in the Pacific . . . [especially] since the codes were outdated and the value of the other information was negligible."[3]

Of course, the Soviet submarine might only have been the cover. Maybe, it was wiser to assume the CIA had grown concerned with finding a new source of minerals to compete with Third World cartels. They could have "awarded Hughes the $350 million to develop an advanced technology for underwater mining — thereby giving Hughes a head start toward a bonanza with more potential than oil. . . ."[4]

The Glomar bonanza could leave Hughes, by some counts already the wealthiest man in the world, an order of magnitude wealthier. But then for two decades Hughes must have been suffering something like the psychosis of a heavyweight champion. (Every heavyweight champion has to be a fraction insane since he cannot know if he is the greatest fighter alive or if some unseen maniac of the martial arts is getting ready to destroy him in an alley.) So Hughes had to wonder whether he was making history or was only a servant of the history the CIA might be making through him.

---

[3] Howard Kohn, "Strange Bedfellows — The Hughes-Nixon-Lansky Connection," *Rolling Stone.*
[4] "Strange Bedfellows."

He could not know, and no one looking on from the outside could know, how much of the CIA was part of his operation or how much of his operation was directed by the CIA. Indeed, was there even a live man named Hughes at the center of it all, or was there a Special Committee?[5] Suffice it that whatever entity was comprised by his name, Hughes had properties. Since we don't know what we are dealing with, let us designate it HUGHES.

HUGHES's corporations earned more than half a billion dollars a year from government contracts alone and thirty-two such contracts were with the CIA. That was the largest number held by any corporate entity with the Company. *Time* fortified such figures: "During the past ten years Hughes Aircraft, which relies almost exclusively on Government work, has won nearly $6 billion in Government contracts. . . . There was also about 6 billion dollars more in secret contracts with the CIA over this period. . . . Asserts one former Pentagon official, 'Their interests are completely merged.' "[6] So, HUGHES, whoever HUGHES was, might begin to look like the pope of Avignon to any director of the CIA. If an enclave needed funds for a special caper, who was better than HUGHES to fund it? HUGHES was Daddy Warbucks to the CIA. HUGHES owned half of Las Vegas. HUGHES, by way of various intermediaries, had absorbed it from Meyer Lansky. Since the CIA already had associations with Lansky, easily as old as their mutual attempts to assassinate Castro, the Company could now, by way of HUGHES and Las Vegas, enter into another majestic interface with the Mafia, that is, with half the labor unions of America, and nearly all of the entertainment industries, the construction industries, the highway, travel, and tourist industries, not to speak of the more celebrated nonlegal industries like prostitution, porny, narcotics, and — the finest operation yet discovered for laundering huge sums of money and evading the IRS — gambling. (If the Mafia had detested the very mood and atmosphere of gambling casinos, it would still have been obliged to get into the business for the legerdemain it offered to heavy sums.) In turn, the high-potential money in the CIA would want to discharge into the great sea of Syndicate wealth. There the take — voices fill in awe — came to $50 billion a year, and

[5] The body of the Hughes who died in April of this year had its fingerprints checked "against genuine Hughes prints on file with the FBI in Washington. It was," *Time* says cheerfully (April 19, 1976), "Hughes, all right." Of course that assumes no one in the mills of identification has ever been able to switch a set of prints.

[6] *Time* also says: "Not until 1971 did the IRS subject the Hughes holdings to an overall audit; the results of that audit have been kept secret."

that was twice General Motors' if only half the size of the defense budget.

> CIA officials asked Maheu to enlist Syndicate men for the Castro murder . . . and authorized him to pay $150,000 for the hit. Maheu told the Church committee he hesitated initially because he feared the project might interfere with his work for Howard Hughes,[7] who also had retained Maheu's services. But Maheu said he agreed to the assignment after informing Hughes of the murder plot — and, according to one source, gaining the billionaire's approval. For the project Maheu called on John Roselli, Sam Giancana and Santo Trafficante.
>
> — Howard Kohn, *Strange Bedfellows*

We could speak of Maheu, an ex-FBI agent on special retainer to the CIA since 1954, as a man of variety and dimension, a veritable fixer, but such words do not elucidate the physics implicit in his personal forces. Rather, Maheu is known in Intelligence as a "pivotal" figure — the roads go through his tollbooth. We will learn for instance from the Pike committee that pornographic movies were sometimes made with CIA funds to blackmail people and "one of these was titled 'Happy Days' with Mr. Robert Maheu as casting director, make-up man, cameraman and director." The detail is cited not to offer us the opportunity to rise in moral height above Maheu so much as to loosen our imagination. He was also for a time the most visible HUGHES representative in public life. "You are me to the outside world," reads one memo to Maheu.[8] "Go see Nixon as my special confidential emissary," says another in the spring of '68. "A Republican victory this year . . . could be realized under our sponsorship and supervision every inch of the way."[9] HUGHES even had a $600,000 French colonial mansion built for Maheu on the Desert Inn grounds.

> The first time he entertained for lunch the casino managers . . . Maheu tapped his water glass for attention. Then, to the astonishment of his Las Vegas colleagues, Robert Maheu said grace.[10]

---

[7] In excerpt, out of respect for the source's punctuation, *Hughes* will appear in lowercase.
[8] David Tinnin, *Just About Everybody vs. Howard Hughes.*
[9] Ibid.
[10] Ibid.

"O'Brien and Maheu are longtime friends from the Boston area. . . . During the Kennedy administration there apparently was continuous liaison between O'Brien and Maheu."
— Memo from John Dean to H. R. Haldeman,
January 26, 1971[11]

There was, of course, the delicate matter that Hughes wanted to hire me but didn't want to meet me face to face. Maheu raised the issue — he said that was simply Hughes's style of operation, that he, Maheu, had worked for the man for years, and was his chief executive officer, but had never met him.
— Larry O'Brien, *No Final Victories*

After Hubert Humphrey's defeat in 1968, Larry O'Brien was relatively at liberty. The new administration might be Republican, but O'Brien had not worked as postmaster general and chairman of the Democratic National Committee nor managed the presidential campaigns of Kennedy, Johnson, and Humphrey for too little. Nobody had more contacts in Washington than Larry O'Brien. From early in 1968 on, even as Maheu was being confidential emissary to Nixon, so was he also being instructed to hire O'Brien as HUGHES's Washington representative; but it was only in October, 1969, after a stretch for O'Brien on Wall Street, that the consulting firm O'Brien Associates was formed and given a HUGHES contract at $15,000 a month. The arrangement, however, soon faced complications. By late 1970, HUGHES had decided to replace Maheu with Intertel.

Although this is not widely known, an increasing number of big corporations in recent years have either established private intelligence units or hired intelligence consultants from the CIA, the FBI, the DIA, the Internal Security Division of the Justice Department, the Treasury, the Secret Service, or the Internal Revenue Service. The purpose is, basically, to protect a corporation's own secrets or acquire other corporations' secrets in the ever-competitive business world. A whole underworld of corporate intelligence has thus developed.

Several organizations in the United States openly offer corporate intelligence services. The most important is Intertel. . . .
— Tad Szulc, *Compulsive Spy*

---

[11] J. Anthony Lukas, *Nightmare — The Underside of the Nixon Years.*

It could be said that Intertel had better CIA connections than Maheu. In fact, they were socially superior. Intertel's owner was James Crosby, good friend and host of Rebozo and Nixon. Crosby was also the chairman of Resorts International, an immense gambling-and-tourist complex in the Bahamas which (with many a camouflage) had been taken over from Meyer Lansky by the CIA. (Brave men grow bold in the Caribbean and gentlemen turn into pirates.) Resorts International came right out of the Crosby Miller Corporation, in which a controlling interest had been acquired in 1958 by Mary Carter Paint, a corporation originally gotten up by Allen Dulles and Thomas E. Dewey.

If the CIA hierarchy had icons analogous to the Mayflower, they were Allen Dulles, Thomas E. Dewey, and the Mary Carter Paint Company. By such cachet James Crosby of Intertel was to Maheu's CIA pornies and assassination capers as Louisburg Square to Scollay Square. In addition, Intertel may also have been in position to offer HUGHES the Glomar Explorer contract if he would take them on. That meant letting Maheu go. Since Maheu knew a lot about HUGHES, it was a big payment for a real peril.

The changeover in 1970 was accomplished with the maximum of mystery. The man, Hughes, six feet four inches, reported to weigh 97 pounds and, by a Las Vegas doctor's report, next to death, gave over his authority to Maheu's most determined enemies with a proxy which enabled these enemies to bring Intertel's security force into the casinos and drive out Maheu's troops, a dramatic night for Las Vegas, whose citizens were learning about this time that a tall thin man, claimed by his proxy-holders to be Howard Hughes, had been smuggled out of his sanctuary in the penthouse of the Desert Inn and been flown to the Bahamas (even though he was next to death and swore he would never fly again). There were some, Maheu among them, who offered the mordant suspicion that HUGHES was now a karmic transplant, but then there were others who had been supposing the same since 1958, when the man, Hughes, stopped seeing anyone but a few Hughes Tool Company executives and/or his rotating male nurse-secretaries (five), who received all messages for him. Maybe, by the time of the move to the Bahamas, HUGHES was going into his second karmic transplant; maybe HUGHES was now a computer not unrelated to OCTOPUS at Langley.

But such speculations take us too fast down the stream. Let us keep to what we may suppose we know. It seems clear that HUGHES, now divested of Maheu, would not necessarily want to keep Maheu's friend in his employ. Of course, dropping O'Brien would hardly be fail-safe. It was not comfortable to estimate how much O'Brien had learned about the CIA from Maheu (if for that matter O'Brien had had a great deal to learn about the CIA).

Nonetheless, the transfers were made. Some time after Intertel took over from Maheu, HUGHES replaced O'Brien with Bob Bennett. The son of Senator Wallace Bennett (R), from Utah, Bob Bennett was a churchgoing Mormon; in fact, he was part of the three-man bishopric of the Church of Jesus Christ of Latter-Day Saints in Arlington, Virginia, a detail of dubious interest until it is fortified with the knowledge that a large number of HUGHES aides, assistants, and top executives were Mormons; indeed, Maheu's most devoted enemies in HUGHES were Mormons. We might·wonder how such religious fellows would comport themselves in Las Vegas, but there is always a tendency to underrate the sects we know least. It seems, consulting the *Encyclopaedia Britannica*, that a secret Mormon society called the Danites was organized for Joseph Smith in October, 1838. They had "the avowed purpose of supporting Smith at all hazards, of upholding the authority of his revelation and decrees as superior to the laws of the land, and of helping him to get possession, first of the state, then of the United States, and ultimately of the world."

It would be an investigator's pleasure to now reveal that there is a modern-day Danite enclave in the CIA reaching out to the Danites in HUGHES, but we shall have to content ourselves with the only Mormon we have — Bob Bennett — and his relations to Chuck Colson and Howard Hunt.

Bennett had been a director of congressional relations at the Department of Transportation, to wit, a public-relations man and lobbyist. Needless to say, both are splendid positions for a mole. In addition, any work Bennett could find concerning highway construction might bring him, if he chose, close to the Mafia; he was thereby twice-connected to voyage out from his one third of a bishopric. Since he had also been friends with Chuck Colson since 1968, and lately of quiet service as the White House contact (that is, informer) in the Department of Transportation, Bennett was on his way to being his own pivotal figure. Consequently, he was in a position to try to do a favor for HUGHES. The good deed (seeking to divert the dumping of nerve gas from the Bahamas ocean floor — a way of protecting future HUGHES investments in the Bahamas) could not be accomplished, but Bennett left a good impression and was hired by his fellow Mormons.

Then "Colson called Bennett to say that Robert Mullen wanted to sell his company. Colson urged Bennett to buy the company and said he would help him find clients."[12] Bennett bought into Mullen & Company, and in one month rose from executive vice-president to president; after nine months he completed the purchase. Earlier than this, sometime "during his first months with the company . . . Robert Mullen told him about the company's relation with the CIA."[13]

This small account of a purchase is invaluable for what it teaches of how to detect a cover story by the incriminating anemia of its narrative. For it asks us to tolerate the idea that a useful CIA front was sold to a non-CIA man who was then kindly informed of the CIA's relation to the company he bought; in return for such courtesy, he proceeded without ado to labor for the agency. Since Bennett will labor long hours, it is comfortable to suspect he has been with the CIA before we have met him.

> It is in the political agent's interest to betray all the parties who use him and to work for them all at the same time, so that he may move freely and penetrate everywhere.
>
> — Galtier-Boissière[14]

Enter Hunt. He has been with Mullen & Company since May, 1970, a little better than six months, before Bennett has arrived, and according to his account, he is furious with Mullen because Bennett came as a surprise. "The switch was as unexpected as it was unwelcome."[15] Hunt had seen himself as eventually taking over Mullen & Company. Accordingly we are encouraged by his account to believe Hunt moved over to the White House out of disgust with his situation at Mullen & Company rather than as part of a more or less orchestrated plan to bring Bennett and Hunt nearer to the administration. It was, in any case, not a shift that was difficult to make, for Hunt was also a friend of Colson's. They had met at the Brown University Club of Washington in 1966. Later, Colson became president of the club and Hunt, vice-president. They met frequently for

---

[12] *Nightmare.*
[13] Ibid.
[14] E. Howard Hunt, *The Berlin Ending* (epigraph).
[15] E. Howard Hunt, *Undercover.*

lunch all through 1969 and 1970, and at one time Colson even thought enough of Hunt to try to make him director of a conservative think-tank, the Institute for Informed America, which would provide intellectual opposition to the Brookings Institution. The scheme lapsed (since Hunt frightened off Jeb Magruder by a proposal to use the think-tank for covert action), but now that Hunt was working for Colson in the Plumbers and Colson was also friends with Bennett, maybe Colson could be forgiven for thinking the prospects seemed fair for a happy family. As early as the beginning of 1971, he even sent a confidential memo to an aide of Agnew's:

> Bob is a trusted loyalist and a good friend. We intend to use him on a variety of outside projects. One of Bob's (new) clients is Howard Hughes. I am sure I need not explain the political implications of having Hughes' affairs handled here in Washington by a close friend. . . . Bob Bennett tells me that he has never met the Vice President, and that it would enhance his position greatly if we could find an appropriate occasion for him to come in and spend a little time talking with the Vice President. The important thing from our standpoint is to enhance Bennett's position with Hughes because Bennett gives us real access to a sort of power that can be valuable, and it's in our interest to build him up.
>
> — *Compulsive Spy*

It is enough to remind us of Tolstoy's opening sentence in *Anna Karenina:* "Happy families are all alike: every unhappy family is unhappy in its own way." Colson's gang, we know in advance, will be unique.

But we can get a look into how closely Hunt is working with Bennett. A couple of years later, it was found out by way of the minority staff of the Ervin committee that Bennett "suggested to Hunt that Hank Greenspun, publisher of the Las Vegas *Sun*, had material in his safe that would be of interest to both Hughes and the Committee for the Re-election of the President," and Bennett also arranged "a Hunt interview with Clifton Demotte [about] the episode at Chappaquiddick. . . . Furthermore . . . Bennett learned of [Dita Beard's] whereabouts from a Hughes Tool Company executive . . . [and] acted as an intermediary between Howard Hunt and Gordon Liddy after the Watergate break-in. . . ."[16]

---

[16] Fred D. Thompson, *At That Point in Time.* The author was chief minority counsel for the Ervin committee.

This encourages the minority staff to the following conclusions:

(1) While Hunt was at the White House on Charles Colson's payroll, Bennett was, at least, suggesting and coordinating many of Hunt's activities; (2) Bennett obviously enjoyed a close and confidential relationship with some of Howard Hughes' top people at a time when they were furnishing cover for the CIA; and (3) Bennett was acting as a go-between between Hunt and Liddy immediately after the Watergate break-in, and during all of these activities he was undoubtedly reporting periodically to the CIA case officer.

— At That Point in Time

We are even offered a bona fide side-bar. An inquiry came in from HUGHES. The Mormons (we may as well assume it is specifically the Mormons) wanted to know "the cost of bugging the home of Clifford Irving at the time he was writing the spurious Howard Hughes biography. Hunt got an estimate from James McCord and reported back to Bennett." The project proved to be too expensive, but HUGHES, whether the man or the karmic transplant, announced by way of a telephone interview with seven reporters that he had suspicions about the origins of the hoax. "To assume that it's all an accident certainly takes a lot of assuming." It seems HUGHES had decided the genius behind Clifford Irving was Maheu. Dare we say that every unhappy family is happy in its own way?

3.
An Exercise in Epistemology

In an ironic twist, the White House's high priest of snoopery, Charles Colson, was himself bugged recently as he uttered some of the Watergate scandal's most indiscreet confessions.

Colson, when he was the top White House hatchet man, was fond of flipping a switch and tape-recording friends and enemies alike. A few days before he went to prison for obstructing justice, however, he was secretly recorded as he bared his soul to Washington businessman and sometime private eye Richard Bast. . . .

Beside Bast's swimming pool, whose fountain made background water music over a "mike" secreted among poolside flow-

ers, the two men discussed how Nixon could rid himself of CIA
and military spying on the White House.
                              — Jack Anderson, July 15, 1974

If we have been entertaining ourselves until now with the illusion
that we are pursuing a narrative, or hovering over a picture that will
soon come to focus, we may as well recognize that we can count, at
best, on no more than a glimpse of a narrative — enough perhaps to
give us hope this is a narrative which exists and not a chaos. But it is
a curious endeavor. The best details often lead nowhere. Nixon, for
example, received campaign contributions in 1972 which were as
large as $2 million from W. Clement Stone and $1 million from
Richard Mellon Scaife of Pittsburgh. Nonetheless, the Nixon administration reacted with excessive anxiety to the disclosure of a gift
of $100,000 in 1970 from HUGHES by way of Richard Danner to
Bebe Rebozo; in fact Nixon fired Archibald Cox only two days after
he had indicated to Elliot Richardson how displeased he was about
Cox's zealous investigation of Rebozo. The break-in at Watergate
was even explained in some scenarios as the measure of Nixon's
need to know how much O'Brien knew about HUGHES's gift.[17] It
made no sense. Rebozo had an explanation which was legally impeccable. He told investigators that he was worried about the "appearance" of the gift and so did not give it to the President but put it in
his own safe-deposit box, and later, in June, 1973, sent it back to
HUGHES. One did not have to believe the story, but in the absence
of evidence that the cash had been passed, why did Nixon react so
powerfully?

> "They must certainly know something very heavy on Nixon,"
> commented Bast. . . .
>   Colson . . . replied, "They must."
>   "I mean, if he knows this stuff is going on and he's not doing
> anything about it . . ." began Bast.
>   "You know what I think?" interrupted Colson. "You want to
> know what I really think? . . . I'm loyal to the guy (Nixon) 'cause
> he's my friend . . . I think Bebe used that ($100,000) for himself
> and for the President, for the family, and the girls. I think that the
> President figures — this is my worst suspicion — that if he really
> blows this, Hughes can blow the whistle on him." . . .
>   . . . Bast asked whether the only thing the CIA had hanging
> over Nixon's head was the $100,000.

---

[17] That would assume it was worth $250,000 to CREEP to find out a little more about
$100,000.

Replied Colson morosely:
"Who knows that that's the only $100,000?"
— Jack Anderson, July 16, 1974

It is a fascinating detail. It is just that nothing comes of it. We still don't know if it is the only $100,000 or no more than the tail of the mouse left in the trap. Since much that we examine will appear, then tend to disappear, it is nice to think there is something iridescent about a view seen for an instant in the fog.

Perhaps it is the effect of such glimpses to leave us with an after-image. On reflection, Nixon's reaction to the $100,000 does not have to be political. Even a political man is entitled to a private emotion. Fighting the attack on Rebozo, Nixon could be expressing the outrage he felt at attacks against himself. Or, maybe the gift just gave him an uneasy feeling from the moment it was proposed. Of course, the hard chancre of an inflamed in-house scandal could also have been sitting beneath the money. We simply do not know to which corner the mouse has gone.

The nature of the difficulty begins to disclose itself. We cannot house an explanation because we do not know which of our facts are bricks and which are papier-mâche painted to look like bricks. We can only watch the way the bricks are handled.

It is painful, nonetheless, to relinquish one's hope for a narrative, to admit that study of the CIA may not lead to the exposure of facts so much as to the epistemology of facts. We will not get the goods so quickly as we will learn how to construct a model which will tell us why we cannot get the goods. Of course, that will never be enough — willy-nilly, the habit will persist to look for a new narrative (and damn the papier-mâche bricks).

In the meantime, however, a short course:

Epistemological Model I:
If half the pieces in a jigsaw puzzle are missing, the likelihood is that something can still be put together. Despite its gaps, the picture may be more or less visible. Even if most of the pieces are gone, a loose mosaic can be arranged of isolated elements. The possibility of the real picture being glimpsed under such circumstances is small but not altogether lost.[18] It is just that one would like to know if the few pieces left belong to the same set.[19]

---

[18] Larry Rivers has taught us as much.
[19] Is this what Robert Rauschenberg is up to?

Epistemological Model II:
Maybe it is the splinters of a mirror rather than the scattered pieces of a jigsaw puzzle that provide a superior ground for the metaphor. We are dealing not with reality, after all, but that image of reality which reaches the surface through the cracked looking glass of the media.

Epistemological Model III:
What is most crucial is that we do not forget that we are interpreting curious actions. Men who seem to be honest are offering cover. We are obliged to remind ourselves that a life lived under cover produces a chronic state of mind in the actor which is not unlike those peculiar moments when staring in the mirror too long we come to recognize that the face looking back at us must — inescapably — be our own. Yet it is not. Our vicissitudes (but not our souls) stand revealed in the mirror; or, given another day, and another mirror, there we are, feeling wretched, looking splendid.

Epistemological Model IV:
Doubtless the difficulty is analogous to writing a poem with nothing but names, numbers, facts, conjecture, gossip, trial balloons, leaks, and other assorted pieces of prose.
For example:

> When we interviewed him in my office on December 10, 1973, he struck all of us as a highly intelligent, highly motivated person. . . . Finally I asked him, "Mr. Martinez, if in fact you were a CIA plant on the Watergate team and were reporting back to the Agency, would you tell us?" He broke into a broad smile, looked around the room, and laughed. He never answered the question; no answer was necessary.
> — *At That Point in Time*

Let us go back to the facts, to the false facts, distorted facts, concealed facts, empty facts, secretly rich facts, and unverifiable speculations of our narrative.

In this connection, nothing we have read about Gordon Liddy explains his long silence in jail so well as the supposition that he is an agent of real caliber. Of his biography we know he was in the FBI in the early Sixties, an assistant district attorney in Dutchess County, ran for Congress on the Conservative party ticket, and got a job with the Treasury Department high up in a Customs Bureau drug campaign called Operation Intercept. It was not a position to leave him alien to certain intimacies of the CIA, the Mafia, and the flow of profits in the drug trade. Liddy came to the White House to work for Egil Krogh, who was trying to organize the Nixon administration's war on drugs with a projected team of CIA men, FBI men, narcs, and private detectives, an undertaking some would see darkly as a most ambitious cover for Nixon's real intent, which was to commence his own Intelligence on a competitive level with the CIA and the FBI — in other words, his unspoken follow-up to the Huston Plan. It is worth mentioning that during this period, Liddy wrote a memo for Nixon in criticism of the FBI, which Nixon described to Krogh as "the most brilliant memorandum" to come his way "in a long time."[20] It is with this background that Liddy comes to CREEP. There is nothing in these details to suggest he could not be a career agent.

We read of how he burns his hand in a flame to impress a girl and threatens to kill Magruder if Jeb touches him on the shoulder again. John Dean describes to us how Liddy offers to commit suicide if that will protect the administration. Liddy offers a lecture on how to kill a man with a finely sharpened pencil. There is nothing in these details to suggest he could not be a career agent.

> "The master who instructed me in the deadliest of the Oriental martial arts taught me that the outcome of a battle is decided in the minds of the opponents before the first blow is struck."
> — G. Gordon Liddy[21]

We have the habit to look on the Watergate burglars as ignorant Cubans led by clowns. Being scorned as ridiculous is, of course, a cover in itself; the CIA can count on such a disguise being provided by the wire services. Simple declarative sentences make curious actions appear automatically absurd.

Under examination, the burglars look better. Gonzales had been a bodyguard for Batista, and fought in the Bay of Pigs. Martinez had been a CIA boat captain and made 354 illegal runs to Cuba. Barker was a member of Batista's secret police, and an FBI contact in Cuba, then an informer against Castro. By Hunt's own description, Barker

---

[20] These details are given in a forthcoming book impressively researched by Edward Jay Epstein, *An American Coup D'Etat* (Putnam's).
[21] As quoted in *Nightmare.*

became his "principal assistant" during the Bay of Pigs, and Hunt was chief of political action.

The fourth Cuban happens to be Italian — Frank Sturgis, an ex-Marine born Frank Angelo Fiorini. He served with Castro in the Sierra Maestra — and would later claim he was already an agent for the Company. In any case, he was good enough to be working as Fidel's personal supervisor in the Havana casinos until the day gambling was eliminated. Then Sturgis decided to defect. To the Mafia and to the CIA. (Or is it simpler to say the Mafia wing of the CIA?) It is a not inconsiderable defection.

Before the Bay of Pigs, Sturgis would act as contact for Santo Trafficante, who with his son Santo Jr. "controlled much of Havana's tourist industry," and was alleged to have received "bulk shipments of heroin from Europe and forwarded them through Florida to New York."[22] During this period, Sturgis joined a CIA unit called Operation Forty, which had been set up to kill Castro and a number of important Fidelistas. Involved in this training were Trafficante and E. Howard Hunt,[23] Frank Sturgis,[24] and Robert Maheu. Maheu and Sturgis must have been reasonably well met, since Sturgis is still pivotal enough eleven years later to be chatting with Jack Anderson in the lobby of Washington National Airport on the morning he arrives from Miami with Barker, Martinez, and Gonzales for the last break-in at Watergate, but then it would be difficult to name an investigative reporter in America more pivotal than Anderson.

> "I don't know if I told you before," Sturgis wrote to his wife [while in jail], "but William F. Buckley used to work for CIA and I don't know if he still does. When he found out that Howard (Hunt) was going to work in the White House, he told Howard it was good that he could be so close to the President but Howard told him that he was there to take orders and not to influence anyone. That was a good answer!"
>
> . . . Buckley frankly admitted he was a "deep cover agent" for the CIA from July, 1951, to March, 1952, but said he had not worked for them since.
>
> — Jack Anderson, September 18, 1973

[22] Alfred W. McCoy, et al., *The Politics of Heroin in Southeast Asia*.

[23] "Strange Bedfellows."

[24] In *Undercover*, Hunt mentions in passing that he did not meet Sturgis until shortly before Watergate. Of course, he also does not mention that there was a plot to assassinate Castro. Nor does he bother to inform us that Hank Sturgis is the name of a character in Hunt's early novel, *Bimini Run,* which Frank Angelo Fiorini liked well enough to modify into an alias.

It was apparent from the documents that in November 1971, a month after he took part in the Fielding break-in, Martinez mentioned his association with Hunt to his case officer who, in turn, took Martinez to the CIA's chief of station in Miami.

We immediately requested that the chief of station be brought from Florida for an interview. The chief, a heavyset man who appeared rather nervous, told us that in March 1972, Martinez had asked him if he "really knew all about the Agency activities in the Miami area." Martinez had dropped hints about Hunt's activities, the chief said, which had concerned him so much that he wrote a letter to CIA headquarters inquiring about Hunt's status. The answer, we were told, was that the chief should "cool it" and not concern himself with Hunt's affairs.

— At That Point in Time

One does better not to rely on that comfortable picture we have of E. Howard Hunt as an unhinged undercover man in a wild red wig impotently badgering Dita Beard on her hospital bed — the wig may have been chosen to make him startling to a fearful woman.

By the rank of the posts he occupied in his career, it is obvious that Hunt, for a long time at least, was well regarded in the Agency. For that matter, he has so many credentials we can wonder how close he came in his own mind to becoming director of the CIA. In his autobiography, *Undercover*, he remarks, "Obviously I was never going to be director of Central Intelligence, nor did I particularly want to be," but the year is 1966 and he says it after more than fifteen years of service and such prime positions as deputy chief of station in Mexico (which is where William F. Buckley, Jr. worked for him); chief of covert operations for southeastern Europe — Albania, Yugoslavia, Bulgaria, Greece, and Turkey; chief of political action for the Guatemala operation which overthrew Arbenz; chief of covert operations for the north Asia command — China, Korea, Japan; chief of station in Uruguay; chief of political action for the Bay of Pigs; chief of Domestic Operations Division (the United States); and chief of covert action for Western Europe.

Before joining the CIA Hunt had been an English major at Brown, served in the navy, the OSS, had been a war correspondent for *Life*, published novels, worked in Hollywood, had a Guggenheim Fellowship for one of his novels, and was in Europe for the ECA under Averell Harriman. Later, within the CIA, he collaborated with Allen Dulles in the writing of *The Craft of Intelligence*. He also worked closely with Frank Wisner, Allen Dulles,

Dick Helms, Richard Bissell, Track Barnes, Tom Karamessines —
there are no larger names in the CIA. If his autobiography fails to
mention Cord Meyer or James Angleton there is no reason we cannot speculate on his concealed relations with them, particularly
from 1966 to 1970, when Hunt neglects to describe what he is doing
for the Company, and the assumption, since he is stationed in
America, is capers, domestic capers.

> A Dutch manufacturer of electronic gadgetry was demonstrat-
> ing some ultrasophisticated electronic "sneakies." The Dutch
> salesman announced that over twenty items of gadgetry had been
> hidden in the exhibition room and invited his CIA guests to find
> them. Then the Dutchman set about to uncover them, and *he*
> couldn't find them. Jim McCord had sneaked into the room be-
> fore the demonstration, found them all, and removed them. "Jim
> is one fine operator," said Helms. . . .
> — Miles Copeland, *National Review*,
> September 14, 1973

McCord was in the CIA for twenty years but he seems like nothing so much as an FBI man. A devout Methodist, abstemious, soft-
voiced in his right-wing opinions, his personality speaks of law and
order rather than espionage or counterespionage. With the CIA
from the first years of its inception (those years when it was raiding
the FBI, and Hoover did not like it, and may for all we know have
been casting about for a career agent who could infiltrate the CIA
for the rest of his working life), McCord worked for the Company
from 1951 to 1970 and became chief of the Physical Security Division of the Office of Security.

As we know, his work had in part to do with finding concealed
bugs and dealing with advanced eavesdropping equipment. He was
good enough to receive a Distinguished Service Award from Helms,
and Allen Dulles once referred to him as "my top man."[25] We do
not know what he was top man in, but it is not mean praise.

His performance during the Watergate break-in is on the consequence fascinating for its incompetence. McCord, according to
Hunt's account, bought only four walkie-talkies where six had been
needed. He delayed charging the batteries. He neglected to discon-
nect a burglar-alarm system. In the course of the first break-in, he

---

[25] Lewis Chester, et al., *Watergate.*

removed his men from the Democratic National Committee offices before the job was done. Then for several days he was unable to process the two rolls of film the Cubans did manage to take because McCord's "man" was out of town. In addition, according to Liddy, McCord "bugged the wrong telephone line. He was supposed to tap O'Brien's."[26] So a second attempt was necessary. On the next try, two of McCord's walkie-talkies had uncharged batteries. McCord retaped the locks after the guard had removed the tapes. He then insisted to Liddy on going ahead with the operation. He also retaped the locks horizontally instead of vertically; the tape was therefore visible at a glance. Hunt would finally decide that McCord was a double agent for the Democrats. A double agent he may have been — for the CIA — and a triple agent for the FBI, but a Democrat? McCord?

Whoever he was, McCord broke the Watergate case by his letter in March, 1973, to Judge Sirica: "There was political pressure applied to the defendants to plead guilty and remain silent. Perjury occurred during the trial. . . ."

He also said, "The Watergate Operation was not a CIA operation. . . . I know for a fact that it was not." It is a retired CIA operative speaking, which is to say, a man who may or may not be retired. Authoritative disclaimers by CIA officials bear the same relation to fact that the square root of minus one bears to a real number. The net effect of McCord's remark, therefore, is to make us more suspicious of the CIA. The possibility that he is an FBI man thereby increases an iota.

The second break-in took place in order that the tap on Larry O'Brien's phone that McCord had not put in well enough to function after the first break-in should now be put in again. Hunt thought the project was odd. "O'Brien's in Miami," he said to Liddy. "Why in hell should we tap the phone in his Washington office? . . . What's the rationale? As a friend, colleague and fellow professional, I'm asking you to go back to Mitchell, Dean and Magruder and reargue the case."[27] Liddy replied, "Okay, I'll try again, but I hate to do it. They look to me to get things done, not argue against them."

---

[26] *Undercover.*

[27] Quoting from Hunt is biting the bullet. Still, it is tempting to quote. From *Undercover.*

Since Liddy is the conspirator who has remained silent, we do not know his "principal," that is, we do not know who told him to break into Democratic headquarters the first time, nor — it may be more interesting — who insisted on a second time when Hunt thought the only logic was to call it off. It is not impossible that Magruder, Mitchell — or could it be Dean? — had an undisclosed relation to the CIA. Let us spin on the vertigo of that thought.

Mr. Haldeman said he had never understood why Alexander P. Butterfield, the aide who disclosed the existence of the White House tapes to the Senate Watergate committee, wanted to join the White House staff. . . .

"He was soon to become an Air Force General. I have never understood why he insisted, against my advice, on dropping his commission or why he suddenly wanted to be part of the Nixon team.

"In view of his subsequent role," Mr. Haldeman went on, "these actions seem even more curious today. Was Butterfield a CIA agent? Maybe. I just don't know."

— The New York *Times*, June 23, 1976

In the early Sixties he [Haig] ran a CIA-financed Bay of Pigs rehabilitation program, preceding Alexander Butterfield in the job.

— "Strange Bedfellows"

Colson complained to Bast that the President was always on the verge of coming down hard on the CIA. But, Colson groused, Nixon was talked out of it by presidential staff chief, Al Haig, who feared it would "take down the whole intelligence community."

— Jack Anderson, July 15, 1974

Haig told us there was "no way" he was working for the CIA.

— Jack Anderson, July 15, 1974

Paul F. Hellmuth, the managing partner of St. Clair's Boston law firm, has been associated over the past decade with . . . Anderson Security Consultants, Inc . . . a CIA front. . . .

Mysterious checks, written for large amounts, would frequently arrive at the office of the firm's secretary-treasurer, Virginia lawyer L. Lee Bean, who would . . . disperse it upon instructions.

The secret instructions often came, say our sources, from James St. Clair's quiet law partner. Some of the mystery money was dispatched to Miami banks and was used allegedly to support the CIA's anti-Castro activities. . . . [Hellmuth] insisted . . . that James St. Clair didn't know "the first thing about the security firm."

—Jack Anderson, July 22, 1974

[Leon] Jaworski had been . . . a director of a private foundation that laundered funds for the CIA.

— "Strange Bedfellows"

We also learned that Paul O'Brien, who had served as counsel to the Committee to Re-elect the President after the Watergate break-in, was a former CIA operative.

— *At That Point in Time*

Among the officers of OSS Detachment 101 was Clark MacGregor, later a Congressman, a White House staffer, and, after the Watergate break-in, the replacement for John Mitchell as head of the Committee for the Re-Election of the President.

— *Compulsive Spy*

"Bob Woodward interviewed me on numerous occasions. I have told Woodward everything I know about the Watergate case, except the Mullen company's tie to the CIA. I never mentioned that to him."

— Robert Bennett: House subcommittee testimony[28]

Because Robert Bennett's CIA ties were exposed by the Watergate scandal, he has closed down the Mullen Agency. He now works for the Hughes organization as a vice-president and CIA liaison.

— "Strange Bedfellows"

During the Bast interview, Colson would name Bennett as Deep Throat. At one point, he would say in pain, "Every story that Woodward won the Pulitzer Prize for was fed to him by the CIA."

An observer of the Company, hearing of this, shook his head. "Deep Throat is a cover in itself. Where is the casual reader who will argue with so agreeable a story — one man's revelation pulling down the entire Nixon administration? If Deep Throat told all, it was only because the information had already been neatly collected

---

[28] As quoted in "Strange Bedfellows."

for Deep Throat to tell." The observer shook his head. "Learn the law of reversal. The victims can be the agents in these affairs. There is as much need to remain suspicious of Colson as to feel sorry for him, since in attacking the CIA, Colson creates good cover for them. The reaction of the newspaper reader who dislikes old Chuck is to think, 'Even if it is true (and I must say I have had my suspicions of the CIA) I won't believe the story if it comes from Colson.' The Bast interview, you see, bothers me. Colson visits Bast, a private investigator, sits down by the pool next to the shrubbery and never wonders if he is being taped? Colson? Pit-bull Colson?

"By the same guideline, the heroes can be the villains. Beware of the heroes of Watergate. I look at the Washington *Post* and think, 'Isn't it a brave paper? Isn't that a heroic editor who dares what no editor of no other major paper will dare? Isn't that right in the vein of major newspaper editors as we have come to know them?' "

On publication of this piece, the editor of the Washington *Post* emphatically denied that he had ever been, or was now, a member of the CIA.

"Never allow yourself," the observer says, "to think you have a fixed platform from which to measure these motions. We're out in the stars with Einstein, I assure you. For instance, you speak of McCord as being inefficient, when what you relate is no more than Hunt's description of how McCord acted in the break-in. Hunt's book could have been written by an enclave."

"Were they wishing to suggest that McCord was dealing with the Democrats?"

"Never look for the answer. Pursue the question into the next question. The answer is invariably smudged, but the questions are beautiful. There is the rapture of the depths descending into the questions."

I also suspected, but could never prove, that the Nixon crowd tapped my telephones. I was only slightly surprised, therefore, by a letter mailed to me on April 15, 1972. It was written by William Haddad, a New York entrepreneur who, until a dozen years ago, had been a prize-winning investigative reporter. Haddad told me he had learned from a private investigator of plans to tap the telephones of the Democratic National Committee. Haddad understood the plot had been hatched by a group of advertis-

ing men, known as the November Group, who had been re-
cruited for the Nixon campaign.
                    — Jack Anderson, *Parade,* July 22, 1973

A letter from William Haddad to Larry O'Brien, March 23, 1972:

> "I am hearing some very disturbing stories about GOP sophisti-
> cated surveillance techniques now being used for campaign pur-
> poses and of an interesting group here in New York where some
> of this "intelligence" activity is centered. The information comes
> from a counter-wiretapper . . . who had come to me highly rec-
> ommended. . . . Can you have someone call me so you can get the
> info first hand and take whatever actions you deem necessary."
>   — *At That Point in Time*

O'Brien sent the director of communications for the Democratic
National Committee to visit Haddad and there was a meeting with
the counter wiretapper whose name proved to be Woolston-Smith.
He was "a short paunchy bald man who spoke with a pronounced
British accent and smoked a pipe." In October, 1973, a year and a
half later, two members of the minority staff of the Ervin committee
took a deposition from Woolston-Smith.

> He testified that he was a private investigator in New York City,
> a citizen of New Zealand with experience in British intelligence,
> and a permanent resident of the United States. He acknowledged
> that he had excellent contacts in the intelligence community and
> said his New York offices had been used by the CIA, after the
> Bay of Pigs, as a clearinghouse for those returning from the inva-
> sion brigades. This information was consistent with what we had
> determined from other sources. Woolston-Smith was a most mys-
> terious person; there were indications that he had connections
> with both British and Canadian intelligence, although we could
> never determine the exact relationship.
>   Woolston-Smith said he had told William Haddad of the possi-
> bility of Republican media control through the November Group
> as early as December 1971, and that they had discussed the
> Group many times before the meeting of April 26, 1972. He
> knew enough about the operation, he said, to know that Gordon
> Liddy "ran the show."
>   — *At That Point in Time*

Since Gemstone, Liddy's first ambitious plan to tap the Democratic National Committee and wire Miami for the Democratic con-

vention, was not even presented to John Mitchell until January 27, 1972, it seems that some undisclosed scheme was already being developed by Gordon Liddy and the November Group in the fall of 1971. Such a probability hardly diminishes the hypothesis that Liddy is an agent of stature. (In fact, the November Group will even be given a million dollars by CREEP before the famous April 7 deadline for campaign contributions. While the majority of this is ostensibly for the November Group's stated purpose, which is advertising, not espionage, the figure is nonetheless interesting. It is equal to the sum Liddy tried to get for Gemstone.)

At any rate, we are left with the following additions:

(1) The Democrats were well aware of the November Group and the possibility that their offices would soon be bugged.

(2) British and Canadian Intelligence can now be added to the soup. Let us think of them as herbs.

(3) Maybe the Democrats were putting in the garlic. Haddad "sent his entire file to Jack Anderson in April 1972" and now "could not remember what was in it. In fact, Haddad said, he sent material to Anderson twice, but had kept no copies." Jack Anderson "had acknowledged receipt of the material from Haddad concerning plans for the break-in, but he said he had since lost it."[29]

Of course, the CIA had infiltrated the FBI, and the FBI had unknown men working for it in the CIA. We must assume both had agents in the Bureau of Narcotics and Dangerous Drugs, the IRS, the National Security Council, the 40 Committee, the Atomic Energy Commission, the Special Operations Division, Naval Intelligence, Air Force Intelligence, the Defense Intelligence Agency, the National Security Agency, the Council on Foreign Relations, HUGHES, plus a number of private intelligence companies whose work extended from military-industrial security to private detectives' offices. In turn, these companies, bureaus, groups, and agencies had to the best of their ability infiltrated the CIA and the FBI. Since the CIA, the FBI, and other major intelligence also had had their authority infiltrated by their own unknown enclaves, it is, in certain circumstances, meaningless to speak of the CIA as a way of differentiating it from the AIA, the DIA, the NSC, HUGHES, or the SOD — let us use the initials CIA therefore like a mathematical symbol which will, depending on the context in which it is employed, usually offer specific reference to a CIA located physically

---

[29] *At That Point in Time.*

in Langley, Virginia, with near to 18,000 employees, understanding that under other circumstances CIA may be no more than a general locus signifying an unknown factor whose function is intelligence and whose field is the invisible government. Students of Einstein's work on tensor calculus may find it comfortable to deal with these varieties of unknowns. In the world of social theory, however, we are at the point where a special and general theory of relative identity in social relations would be of inestimable use since the only situation for which there can be no cover is *anguish,* and the operation of the twentieth century may be to alienate us from that emotion in preparation for the ultimate destruction of the human soul as opposed to the oncoming hegemony of the technological person.

Generally, his enemies and friends agreed that Nixon was a fool not to destroy the tapes. They may not have understood the depth of the pot in which he was boiling. There was reason to believe there were copies of the tapes. If Butterfield would reveal their existence, he could be an agent; if one agent was near those tapes, then more than one; what reason to assume duplicates of the damaging tapes were not being systematically prepared all the while he was being set up? Impeachment was certain if he burned the evidence and a copy appeared.

"You do not understand. This man stood at the threshold of his own idea of greatness. He was going to write the peace with Communism. He was going to be immortal. Now, as he loses respect, it is slipping away from him inch by inch." Kissinger smiles sadly over his salad. Across the city, the Ervin committee is holding a hearing in the hot summer afternoon. "People criticize Nixon for being irresolute about Watergate. Why does he not confess what is wrong and end it? they ask. They do not understand that he cannot make a move because he is not in possession of all the facts. He does not know what is going to happen next. He does not know what is going to break upon him next." Kissinger sighs. "Nobody will ever know how close that man was to getting the foreign situation he wanted."

Nixon is not only a Shakespearean protagonist in the hour of his downfall, but Macbeth believing that Birnam Wood will never come to Dunsinane. Of course, he is as appealing in his travail as Ronald

Reagan might be playing Lear, but the echo nonetheless of a vast anguish comes back — who else has known such anguish and managed to live in the American world? Birnam Wood will come back to Dunsinane as the tapes one by one get to be taken.

Epistemological Model V:
"Sometimes," said the wise observer, "I think of that story of Howard Hughes being so fearful of bacteria that he kept Jean Peters across the room from him, and then I think, what if the fear of bacteria is the cover, and the double dare not get too close to Jean Peters?"

Epistemological Model VI:
There is hardly an episode in Watergate which was not presented to us in a way that makes it seem more stupid than it ought to have been. Or, is it closer to say that what we hope to perceive is more brilliant than the level at which we have been encouraged to perceive it?

The tapes, for example. If a tape can be made, a copy can be made. Until we brood upon the matter, it is natural to assume the copy is equal to the original. We do not stop to think that the poor tapes we thought were the originals could in fact have been inferior copies. The remarkably bad quality of the tapes might have been produced by design. There are advantages to a tape which can hardly be heard: The affair is downgraded, and seems less sinister. No cover is more comfortable to a clandestine operation than the appearance of ineffectuality. Let us remind ourselves of how inept the Secret Service seemed in its taping operation. Possessing all that White House power, all those funds, all that available electronic equipment — yet the product sounds like it was recorded in the glove compartment of a moving car. Admittedly, there were technical difficulties to the taping, but the product still seems inadequate. Nixon must have suffered another turn of the screw. Since he cannot know if the tapes he hears are the unique, original, and only tapes, or a debased copy prepared by his enemies, he cannot even be certain whether it is a trap to encourage him to take advantage of the garbled sound and rephrase the transcripts in his favor. He takes the plunge. But his emendations are discovered later by the House Judiciary Committee. A corrected transcript is presented to America.

How can Nixon not wonder whether somebody substituted a subtly clearer version of the tapes to John Doar's staff?

All the while, Nixon has to confront another question. If he
evades every snare, pit, impressment, and delusion, if he even manages to work his way through the Senate to the edge of being declared not guilty in the impeachment, how can he be certain that in
the last minute after the very last of all these abominably unexpected breaches in his cover-up, the missing eighteen minutes will
still not appear? Then he can envision how America will spank the
horse, and he will twist forever in the wind.

4.
A Crisis in Criminology

I received a telephone call from L. Patrick Gray, the Acting
Director of the FBI — a man I had never met. Gray told me he
was disturbed by reports suggesting the FBI was not conducting
a thorough investigation. "That is simply not true," Gray told
me. "I assure you this matter will be pursued wherever it leads,
regardless of my position in the Administration. Let the chips fall
where they may." I told Gray I appreciated his call, and he concluded our talk with an unexpected comment: "Mr. O'Brien, we
Irish Catholics must stick together."

On July 7, following Gray's call, I was visited by two Secret
Service agents. . . . They told me they had been instructed to report to me that the FBI's exhaustive examination of the National
Committee offices had uncovered no telephone bugs or other
electronic devices — that "the place was found to be clean." I accepted their report without question. I knew the FBI had torn the
place apart — removing ceiling panels, dismantling radiators, and
the like — and if they said there were no bugs, then I assumed
there were no bugs. Later evidence, of course, revealed that bugs
had been placed on my phone and that of Spencer Oliver, Executive Director of the Association of State Democratic Chairmen.
To this day I cannot explain the discrepancy between those facts
and the report I was given.

— *No Final Victories*

When Hunt's team was caught, McCord had already removed a
few panels from the ceiling of O'Brien's office. It is not so very well
known that an excellent and advanced kind of eavesdropping can be

achieved by driving a nail into the flooring of the office ycu wish to monitor from the ceiling of the office below. A listening device is then attached to the nail. The sophistication of this method is that it is not possible to detect the bug from the office being taped, since the listening device attracts no more attention than *any* nail in the floor. The first question to ask of many a break-in is not therefore which office was entered, but who is working in the office above. By this logic, a real interest in O'Brien's conversations could best have been satisfied by a break-in on the fifth floor — in order to tap the sixth. Since we are already on the sixth, who inhabits the seventh?

That part of the seventh floor of the Watergate Office Building, which rested unmistakably over Larry O'Brien's quarters, was occupied at the time by no less than the office of the secretary of the Federal Reserve Board. Can matters be this simple? It is not seemly that great financial secrets should be discussed in an office of a building which looks to have been designed by an architect with a degree in Mafia Modern, but interest augments when we learn that one of the computers of the Federal Reserve Board is located in the basement of the same Watergate Office Building. If, on a given day, the Federal Reserve Board had sealed itself in to discuss a change in the discount rate, is it wholly inconceivable that a CIA man (a veritable Grand Mole of a banker) installed for years on the Federal Reserve Board might have phoned in to the computer in the Watergate Office Building basement an apparently routine question that would yet manage to tell his undercover assistant in the basement what the shift would be in the discount rate? Assuming that this assistant has been sequestered with the computer to maintain his discretion during these important deliberations of the board, the question is whether the basement assistant could not manage to make an innocent phone call to somebody on the seventh floor. Since we are assuming the man on the seventh floor is not part of the team to which the man in the basement belongs, the conversation would have to go something like this:

BASEMENT: I hear Vida Blue is pitching today.
SEVENTH FLOOR: Impossible! He pitched two days ago.
BASEMENT: (Indignantly) Who did?
SEVENTH FLOOR: (Triumphantly) Vida Blue!

That was what the basement wanted to hear said on the seventh floor and said loud enough for the nail in the ceiling of the sixth floor to pick it up — the names of baseball pitchers having been geared to the rise and fall in the discount rate. Now, whoever monitored that conversation could pass the information along. Since more than one team would presumably be working to get advance information on the change in the rate, let us assume our team got the word out with a possible lead of three hours over all the others.

"How much would such information be worth?" a banker was asked.

"Conservatively," he replied, in the rich and pompous voice which is privy to large sums, *"billions."*

"For just a few hours' lead?"

"That is time enough."

The possibility is now open that the CIA was using the break-in to the Democratic National Committee as its elegant cover to the real operation, which was to tap privileged Federal Reserve Board information. Elegance offers its exquisite use of resources, so one would not claim the CIA had no interest in O'Brien nor in Oliver. O'Brien and Oliver had had their propinquity with the CIA, after all. While we know they cannot be in Intelligence — since how may we conceive of a good liberal Democrat who is? — nonetheless, they might attract an enclave in the CIA (if, of course, it is an enclave performing the break-in under the auspices of CREEP and not just a burglary by red-hot amateurs executed at the third rate of CREEP stupidity). Yes, some enclave might legitimately have been curious to know more about what O'Brien and Oliver knew of Chappaquiddick, or Eagleton's secret medical file, or HUGHES in relation to Maheu, Lansky, Rebozo, and Nixon on one side, or HUGHES, Bennett, Hunt, and Helms on the other. Name the teams; HUGHES is on all of them. Recognize that with the Democratic Committee break-in as cover, the operation has power over CREEP — which is to say ultimately over Nixon — even if its burglars are caught. That is elegance. Obtaining neither their first objective — the Federal Reserve tap — nor the second — lines on O'Brien and Oliver — the entrepreneurs still end with more power over the presidency than before. Once everybody made certain the election was won in spite of Watergate, there would be even more power.

Of course, a risk was taken. If Watergate had broken too early, McGovern might have been able to get his campaign turned around (although the thought does not ring loud in the lost ether) but then

Watergate never burst until the election was safe and the operators could begin to apply that wrenching pressure on the bones of the Nixon administration.

It must, however, be immediately visible that while this last scenario violates no facts, it is only a literary fancy — not an iota of proof. Just another model. Perhaps we can modernize William of Ockham's razor by saying: The simplest model which satisfies all the facts is likely to lead us to inexplicable facts.

Four of the five men arrested in the bugging attempt at the Democratic National Committee headquarters Saturday morning were registered as guests at the Watergate Hotel on April 28, the same night that two other firms in the Watergate building were broken into. . . .

The firm of Freed, Frank, Harris, Shriver and Kampelman, located on the 10th floor of the Watergate Building, 2600 Virginia Ave. NW, was broken into on May 18, but officials of the firm did not report the incident to police until yesterday. . . .

A spokesman for the Freed law firm said yesterday that the burglary was not immediately reported to police because nothing appeared to be missing, and employees did not associate the incident with political espionage until disclosure of Saturday's break-in. . . .

On April 28, the night four of the five bugging suspects were registered at the Watergate Hotel, according to police, the 11th-floor offices of the Sterling Institute, a management consulting firm, were broken into and $1,100 worth of typewriters and calculating machines was stolen. . . .

The same night, police records show, the law firm of Boykin and DeFrancis, located on the eighth floor of the Watergate, was forcibly entered and $525 worth of office equipment was stolen.

— The Washington *Post*, June 21, 1972

Maybe if our scenarios have had a purpose, it has been to flavor our reading with the temperament of an agent, a way of saying that we have become sufficiently paranoid to see connections where others see lists. So let us look at a list of the offices in July, 1973, on the seventh and eighth floors of the Watergate Building, and take the pleasure of wondering how many of those names and corporations have no relation to Intelligence.

701 Defense & Aerospace
Center of Sterling
Institute, Inc.
H. F. Dean
Human Factors Re-
search Associates,
Inc.
Inst. for Psychiatry &
Foreign Affairs
704 Harris Intertype Corp.
Harris Shire, Con-
ductor
Radiation, Inc.
R. F. Communications,
Inc.
707 EDP Technology
Systemed Corp.
711 Federal Reserve Board
Office of Sec'y

805 Division of Federal
Reserve Bank
Operations
808 Foreign Banking
Authorities
Office of Defense
Planning
Securities
Stat Methodology &
Procedures Section
811 Interstate General
Corp.
L. E. Steele
812 Armistead I. Selden, Jr.
Boykin & De Francis
815 Perkin Elver Corp.
Joseph Dixon,
Manager

When we add the three robberies in the last news story and in clude the possibility of break-ins to other offices we know nothir about by burglary teams who were removing taps that others ha been putting in, there is now posed to our brand-new agent-typ brain a further question: What part of the Watergate Office Buildir was not being tapped?

Our procedure has conducted us to the point where we have t recognize that we have used up our last scenario in order to bring u to a place where we have no scenario to replace it. Now, we kno less than before of what might possibly be going on.

5.
A Tension in Teleology

Said the CIA:
Authority imprinted upon emptiness
   is money,
     honey.
Bang bang Howard.
We don't need you.
We need
The space where you were.
           — Anonymo L'Rivera

Like a main gear in the clockwork is Nixon's anguish. As we hear the tick, we dwell in the fascination of the inexorable.

Next to Nixon, Hunt is an idler gear. His anguish is all of his existence, but it moves us less. The main gear goes until the last of the tension in the spring runs down, but the idler gear never runs down — it is merely attached to the alarm. So its end is not inexorable but catastrophic — as when the clock is dropped and the idler gear is broken.

Hunt was broken. The style of *Undercover* has that numbness of affect which comes from a fall. He writes without feeling more for one period in his life than another as though he is saying it is costly enough to locate the episodes. He is like a semiconscious victim who senses that coming awake will be equal to crawling up a slope of broken glass. The horrors to come will be greater than the ones he has known already.

Yet, as with Nixon, there is no danger of getting to like Hunt too much. We can decide that Nixon was set up by Watergate and feel no great pity because we can also remember the war in Vietnam he kept going for four years in order to assure his reelection. One can always recall the voice Nixon used when he spoke of the North Vietnamese as "my enemy," on the day he ordered the Christmas bombing. He had always wanted to be an actor and he ended by playing the classic role of the criminal who is convicted for the wrong crime. So one does not have to feel an overcharge of compassion for Nixon — just enough to water our imagination. Your enemies succeed after all when they dry up your imagination.

By the same token, there is a built-in limit to how much compassion we can feel for Hunt. We have only to read his account of his own methods on a caper in the early Fifties:

> The Mexican Communist leader was then visiting Peking. On the day of his departure Bob North airmailed me a copy of a Chinese newspaper announcing his departure, sending a duplicate copy to CIA headquarters. To replace the departure announcement I fabricated a story in which the Mexican Communist was quoted as deprecating fellow Mexicans and saying, among other things, that Mexican peasants could never hope to achieve the cultural level of the superior Chinese. I cabled the fabrication to headquarters, where a special type font had been made by reproducing samples from the local paper. My fabricated story was set in this duplicate type and the entire front page of the local paper re-created by technical means. A dozen copies were pouched to me and were received before the target Communist returned to Mexico.
>
> The fabricated newspapers were made available to local journalists who published facsimilies of the offensive interview together with a translation into Spanish. The target's protestations of innocence gained no credence whatever, for technical tests conducted on the duplicated Chinese paper affirmed that the type in which the story was printed perfectly matched other type samples in the same newspaper and so had to be authentic.[30]
>
> *— Undercover*

A footnote says, "It was this sort of technical assistance from CIA that I lacked when I undertook to fabricate two State Department cables in 1971."

No, we do not have to like him too much. Self-pity is Hunt's companion, and bitterness is his fuel. He writes with the tightly compressed bile of a disappointed man; the reader is to be reminded that his early prospects were happier than his later ones. Photographs taken of him on the beach at Acapulco a few months out of OSS show the would-be screenwriter looking well built in bathing trunks. He bears a bit of resemblance to Hemingway, and is at pains in *Undercover* to show pictures of himself skiing and hunting. For that matter, he is also adept at fishing, squash, golf, tennis, riding, boxing, and screwing — so the autobiography suggests.

---

[30] This story is a perfect example of how a fact can be wiped out by an artifact.

It would be a bet Hemingway is his hero, and that Hunt in the late 1940s was torn between a life as a great novelist and a social life as a spy. We can guess how he chooses. He is, with everything else, a social climber, and drops on the reader every big name he knows from Eisenhower and Nixon down, making a show of his good WASP family origins (Hunt's Point in the Bronx is named after a relative who goes back to the Revolutionary War, and Leigh Hunt is on the family tree) as well as his wife's sterling ancestry ("In addition to being descended from the Presidential Adams and Harrison families, my wife was one-eighth Oglala Sioux . . ."). Before Hunt, she has been married to the Marquis de Goutière. No matter that her maiden name is Wetzel and Hunt is from Brown, not Princeton (a full demerit in the early CIA), he will still look to climb high into the good life of Oh So Social. "The service plates were Revere gadroon, the crystal was an opaline . . ." is a line from one of his novels, and he will make a point of asking Bill Buckley to be godfather to his children. At the end, when tragedy strikes, he and his family are living in a house called Witches Island in Potomac, Maryland, in "what was to be our final family home. On its ample acreage were paddocks, a stable, outbuildings and woods." He is the perfect reader for the magazine edited by the godfather of his children.

Still, he is not just one more anti-Communist with nothing but the righteous moral equivalent of tunnel vision. He has also had a life. It is almost an appealing life. He has had dyslexia as a boy and played trumpet in a high-school dance band. What is most irritating about Hunt is that he is nearly large enough to be a protagonist in a good and solid novel, and yet — hatred has certainly dried his imagination — he is never large enough. No moment of wit will ever separate his soul from his disasters.

All the heavier must those disasters sit on him. Those disasters pose insoluble questions. Their lack of an answer promises insanity.

What, for instance, can he make of that list of offices on the seventh and eighth floors of the Watergate Office Building? Or of those extra break-ins he may now be hearing about for the first time? With his sophistication in the infiltration of one group of Intelligence by another — he has after all been chief of covert action in the Domestic Operations Division — how could Hunt not entertain the hypothesis that a species of trench warfare in bugging and counter-bugging had been going on in the Watergate Office Building long before his operation ran into its peculiar trap? Let us even assume that everything he has told us is only a cover story for the more serious job he assumed he was doing. After the arrests, how can he be certain he was told anything accurate?

There is a tool of inquiry provided by Lenin. He suggested that when a political event occurred whose origin or motive seemed incomprehensible, then ask the question: "Whom?" Whom does this benefit? Whom did Watergate benefit? Hunt would ask the question. And he would have to face the nightmare that the Nixon-Kissinger wing of the CIA, which by now for practical purposes could be described as the Rockefeller-Détente wing, had been mangled at Watergate by the Cold War wing. If so, however, then he, Hunt had also been set up in the process, had been sacrificed by his own people to implicate Nixon. There was a centrality to such a hypothesis no agent could ignore.

There are not only dimensions to paranoia but degrees. Cold paranoia can serve as the assistant to brilliance, but fevered paranoia (where the heat comes from the thought that one is being done in by one's friends) is the true hellion of hysteria. All panics are loose, all proportions are lost. In such a fry, how can one ignore the smallest detail?

Hunt could even begin to brood over people like R. Spencer Oliver, whose phone happened to be the other line tapped at the Democratic National Committee. Hunt could remember a dinner with a young Democrat named Spencer Oliver who had been out with Mullen, Bennett, and himself back in 1970 or 1971. During the meal, Oliver had made a point of mentioning the names of a few CIA officers Hunt knew personally. Oliver had been surprisingly knowledgeable. Mullen and Bennett had even wanted to take Oliver into Mullen & Company as a partner! But Hunt had disapproved.

Now, he had been caught on an operation which had for one of its tasks the tapping of Oliver's phone. Hunt could mention Oliver casually in his book and make no connection between the Spencer Oliver with whom he had dinner and the R. Spencer Oliver whose phone was tapped. He does not ask if they are not most certainly the same man. Such calm, however, is for his book. From Hunt's point of view, Oliver might have little or a great deal to do with Watergate. In the ongoing crisis of trying to solve the mystery of his life with all the working experience of his career, how is Hunt to measure the relevant importance of that detail, or of McCord and Fensterwald? McCord, for instance, has taken Bernard Fensterwald for his lawyer to go before the Ervin committee, Fensterwald who is chairman of the Committee to Investigate Assassinations. The unspoken shock to the media would not be small. It is a way of saying Watergate is related to Dallas. Which enclave now wanted the media to think that way? Dallas and Watergate. That would be the scoop of the century. The people behind McCord might be serving some kind of notice.

We are trying to live in the measure of Hunt's anguish, but it is impossible to speculate here. We do not know, after all, whether he had anything to do with Dallas. The photograph of the two bums arrested by the police in Dealey Plaza shortly after the murder does show a resemblance to Hunt and Sturgis but there is an indigestible discrepancy in the height. On the other hand, Hunt was chief of covert action in the Division of Domestic Affairs at the time; that is a perfect desk from which to have a hand in such an assassination (especially if it has been brought off by some variant of a Mafia and anti-Castro Cuban team). At the least, we have to assume that Hunt would have been in position to pick up enough to embarrass the CIA profoundly. But then it is staggering to contemplate how much Hunt may have found out about matters he had not necessarily been active in himself. If no one in the CIA could locate to a certainty the details of other operations, still a tremendous amount might be learned through gossip, or by reconnaissance through those more or less secret files which would be more or less available on long, dull office afternoons. And he was a writer of suspense novels, no less. What material might be at hand! To the degree the CIA is bureaucratic and not romantic there would be formal procedures in getting to the files which could be winked at, breached, circumvented, or directly betrayed. To the degree the CIA was a culture, then Hunt was a living piece of inquiring matter, and in the years from 1966 to 1970 as his career in the CIA was ostensibly winding down, he had time to do a little research on some of those hundred and more murders in Dallas supposedly connected to witnesses of the assassination, time to get a line on who might be doing the job. For the CIA, whether implicated or not, could hardly be without interest in a mop-up operation of such magnitude. Over a hundred murders to keep the seepage of information under control!

So Hunt may have known a great deal about Dallas. We have to hold this in our attention when we begin to think of the nightmare within Hunt's nightmare — the death of his wife in the crash of United Air Lines Flight 553 from Washington to Chicago on December 8, 1972. The plane had crashed on landing at Midway and she was one of forty-five people who were killed. We do not know how much Hunt knew nor how much he had told his wife. We know that she was making payments to the Cubans with White House money, but that is hardly a piece of information worth silencing by the risk and carnage of sabotaging an airplane. An investigator, Sherman Skolnick, in Chicago, would lay the claim that twelve people in one way or another connected with Watergate were on the plane, and he would remind us that White House aide Egil Krogh, Gordon Liddy's old White House boss, was appointed under secretary of transportation the next day and would supervise the National Transportation Safety Board and the Federal Aviation Administration in their investigations of the crash. That is not an automatically insignificant detail. On December 19, Alexander Butterfield would be appointed the new head of the F.A.A.[31]

If Hunt and Dorothy Hunt had known a great deal about Dallas and were threatening to tell the world, then Hunt would not have to brood over such details. He could assume his wife's plane had been encouraged to crash. Of course, we would no longer be talking about anguish, but masterplots and last-reel peril. The likelihood is that Hunt and Dorothy Hunt were trapped in a smaller game, and the crash was a mixture of inefficiency, cynical maintenance, and who knows? — some overload of psychic intensity among the passengers. (Why else do great athletes live in such fear of traveling by air but that psychic intensity is also a species of physical charge and can even distort the workings of an electronic system?)

No, it is more likely Hunt was living with the subtle horror that attends every inexplicable crash — is there a psychology to machines? Had there been an intervention of moral forces, a play of the dice from the demiurge? At the least, Dorothy Hunt's death was evidence of the raised law of coincidence in dramatic and dreadful events. Great or livid events could indeed be peculiar in their properties, and maybe no perfect conspiracy ever worked, since people were so imperfect — only imperfect conspiracies succeeded and then only when a coincidence drove the denouement home. Was it possible that Hunt was finally obliged to look over the lip of tragedy itself — a view which leaves us, the Greeks were certain, babbling and broken? Did he come to think that a psychic vortex pulls in a higher incidence of coincidence itself?

---

[31] For that matter, Dwight Chapin, appointments secretary to Nixon, moved over two months later to an executive position at United.

"A man may defend himself against all enemies save those who
are resolved that such a man as he should not exist."
— Tacitus, epigraph to *Undercover*

Reflect on the phenomenon: A higher incidence of coincidence itself. The more central the dreadful act, then the greater is the number of accidents, disasters, and astonishing connections which surround it. By such a cosmic thesis, more than one assassination plot
would come to collision on those murderous days of our history
(when Americans began to live in fear of more than the atom
bomb) and so, too, more than one agency, more than one enclave,
more than one motive, yes, more than one plot have been set up, or
unhinged, at Watergate. We have to free our minds of a hundred
certainties we have been provided (and have provided ourselves) on
that third-rate burglary. We have preferred to rely on the testimony
of a hundred skilled and professional liars rather than face into a vision of reality which would recognize that Franz Kafka is the true if
abstract historian of the modern age, and the Möbius strip is the
nearest surface we can find to a plane.[32]

To free our minds! We live in one existence, but have the overlay
of another upon us. We strive to make our history, and sense, with
the uneasiness of confrontations never faced, that we may dwell
under the overall domination of an invisible second government (at
odds with itself?) whose touch is subtle, but whose scenarios sit like
an incubus upon Intelligence itself.

Of course we also live in a world more dazzling with the montage
of startling connections than a Kenneth Anger film. Maybe, it is our
reward. During that season when Bobby Kennedy, weary from
stalking Jimmy Hoffa, would relax with Marilyn Monroe, we find
out Hoffa, in his turn, hired a wiretapper, Bernard Spindel, to listen
in on Bobby.[33] Spindel, who must have been as proficient as Gene
Hackman in *The Conversation*, was going to be arrested eventually
and would die in jail. There is reason to think the Kennedys never
forgave him, for Spindel seems to have gotten some tapes on Bobby,
and the wiretapper's widow appears to have kept and concealed
them. She rose up to the polluted surface of the news a year or two
ago, Mrs. Barbara Fox Spindel. A small munitions company she

---

[32] A Möbius strip is like a paper band curved into a circle, but twisted a half turn before it
is glued. If you start drawing a line down the middle of the band your pencil will end up on
the opposite side of the paper once you have circled the ring. Stated by it s paradox, the top
surface of the plane is now the bottom surface.

[33] Robert F. Slatzer, *The Life and Curious Death of Marilyn Monroe*.

owned had been offering (by the claim of its promotion material) to be able to produce fatal exploding cigarette packs and other small works of surprise for the use of the CIA and other espionage. Her company and her name became connected by way of the newspaper story to Lucien "Gus" Conein, an old CIA hand who had long worked for General Lansdale, the CIA station chief in Saigon. Conein denied the connection vehemently, of course, but then we can imagine how quickly somebody in his line of work is going to admit a professional association with Mrs. Spindel.

Now, it happens to be Conein, an old Company associate, whom Hunt interviewed when Chuck Colson was looking for a way to cook up a few false Kennedy cables on the assassination of Diem. It is a long trail which leads from the tragedy of Marilyn Monroe to E. Howard Hunt and his thunderstruck fun and games, and there is not much voltage in these connections. No shock comes across the gap. It is just that like Agatha Christie's characters we all seem to end up knowing one another. Before too long, if irony does not paralyze, we may be singing, "No man is an Iland, intire of it selfe" in the godawful music of Ernest Hemingway's final whiskey-cracked voice. Listen to his record.[34] What a crazy country we inhabit. What a harlot. What a brute. She squashes sausage out of the minds of novelists on their hotfooted way to a real good plot.

Bibliography

Anderson, Jack. "My Journal on Watergate." *Parade*, July 22, 1973.

Anderson, Jack. The Washington *Post*, September 18, 1973; May 23, June 6, July 15, 16, 22, 1974.

Chester, Lewis, et al. *Watergate*. New York: Ballantine, 1973.

Copeland, Miles. "The Unmentionable Uses of the CIA." *National Review*, September 14, 1973.

Fay, Stephen, et al. *Hoax*. New York: Viking, 1972.

Hunt, E. Howard. *The Berlin Ending*. New York: Putnam's, 1973.

Hunt, E. Howard. *Undercover*. New York: Berkley, 1974.

Kohn, Howard. "Strange Bedfellows—The Hughes-Nixon-Lansky Connection." *Rolling Stone*, May 20, 1976.

Lukas, J. Anthony. *Nightmare*. New York: Viking, 1976.

Magruder, Jeb Stuart. *An American Life*. New York: Atheneum, 1974.

Marchetti, Victor, and Marks, John D. *The CIA and the Cult of Intelligence*. New York: Knopf, 1974.

---

[34] Ernest Hemingway Reading, *Caedmon Records TC 1185.*

McCoy, Alfred W., et al. *The Politics of Heroin in Southeast Asia.* New York: Harper & Row, 1972.

O'Brien, Lawrence F. *No Final Victories.* Garden City, N.Y.: Doubleday, 1974.

Prouty, L. Fletcher. *The Secret Team.* Englewood Cliffs, N.J.: Prentice-Hall, 1973.

Skolnick, Sherman H. *The Midway Crash and Watergate.* Chicago: Citizens' Committee to Clean Up the Courts, 1974.

Slatzer, Robert F. *The Life and Curious Death of Marilyn Monroe.* New York: Pinnacle, 1974.

Szulc, Tad. *Compulsive Spy.* New York: Viking, 1974.

Thompson, Fred D. *At That Point in Time.* New York: Quadrangle, 1975.

Tinnin, David B. *Just About Everybody vs. Howard Hughes.* Garden City, N.Y.: Doubleday, 1973.

Acknowledgments

*

"Our Man at Harvard" originally appeared in *Esquire*, March 22, 1977.

"An Advertisement Advertised" was written for the reissue of *Advertisements for Myself* by Norman Mailer. Reprinted by permission of G.P. Putnam's Sons. Copyright © 1976 by Norman Mailer.

"Are We in Vietnam?" was written for the reissue of *Why Are We in Vietnam?* Reprinted by permission of Holt, Rinehart & Winston. Copyright © 1977 by Norman Mailer.

"Of a Small and Modest Malignancy, Wicked and Bristling with Dots" originally appeared in *Esquire*, October 20, 1977.

"Two Letters From Frank Crowther" originally appeared in *The Paris Review*, Volume 17, No. 67.

"Miller and Hemingway" has been adapted from *Genius and Lust*, copyright © 1976 by Norman Mailer. Reprinted by permission of Grove Press, Inc.

"Papa & Son" originally appeared as the preface to *Papa: A Personal Memoir* by Gregory Hemingway. Preface © 1976 by Norman Mailer. *Papa: A Personal Memoir* © 1976 by Gregory Hemingway. Reprinted by agreement with Houghton Mifflin Company.

"My Friend, Jean Malaquais" is reprinted by permission of Warner Books/New York from the introduction by Norman Mailer to *The Joker* by Jean Malaquais. Copyright © 1974 by Warner Books, Inc.

"Narcissim" originally appeared in *American Review*, No. 24, April 1976, published by Bantam Books, Inc. Copyright © 1973 by Norman Mailer.

"Tango, Last Tango" originally appeared in *New York Review of Books*, May 17, 1973 as "A Transit to Narcissus." Copyright © 1973 by Norman Mailer.

"The Faith of Graffiti" originally appeared in *The Faith of Graffiti*, an Alskog Book. Copyright © 1974 by Norman Mailer.

"A Harlot High and Low" originally appeared in *New York* Magazine, August 16, 1976. Included in that piece were a number of quotations from other works, a bibliography of which appears in the piece itself. The only sources requesting permission were:

The Rolling Stone for excerpts from "Strange Bedfellows — The Hughes-Nixon-Lansky Connection: The Secret Alliances of the CIA From World War